BITTER SECRETS

PATTY BRANT

BITTER SECRETS

iUniverse, Inc.
Bloomington

Bitter Secrets

iUniverse books may be ordered through booksellers or by contacting:

iUniverse
1663 Liberty Drive
Bloomington, IN 47403
www.iuniverse.com
1-800-Authors (1-800-288-4677)

Because of the dynamic nature of the Internet, any web addresses or links contained in this book may have changed since publication and may no longer be valid. The views expressed in this work are solely those of the author and do not necessarily reflect the views of the publisher, and the publisher hereby disclaims any responsibility for them.

Any people depicted in stock imagery provided by Thinkstock are models, and such images are being used for illustrative purposes only.

Certain stock imagery © Thinkstock.

ISBN: 978-1-4620-7156-2 (sc)
ISBN: 978-1-4620-7154-8 (e)
ISBN: 978-1-4620-7155-5 (dj)

Library of Congress Control Number: 2011961812

Printed in the United States of America

iUniverse rev. date: 5/7/2012

CHAPTER 1

I SEE FACES.

I can't quite remember when I first started seeing them. They were so faint, so unobtrusive, like mist gliding above the sand. More like a sigh, really, flitting just at the periphery of vision, or tangled among leaves like low-lying clouds. At some point, they began to register in my consciousness like little feathers gliding across the bottoms of my feet. Almost imperceptible, but not quite.

I had been in this small town since high school, coming as a brokenhearted thirteen-year-old orphan to live with a widowed great aunt I barely knew. Now a reporter with the *Oxbow Independent*, our local mullet wrapper, I, Molly Martindale, had settled quite comfortably into my life. This town had become my own.

I remember quite clearly the day I could no longer ignore these faces. I had just spent the better part of my day wrestling with an absentee boss—you know, the kind who rarely shows her face and still manages to give you grief. As I finally hung up the phone for the last time and switched off the light, it was just about dusk. When I pulled the key from the front door lock and turned to the darkening street, it must have been bedtime for the birds. They were swishing through the air, calling to each other, making quite a ruckus. At first I hoped the waning light was playing tricks on my strained eyes.

But no, I was certain. There really was something up in the branches of that old orchid tree. All my instincts said there was.

Then the birds were gone, and a deathly stillness took the place of their cries.

Although I'd seen that tree almost daily for nearly twelve years as I entered and exited my office, it demanded my attention that evening. It wasn't the lavender blooms that were once again painting that corner as they do for weeks every winter before falling softly to shrivel like limp stars on the ground. It was something else … something barely there. Something that wouldn't be ignored any longer.

For a long time I had done an admirable job of doing just that—denying there was anything out of the ordinary there. Maybe because there was no sound—not a whisper. Strange that should occur to me now, but there was no sound, at least no natural sound. Even the traffic noises faded away. Then they were there again—my faces—a twist of leaves in the breeze, undulating shadows, just the mere outlines of ghostly countenances, sad and waiting. Waiting. But for what? Or for whom? Were they there at all?

Slowly I felt myself being drawn to that orchid tree. I was almost across the street when I noticed the man with slightly glazed eyes just sitting there, hunched against the trunk of a giant oak, just about twenty feet from the orchid tree—what I was beginning to think of as "my" orchid tree. I prepared myself for the now-familiar stench of stale alcohol I knew would soon be assaulting my nostrils. Any thoughts of unearthly faces evaporated as quickly as they had formed.

"Hi, Dennis. Gonna be a nice evening, looks like." My words echoed unnaturally loudly in my ears as my raggedy fingernails reached my lips. I'd been trying to stop biting my nails since I was a teenager. It was not the night I was finally going to conquer that bad habit.

Dennis Blankenship had been what is commonly known as the "town drunk" for about as long as I'd been working at the *Oxbow Independent*. He just sort of came with the territory. In his fifties, was my guess, with a weathered face and empty eyes. The faded scars, more pronounced on one side of his face than the other, gave mute testimony that something horrific had happened to Dennis at some time in his life. It was his disfigured face that struck you most about the man. Well, that and the almost overpowering reek of alcohol that floated around him like an invisible cloud. He was grinding a cigarette nub into the musty ground.

I'd see Dennis at least once a week, sometimes at the post office, sometimes coming out of the bank. Most often his little dog pranced alongside him. Li'l Bit, he called him. The scruffy critter looked like something put together with spare parts from other dogs—I would defy even the American Kennel Club to find any part that matched another. As improbably ugly as the mutt was, he was a lively little fellow—and cute in an odd sort of way. A well-behaved, drab-colored little orphan whom Dennis miraculously kept clean. The two had apparently adopted each other, and the pair of them lived in the woods behind the bank on the other side of River Street. When it was really cold or rainy somebody always found an empty room or a garage for Dennis—Li'l Bit by his side. It was one of those things that make a small town comfortable. Dennis might have been just a drunk, but he was our drunk. He'd been around for about twenty years, near as I could figure—since the '60s—and folks took care of him, well, as much as he'd let them. Li'l Bit was just part of the deal. Maybe the little guy made Dennis more acceptable to the good people of Oxbow. Anybody who could engender that kind of devotion from a dog just had to be worth something.

"Hey there, Molly. Think you're right," Dennis responded, stroking Li'l Bit with one scarred hand and raising a beer bottle swathed in a brown paper bag to his lips with the other. "March nights can still get awful damn cold, but it don't look bad tonight. Anyway, I got a place fixed up in Mattie Lou's garage. Real nice. If it gets too cold, I'll just head on over there," he told me.

Bless her heart, Mattie Lou just couldn't turn away any stray.

Dennis was always polite, always spoke when I spoke first, but he never looked at me. In fact, I noticed that he never seemed to really look at anybody. I always figured he was ashamed. Or maybe he was afraid he'd see pity in people's eyes. My "faces" melted away as Dennis spoke—as though they were never there at all. *Thank God,* I think. *I must be cracking up—or I'm just way overdue for a vacation.* Our conversation continued.

"Put the paper to bed, did you?" Another swig.

3

"That was Tuesday, Dennis," I reminded him.

"Yeah. Guess I forgot. Days sure are a lot shorter than they used to be," he said, glancing around the lot. "Can't say that's necessarily a bad thing."

Dennis was always kind of quirky. Jumpy, as though he always expected something, or somebody, to be sneaking up on him. Drink does take a toll on a person.

Speaking of being jumpy, I was well aware of my own raw nerves, keeping an uneasy eye on the profusion of lavender petals and green leaves in the low-hanging branches of "my" orchid tree, searching for any trace of those feathery faces overhead.

Just then a few notes of "When the Saints Come Marching In" broke into our conversation. Oliver St. Claire, rake in hand, was approaching the lot.

Nodding his good-byes, Dennis stood up—a lot more steadily than I would have thought possible—and headed off toward Mattie Lou's place. Dennis always liked his space—for him, three was always a crowd, and he avoided people as much as he could. With Li'l Bit's tiny paws making little clicking noises on the sidewalk, he ambled off in the opposite direction from Oliver, rocking slightly from side to side with his peculiar rolling gait, mumbling about a walk and then a nice hot cup of coffee. Mattie Lou could always be counted on for a nice hot cup of coffee.

One more glance around the treetops—*no more faces!*—and my brain went into high gear. Could I make it over to my nine-year-old '74 Oldsmobile without Oliver seeing me? After all, darkness was just beginning to gather, maybe if I stay real still …

Damn! Here he comes.

Oliver St. Claire and his family owned the building across and down the street from my office—right next to "the lot." Except for that empty lot with the orchid tree, the landmark building took up that entire side of the street. The St. Claire Building, built in the mid-thirties, was one of the centerpieces of downtown Oxbow. In addition to Ruby Mae's Café, it housed rental offices and an upstairs apartment. Only the courthouse eclipsed it in architectural elegance. It was as if one of the Old South's grand plantation homes had been transported and rooted to that spot. After almost fifty years, it still attracted the eye like a single lily in the middle of a green field.

I noticed that the birds were back at it, swooping and screeching. Rake in hand, Oliver was leading the imaginary parade of saints, coming out to rake up the fallen debris—fragile lavender flower shells, leaves, and the assorted detritus that constantly requires attention on a wooded lot.

In midstride, he spied me, as I unsuccessfully tried to be inconspicuous. From his vantage point I probably looked as though I were contemplating the glories of nature, not trying desperately to gather my wits.

Oliver was a hard worker—one of the original members of the town's premier family. Everyone in Oxbow was familiar with the St. Claire family history. Long gone, James St. Claire was the patriarch who brought the clan to Oxbow. A successful businessman and restaurateur, James was beginning to take things easier by the time they came to Oxbow. His eldest son Anderson, also long gone, ran the family businesses by then. He was most like his daddy. The mayor of Oxbow for most of the '40s and '50s, Anderson was a legend in our small town. Anderson St. Claire had been a man of influence. Oliver, the middle brother and whistler, helped manage the family's properties and businesses. If Anderson had been the "brains," Oliver was the worker bee—the one who rolled up his sleeves and got the job done. The third son, Elwood, got the benefit of the family's success. His daddy sent him to the University of Florida, and he eventually became a lawyer. His son, Kyle, followed in his footsteps. Their law office was in the St. Claire Building.

Oliver was in his seventies or thereabouts and still a large man. In his prime I imagine he must have been quite an imposing figure, well over six feet tall and probably approaching three hundred pounds. These days his weight was spilling over his belt more than a little, but his arms were still powerful, and he still had a full head of gray-streaked hair.

Oliver was probably the best whistler I had ever known. He could imitate any bird he heard and do a fine rendition of just about any popular song you could name—provided it had come out before 1960. And he was a talker. In my mind, it was the only thing he did better than whistle. That man could talk you right into a stupor. Once he snagged you, it was a minimum twenty-minute "conversation." I prepared myself for it.

"Well, hi there, Molly! Enjoying the orchid blooms, eh? Nice evening for it," he said, planting himself next to me, both hands resting atop the rake handle. His glance took in the profusion of lavender blossoms. "Sure are pretty this time of year," he observed. Then he sighed and launched into the usual small talk ...

"Did you hear how Jane Hauley's little boy broke his arm? It was just a matter of time, you know. Jane just doesn't keep track of that boy ... You know they're going to tear down the old skatin' rink ..." For the hundredth time, he launched into a tirade on how he'd been abused by his latest tenant, the pizza guy. *Thus the vacant rental space between the lawyer's office and the orchid tree lot.* "Shoulda known better than to trust that Yankee so-and-so."

He fell silent for a few seconds, and I thought maybe it was my chance to take my leave, but then he came to his point.

"I know you're supposed to be heading over to the county commission meeting, Mol, but if you've got a minute, I'd really like to show you something." I could see the excitement in his kindly blue eyes, and so I said, "Yes, of course." *Wimp!*

Pleased, he led me over to Ruby Mae's. The restaurant was closed, and the place was deserted, but I followed him in when he opened the door, my curiosity rising.

"Wait here for just a minute," he told me, moving to the back room and then returning just a few seconds later, muscling in a huge picture frame. He turned it around, leaned it up against a blank wall, and pulled a sheet off, smiling all the while like a kid at the circus.

I couldn't help but smile too, just looking at him—till my eyes took in the painting he'd just unveiled.

"My granddaughter, Callie, you know—the one studying art down in Lauderdale—she painted it. Gave it to me over the weekend for the restaurant," he said, eying the painting lovingly. "When she was little she used to just love to play over there. I'd set her up with a little table and chairs, and she'd have tea parties ..."

His words faded as I stared at a richly colored, faithful reproduction of the lot—"my" lot. A profusion of lavender petals clung to sweeping branches, twisting with deep-green leaves in a gentle breeze. Shadows teased the eye, bringing it all alive.

Oliver was going on—something about art classes and Paris—but

I couldn't tear my eyes or my brain away from that painting. Achingly beautiful but dark, with an undercurrent of restlessness.

"Oh, Molly! I've got to get my books done—didn't realize how late it was getting! Guess you'd better head over to the commission meeting too." His words felt like a splash of cold water on my face.

"Yes, I do have to go. The picture's beautiful—just what this place needed. Callie's got a lot of talent," I heard myself stammer. I forced my legs to move, glancing once more at the painting as I opened the door to leave, Oliver right behind me with the key, ready to let me out.

Outside, the evening breeze cooled the heat on my forehead. As Oliver switched off the light inside, I caught a glimpse of my reflection in the window. What I always thought of as my best feature, a full head of shiny, chestnut-brown hair, just brushed my shoulders. Underneath that chestnut mane I was the picture of "average." Average height, average build, average weight—right down to the extra five pounds that clung tenaciously to my backside. I always thought "average" should be my middle name. Molly Average Martindale, that's me. But that evening my average face looked haggard and drawn, as pale as the blue eyes I inherited from my grandmother.

I knew very well I was not the fanciest jewel in the jewel box. My mom always proudly pronounced me "wholesome," but I could see nothing wholesome in those eyes that night. All I could see was penetrating, unthinking panic threatening to overwhelm my average brain.

Inside the café that dreadful painting almost glowed. I tried to steady myself but could not force my eyes away from the painting. Oliver turned out the last light as he went upstairs, leaving only stray rays from the streetlight to illuminate the dining room. A kind of murky shadow took over the room as I stared at the painting, horrified and fascinated at the movement it projected. That movement became more pronounced as I watched till my faces emerged again, pulling at me, reaching out to me—coming for me.

Fascination became fear and was rapidly turning into panic. One foot moved forward and then the other. The streetlights had little effect on the gloom closing in on me.

Faster. A glance behind me. They were still there, gaining on me. I knew I was running in the wrong direction—my car was the other way—but instinctively I understood that I could not outrun these misty pursuers, even in my old car. Still, there was no choice but to keep going. Retreating blindly in search of safe haven, I passed Sunny's Shoe Store (*"We treat your feet right"*) and Shirley's Beauty Emporium, where Oxbow ladies had gone to look their best for nigh on twenty years now. Shirley's styles might have been a trifle behind the times, but she always had the very best gossip and the most exclusive shops in New York City would have envied the loyalty of her clientele.

The absurdity of it kept nagging at the furthest outreaches of my brain, but there was no stopping my mind or my feet, the primal fear far stronger than any limited idea of "reality."

I wasn't seeing anything anymore—just a blur of passing stucco walls and signs—when I was jolted back into what I had always believed to be my real world. I was sprawled on the sidewalk looking up at Dennis, his misshapen eyes concerned as he offered me his hand.

"You okay, Molly? You don't look so good."

Now there was a question I sure couldn't answer. Was I okay? What had just happened to me, anyway? I looked behind and all around and all seemed to be normal—no sign of those hazy faces, more vessels of conflicting feelings than substance.

"You came charging up to the corner here, hell bent for leather, just as I was coming out of the alley. Sure hope I didn't hurt you none," Dennis said. "Don't worry none about my bottle—ain't nothin'."

For the first time I noticed the splash of liquid streaming down the beauty shop's stucco wall and puddling around shards of brown glass glittering on the sidewalk next to me. The smell of malt hung in the air.

"Looks to me like you best get on home, Molly. You just don't look good," he said.

"I think you're right, Dennis," I agreed. I would miss the meeting and catch up with the commissioners the next day. I couldn't get home fast enough.

When I pulled into my driveway, my brown Labrador retriever, Dutch, met me as usual, wanting to play and get fed all at the same time. I filled his water and food bowls, but playtime would have to wait. I looked around carefully—everything looked just as I had left it that morning. I breathed a shaky sigh of relief. All I wanted was a nice glass of wine to calm my shattered nerves, but my cupboard disappointed me, so I settled for a hot cup of Earl Grey tea. I was long since past feeling hungry. I wanted to stretch out on the couch and find a way not to think, but the phone rang as I brought the teacup to my lips for that first satisfying sip.

Everyone in Oxbow knew Miss Jolene. As one of the two founding sisters of Ruby Mae's Café and the town's unquestioned top society matron, Miss Jolene was absolutely everywhere; she had a guiding hand in every notable social event in town. Now in her seventies, she showed few signs of slowing down. Her parents had been pioneers in Oxbow, long before the St. Claires, and both families continued to work hard. It was definitely her soft and cordial voice that came through the receiver.

"Have you heard that the St. Claires are going to be leasing that property across the street from the *Independent*?" she asked.

"No, Miss Jolene, I haven't heard that," I responded. Now that was a surprise—they were leasing my lot? And I had just talked to Oliver, and he hadn't said a word about it. I had hoped this would be a short conversation, but suddenly I wanted to know everything. Dutch had finally finished saying hello and was lying quietly at my feet.

"I understand the St. Claires are going to build an office for a doctor there, from over in West Palm Beach, or so I hear," she informed me. Then, almost to herself, "My, it's been a lot of years since the Parkers lived there." *Parkers?* I thought. I was exhausted but felt my reporter's instincts ratcheting up. I was disappointed, though. She either didn't know anymore or was unwilling to tell me.

It was obvious that Miss Jolene was in the mood to talk, and people simply did not cut off Miss Jolene. She was arguably the nicest lady in town—unless you cut her off—so I settled in with a sigh, mentally congratulating myself on my forethought at bringing my tea with me to the phone. I settled in for a long conversation, wishing I'd fixed myself a bigger cup of tea.

CHAPTER 2

FRIDAY MORNING. THE FIRST thing on my calendar was the fiftieth-anniversary celebration at the Sweet Chariot African Methodist Episcopal Church at ten o'clock. In the afternoon the city would have a public hearing on a special exception request for a small parcel of land on the main east-west road through town. I had plenty of time to sort through the piles of information, phone calls, and all manner of chicken dinner and carwash public service announcements hurriedly scratched on the backs of envelopes and napkins. The high school cheerleaders were having a carwash at the firehouse next Saturday to buy new uniforms. The American Legion was planning another one of its ever-popular fish fries. None of us in the office could get much done for answering the constant phone calls. It was a typical Friday.

All this activity built up to Mondays and Tuesdays—the big "crunch" days when all the week's copy and photos had to be compiled into something cohesive, since the paper came out again on Wednesday. It was a free weekly that it seemed everybody in town grabbed up as soon as it hit the stands, if only to find out whether we "got it right this time."

As someone once told me, writing is 90 percent the art of applying the seat of the pants to the seat of the chair. In other words, it just begins with gathering facts and information. The real work comes when you sit down to put it all together—a weekly process at the

Oxbow Independent and countless other papers around the country. In 1983 the process still included developing film and printing actual photos, as well as banging out copy on a typewriter to be edited and reset by a typesetter and then pasted up on large pieces of paper called grid sheets.

As I began to type up a piece submitted by the health department describing the very real threat of a head-lice epidemic in the local schools, I couldn't keep my mind from going back over Miss Jolene's phone call. It was the same head-lice warning I typed every year, and I could almost do it by heart anyway.

I'll probably never know just what made Miss Jolene so talkative that night on the phone—well, talkative might be a little too big a word for the amount of real information she entrusted to me. Meager though it was, it was my introduction to the Parker family, which had lived in Oxbow years before. I thought I'd heard about every old-time Oxbow family there was, but I'd never heard anything about this family in the nearly twenty years I'd lived in town.

Oh, man! 9:45! Grabbing my reporter's pad and making sure I had fresh film for my 35mm, I headed out the door to the Sweet Chariot AME Church.

Outside the door, I deliberately checked my watch again so I wouldn't see the lot across the street. Still, it was there in my consciousness. Like a stone in my shoe. Out of the corner of my eye, I saw a few more shriveled lavender stars floating down, adding to the pattern on the carpeted ground. That unobtrusive corner lot taunted me, quietly exuding an ominous magnetism that it seemed only I could feel.

The congregation at the black community's largest church was celebrating its fiftieth anniversary. For half a century that plain wooden building had been the heart of Oxbow's black community. One of my first big assignments at the *Oxbow Independent* was to cover the Sweet Chariot AME's fortieth anniversary back in 1973. I was just out of high school and working for the paper full-time.

For years the black section had been referred to as "The Quarters." In recent years, though, the residents shunned that name and preferred its official designation—"Oak Park." In the early '20s, a Mr. Jackson Booker, who was one of the city's first black leaders, petitioned the city commission to set aside a section for a "Negro Town," where his people could enjoy their own neighborhood and build a place where they could be comfortable. The subdivision included lots for two churches and a school and was covered in some truly spectacular old oaks.

The fiftieth-anniversary ceremony at the church was well attended—mainly by Oak Park residents, but a few city commission and civic leaders also showed up. As I listened to the speeches, I juggled taking notes and pictures, stopping to join in intermittent prayers. It was a beautiful day, and the ceremony was held outside, by the church's little cemetery. The children's choir provided the music enthusiastically.

Whenever I'm over in Oak Park, I always spend a few minutes at the little park right there on the other side of the church cemetery. Two stately oaks stretch huge branches in all directions, overhung with Spanish moss, providing shade for a lovely little bench. A small brass plaque notes that the little park was dedicated in 1943, ten years after the church was dedicated. The plaque promises the park will remain "A place of peace and serenity for all."

After the last "Amen," everyone went over to the old Booker School for refreshments. The tiny wooden building had harbored every child from that neighborhood as the youngster earned his or her basic education in segregated times. Since the '60s, when the schools were integrated, the Booker School had continued to serve as a community center.

I held back, though, for a few minutes, seeking the cool shelter of that peaceful bench under the trees.

CHAPTER 3

I<small>T WAS MIDAFTERNOON, AND</small> I was sitting on a hard chair in the city commission chambers, surreptitiously trying to stretch. As always, the public hearing dragged, but everybody who wanted to have their say got their chance.

Ol' man Sedgeway lived off the highway, just southwest of the parcel on the highway for which the St. Claires wanted a special exception. The old man had just finished building his tiny, one-story cinderblock square of a house the previous year. That little piece of ground had been in his family for years. It was just barely inside the city limits and just one block off the highway. It had some of the biggest, prettiest oak trees in a city that prided itself on one-hundred-year-old goliaths dripping with Spanish moss. Ol' man Sedgeway had finally made good on his dream to retire there.

The St. Claires wanted to put in a strip mall on their property facing the road, which was still zoned residential, even though it was on the highway. It was "progress versus one man's dream."

The wrangling went back and forth for hours. By five o'clock the commissioners were no closer to a decision than when they walked in, so they finally tabled the whole issue. It's amazing how long the cogs of the American government can grind without really getting anywhere.

I resisted the temptation to head on home after the commission meeting, opting instead to go to the office to finish up a few things.

The police scanner normally faded into the background noise at the *Independent*, but the irritating scratchy squawks had been silent for some time. I hadn't really paid much attention until the dispatcher calmly intoned the codes "signal four, signal seven." Then I took notice. It was code for a traffic fatality, and she was sending officers to the corner of Third and Baines Street. Naturally, I dropped the engagement announcement I had been working on, reluctantly grabbed my camera, a reporter's pad and pen, and headed out the door.

Working fatal accidents was always an ordeal for me. I avoided it whenever possible, providing myself with a variety of excuses: the crash in question was too far out—by the time I got there traffic would be so backed up I'd never get close enough to get a picture, or I was just too busy to break off—I'd get the information later. A fatal crash always had a sad, surreal kind of quality, a sense of unnaturalness for me.

There would be one or more twisted piles of ragged metal and shattered glass strewn around the road like grotesque dice thrown by some giant hand. It always brings home to me the harsh realities the world can hit you with without warning. It always brings home to me the day my parents died.

I felt that same sick uneasiness in the pit of my stomach whenever I headed out to one of these, but I was also pushing myself. *It's part of the news, after all, and it's my job. So stop being such a wimp and just do it,* I chided myself.

As I approached Third and Baines, an ambulance came screaming and flashing its way through traffic. I could see it was the third ambulance to arrive. Three other drivers and I pulled over to let it pass, while a fourth just stopped in the middle of the street, forcing the ambulance driver into the opposite lane to weave around him.

Coming up to the scene, I saw that I could pull into the pharmacy's parking lot and walk over to the corner. My car would be out of the way, and I'd still have easy access. Jeff Warren was already in the middle of Baines Street, directing traffic around the crash. I motioned to him where I wanted to go, and he waved me in. Jeff had been in the Oxbow Police Department about six years. He was smart, eager, and would probably end up chief before it was all over.

The paramedics were working on someone—I couldn't tell whether it was a man or woman, but it looked like an adult. Jeff turned traffic duty over to another officer and walked over to where I was standing on the side of the road. The scene was organized chaos. Two mangled vehicles were strewn across the intersection. Firefighters were muscling the Jaws of Life, working to slice the top off a new-model Chevrolet that had ended up across the middle of the intersection. The front was smashed in like a pug dog's face, and there were jagged holes where the headlights should have been. Bits of glass sparkled all around like little diamonds in the road.

I could hear the woman pinned in the driver's seat moaning softly, occasionally saying something to the firefighters, although I couldn't make out the words. A body bag lay ominously on the side of the road, ignored by all the emergency workers. Paramedics were tending to an older man and woman I judged to be in their seventies, apparently passengers from the Chevy. They were strapping the woman on a backboard, neck collar in place, to be lifted into the back of the ambulance. Other paramedics had finished placing the man on a litter and were pushing it into the back of a second ambulance. I could hear the man's cracking voice, asking about someone named Phyllis. The first ambulance driver hit a button inside the cab as he pulled out, and a siren screamed in accompaniment to the garish red lights scattered throughout the scene.

A dusty brown van was off to my left, radiator hissing and steam rising. The left front of the chassis was practically resting on the pavement, the left tire jammed underneath at almost a ninety-degree angle. The driver's door hung precariously by one hinge, displaying a jumble of cups, wrappers, and personal items scattered all over the front seat. A spider-web crack split the windshield, centered right about where the passenger's head must have hit.

A young man, twenties probably, was sitting on the ground with two paramedics checking him out. He had blood dripping down the left side of his face, and his left arm was cocked at an unnatural angle. I couldn't see his legs, but that's what seemed to concern the paramedics most. Behind him two young women sat on the ground. Slightly pudgy, with dark-blonde hair, they looked like they might be sisters. One wept softly with her head in her hands, crying out every once in a while. The other one had her arms around the weeping woman, rocking her back and forth like a child. Knots of bystanders were, for the most part, quiet.

"Hey, there, Miss Molly," Jeff called out as he hustled across the street toward me. Jeff and his wife had divorced the previous year, and she had gone back home to Philadelphia. Small-town life just didn't agree with her, and Jeff wanted no part of the big city. He was on the prowl and always made it a point to speak to me. He sort of asked me out once, but the invitation was vague enough that I could duck it with ease. Jeff was a "good catch"—nice guy, good looks with eyes like melted chocolate, a hard worker, but I just wasn't ready for anybody. Not since … well, not since what I always refer to as "the Greg Richards experience."

"How does it look? Anybody serious?" I asked Jeff. "Besides that one," indicating the body bag at the side of the road.

"Looks like the lady they're cutting out of the Chevy's in big trouble. She's elderly, and they're having a hard time popping the top on that thing. She's getting weaker. If they don't get her out soon … well, it won't be good," he explained.

I felt my stomach tighten, but I said, "Can you tell me what happened?" and took some pictures of the firefighters using "the Jaws"—careful not to get the victim in the frames.

"Well, looks like the Chevy blew the stop sign and hit the van on the driver's side, but we better let you get it from the trooper. He's on his way—fortunately he was cruising just a couple miles down the highway and should be here in just a minute now," Jeff explained, inching a little closer to me than was actually necessary. The Florida Highway Patrol always works serious crashes on state roads, and Baines Street qualified. So the local law secured the scene and kept a lid on everything till FHP arrived to investigate.

"It's the new guy, Trooper Blair. Have you met him yet?" Jeff asked. I admitted that I had not and was trying to ease away from Jeff subtly when the brown and tan FHP cruiser pulled up. Tilting his head confidentially toward mine, Jeff said, "He seems okay—new and still a little impressed with himself, but I think he'll be okay once the shine wears off."

The new trooper took his time, marking something on a clipboard and talking into his radio before opening his door. Out of the cruiser stepped a heavily muscled man with a barrel chest and huge biceps. Trooper Blair obviously worked out. Before closing his door, he carefully adjusted his flat-brimmed Mountie-style hat and walked toward us, his ebony skin shining in the sun.

Ignoring Jeff, he glared at me and said in a forced-polite tone, "You'll have to leave, ma'am. This is an accident scene, not a sideshow."

Jeff stuck up for me. "This here's Molly Martindale from the *Oxbow Independent*. She's okay, just doing her job," he explained. *Well, maybe he isn't so bad after all.*

Trooper Blair started to give Jeff a challenging look and then apparently decided it wasn't worth it.

"Just make sure you stay out of the way, ma'am," he warned me, striding past. As he did, a slight breeze picked up, wafting a subtle yet familiar scent into my nostrils. The musky, male, slightly tangy scent of men's cologne caught me unprepared. That scent hit me like a freight train. It always did—ever since I sent Greg Richards packing a year ago.

Reluctance to go forward with this registered in my brain, but it was too late. The memories had taken over …

Instantly my heart sank, and my knees almost buckled. *Please, memory, don't double-cross me again.* No such luck. In an instant there I was again, standing by a rain-filled ditch along the highway. I was starting the trek back into town to the mechanic, fuming not just from the midsummer heat but from the frustration that my old Oldsmobile had failed me once again. It was the first time it had conked out on me outside of town, though. Of course, it would be on the hottest day of the year beside a mosquito-infested ditch. A blue heron glared at me as I passed, apparently warning me off his territory, letting me know I'd have to find my dinner elsewhere. That was okay by me. A motorcycle flashed by me, got maybe fifty feet past, and "hung a U-ey," pulling up directly in front of me.

The afternoon was beginning to look up after all. It was Greg Richards—a new and very interesting guy in town. I had met him a week or so earlier. Not tall, but well built, he could have stepped out of any one of my dreams. Dark-blond hair curling slightly at the nape of his neck, mischievous, soft-green eyes with brown-gold specks that always hinted at some delicious secret, good job—and he smelled even better than he looked. That smell still took my breath away. Oh, yes, Greg Richards was something, all right.

"Not a very nice day for a walk," he said, his soft eyes smiling like the devil's own.

Flustered at this unexpected meeting, I did my best to sound cool and easy. "'Course it is. I figured my old car needed a rest so I just put 'er in park and decided to walk."

He chuckled a little before saying, "So, you need a ride somewhere? The garage? The car cemetery?"

"I was just headed to the garage to get a tow," I told him. He offered to take a look at the old heap, and I said sure. Why not? If he could get it started, it might save me a towing bill. So I popped the hood, and he dove in headfirst. He poked around for a little while; had me try to start it up several times; then gave up.

"Sorry, Molly. It's way past anything I can do for it. If you'll hop on the back of my bike, I'll be glad to take you wherever you want to go," he said with a slightly wicked smile in his eyes.

No doubt noting my uneasy look, he asked, "Ever been on one of these?"

I confessed I had not.

"Well, don't worry. I'm a very good rider," he assured me. "Can't remember the last pretty young lady I lost off the back." What a smile this guy had!

So what choice did I have? I could continue to walk in the sweltering heat for the couple miles back to town, mosquitoes buzzing around me. I could wait to see if someone else stopped. Or I could jump on the back of a Harley with a guy who just could be the best thing that ever happened to me. It didn't take long to decide …

Suddenly I felt a hand on my shoulder, jerking me back to the present.

"Watch it, Mol'!" It was Jeff's voice. I came out of my little dream world as a couple firefighters passed by, heading back to their truck.

The crash scene came back into focus. I tried to get my head back into my work, but fear of the monster Greg had become enveloped me once again, just as it had during the ugly scene that ended our relationship. Greg was not the man I thought he was when we met. Deeply involved in drugs, Greg had hidden his dirty shadow-life well until I finally found the evidence that forced me to face the painful reality. Greg was not only caught up in that life, he was perfectly happy in it. He was wrapped up in the "good life" that selling drugs promised and hell-bent on dragging me into it with him. He was just as willing to destroy me as he was himself, but he refused to see it. Only Dutch—good ol' Dutch, my beautiful, four-legged protector and friend—had kept him from physically hurting me that final day we were together. *Why don't they make men like that?*

Trooper Blair was measuring tire tracks as I took a couple more quick photos of emergency personnel doing their jobs. The queasy sickness in my stomach had suddenly exploded, my head hurt, and my heart was in worse shape. I decided to call FHP headquarters later for the crash report and headed home.

CHAPTER 4

IT WAS OVER A week after her call before I saw Miss Jolene. It was Saturday afternoon, and the Ladies' Social Club was having a tea. All the local women were invited, and they brought their daughters. It was an annual affair, giving mothers and daughters a chance to get all prettied up and play at being society ladies.

Time was when every young lady wore white gloves and patent leather shoes, but now about the best you could hope was that no one showed up in holey jeans and a T-shirt with a ring in her nose.

Still, the tea was perfect, as always. The ladies of Oxbow knew how to put on a nice social gathering. The ladies had a pleasant afternoon out, and the menfolk had the whole afternoon to sit around the TV watching their favorite team slam that week's opponent—or be slammed by them. It worked out just right.

As always, Barbara, Miss Jolene's daughter, scurried around trying to keep up with her mother. They had spent hours setting the clubhouse to rights and putting the finishing touches on the hand-decorated tables before the tea. Between the pair of them and a small group of dedicated ladies, they kept the delicate little crustless sandwiches coming, ceaselessly replenished the punch bowl, and generally made sure everything went according to plan.

As the afternoon went on, I managed to get a few candid pictures and staged a few, because you never know how much space you're going to have to fill in next week's issue. Besides, everybody likes to see local faces in the paper. I stayed on afterward to help clean up and pick Miss Jolene's brain.

Miss Jolene was looking a little frazzled by the end of the afternoon, her slender shoulders sagging a little. I guess the years were finally beginning to weigh her down a bit after all. Her soft gray curls drooped a little around her ears, and the glint in her normally lively blue eyes was slightly dimmed.

Grabbing up salt and pepper shakers to replace in their storage box, I cautiously tiptoed up to the subject of the Parker family again.

"Miss Jolene, about how many times do you think you've pulled out these salt and pepper shakers and replaced them in this box?" I began.

Her hand, filled with more of the shakers, stopped in midair as her face, amazingly smooth and young-looking, wrinkled slightly. She thought for a few seconds. "Well, I don't have any idea. I am sure I don't really want to know, anyway! Too many times to count," she recalled with something that sounded like a half sigh, half chuckle.

The salt and pepper shakers safely encased in Tupperware till the next event, I moved on, helping clear Miss Jolene's homemade centerpieces off the tables. The little votive candleholders went into another container, the delicate strands of green asparagus fern from Miss Jolene's own flowerbeds, into the trash.

"You know, ever since our little talk the other night about the Parker family, I've been curious about that property."

Did Miss Jolene's hand quiver just a tad? I pressed on, nonchalantly continuing the clearing process. "I've heard stories and read about nearly every old family in Oxbow, but the Parker family is kind of a blank for me," I began.

"Well, you know, they weren't here all that long—and it was so long ago," she said, as she too cleared the tables for what had to be at least the thousandth time. "It's kind of hard to remember that far back. I'm not getting any younger, you know," she said, keeping her eyes on her work.

Now that was a first—Miss Jolene saying she couldn't quite remember something about an old Oxbow family. She was the one everybody went to with questions about our little town. If you wanted to know something about Oxbow, especially something about its history, you would ask Miss Jolene. Nine times out of ten, she had the answer and didn't even have to think about it.

For the first time in almost twenty years in Oxbow, I had the unsettling feeling that Miss Jolene was avoiding a subject. She always wanted to talk about "the old days." In fact, just try to keep her from it! The town's history was a passion with her. Maybe because she had seen so much of it. Maybe because her family had always played such a central role in it. Maybe it was just her nature. Whatever the underlying reason, Miss Jolene was an absolute treasure trove of Oxbow history and was always anxious to share it. Even on the rare occasions when her memory really was vague on a subject, she always had a suggestion about who else might know or where to check in our tiny museum files. Yes. Miss Jolene was a marvel.

And she did not want to talk about the Parker family. But I couldn't let it rest. You know how nosy reporters are.

"Well, I was just wondering. I checked with Oliver about that lot across from the *Independent,* and—as always—you were right. Somebody's interested. Some doctor from West Palm wants to "retire" here. I guess it's good they're finally going to get some money out of that lot, but I sure hate to see that pretty little corner go. It's the only vacant one on that block and been in his family for … how long?"

"Oliver's daddy bought near 'bout that whole block sometime after the fire in '30," Miss Jolene told me. "I know you've heard about that."

Oh, yes, everybody knew about the fire that gutted the entire downtown area and nearly took the rest of the town with it. All the buildings were wooden back then, and it took the entire town working together in a bucket brigade to keep the whole place from turning to ashes.

"Yes, I've heard a lot about the fire. That old cypress wood goes up in a flash," I said and then, trying to nudge Miss Jolene into revealing something about the family that had lived on that lot, I asked, "Do you remember the family? Did they have kids?"

Maybe it was the mention of the children that made her kindly blue eyes shine, softening her beautiful little face even more. Miss Jolene just loved children.

So she began, "I don't recall much about old man Parker. Cecil, his name was. He brought his wife here from Georgia, and he worked with my daddy some. He was a carpenter, and a darned good one, too, my daddy told me."

Miss Jolene's father had been an army officer before coming here and had started a mercantile store on River Street, just a few doors down from where Ruby Mae's Café would later be located. Captain Clarey did a brisk business with townsfolk and also with the Seminoles when they ventured up from the swamps to trade.

"Cecil bought that corner lot across from the newspaper and wouldn't ever sell. He did a lot of cabinet work for people around here and just about anything that involved wood. Built a lovely two-story house on that lot. I think his wife died early. I can just barely remember her. I can't even remember her name."

Miss Jolene stopped there, engrossed in fiddling nervously with a salt shaker she found hiding in the asparagus fern. It slipped out of her hand as she reached over to place it in its container, sprinkling little crystals all over the tablecloth. Helping her remove the tablecloth to empty the loose salt into a trash can, I gave her another little nudge. "So, Miss Jolene, Cecil and his wife must have had a family there with them, right?"

"Milton was their son," she said, "born the same year as I was, 1909. We went to school together—well, when Milton showed up, that is. He didn't like school much, but he inherited his daddy's woodworking skill. As a boy he helped his daddy build their house … learned about woodworking that way. Too bad he never really used his talent much. Milton didn't go out of his way to work, you see. When he needed money, the St. Claires always put him on at their sawmill down south of town a ways. Milton could also pick up carpentry jobs on the side. I think Anderson passed some work his way too," she told me.

Sitting at a half-cleared table, clutching a rumpled and soiled tablecloth, Miss Jolene became thoughtful. I thought I would have to push her along a little more, but then she started again, as though she were in a dream. "Wife's name was Hannah," she said. "Milton's wife. We saw a lot of the family. Guess you know that we lived up on the second floor over the store just around the corner, there."

That was odd. Miss Jolene had told me earlier that she couldn't remember much about the family—but they just lived around the corner and "saw a lot of the family." She had even gone to school with Milton.

"Hannah was a kind of surprise to all of us here. Milton brought her back with him from Georgia when he came back from buryin' his daddy up there with his kinfolk. Before that it was just him and that little boy of his, Buddy. Cute little fella. Milton and his first wife—Buddy's mother—got married real young. She was part of a bunch that used to live way out at Devil's Kitchen. She was kind of a wild one, she was. Anyway, she upped and left them—ran off with a salesman when Buddy was just a baby. It hit her folks pretty hard, and they left before too long. Anyway, when Milton came back from buryin' his daddy, he had a brand-new wife, and Buddy had a new mama. She was the best thing that ever happened to that child. Lord knows his daddy didn't ever give him any attention. But Hannah, she loved that boy like he was her very own, and he loved her right back."

Miss Jolene's pump stalled again and I primed it a little more. "So, Hannah was kind of a special lady?" I asked.

"That's God's own truth." Miss Jolene looked at me, and I could swear there was the tiniest tear shimmering in her tender blue eyes. To hear Miss Jolene tell it, poor Hannah held the weight of the world on her slim shoulders.

"She didn't hardly have enough meat to cover her bones, but she was a hardy soul just the same," Miss Jolene said. "She took in washing and cooked at Ruby Mae's Café off and on, right there by their house next to the St. Claire Building. Kept a nice vegetable garden in the back of the house, like most of us women at that time. We all spent hours in a sweltering kitchen canning what we grew to feed our families. Lordy, but those kitchens could get hot!" she recalled. "Many's the day I'd leave the kitchen, my ol' dress just wringin' wet from sweatin'. We all did.

"Anyway, Hannah was also good with healing herbs and lots of the townsfolk came to her when they were feelin' poorly. At one time she was the closest thing Oxbow had to a doctor. The war was on, you see, and most of the young men were gone into the service, including

Dr. Jensen. Old Doc Bradford—he was way past retirement, but he came down from Arcadia once a week, to take care of the worst cases. That left Hannah to do what she could in between.

"Folks had a hard time getting her to take payment for her doctoring, though. She saw it as a calling, a gift from God she was meant to share. So her neighbors would find other ways to repay her kindness."

Another halt. I knew she had to be getting close to talking about the Parker children, and that could be interesting, especially since it was the thought of them that had gotten her started in the first place. *Just add a little more water to the pump, Molly.*

"How many children did Milton and Hannah have, Miss Jolene?"

Still dreamlike, she began, "The boy, Buddy, was kind of big for his age, looked a lot like his daddy—sandy hair and gray eyes. Like most of the boys in these parts, 'specially in those days, he loved nothing better than hunting and fishing. He was a good shot and managed to put wild turkey and deer on the family table regular. Good thing, too. Old Milton wasn't much of a provider in spite of being a good carpenter. Liked his drink too much, you know. Milton wasn't much for the manly arts of hunting and fishing, either."

In fact, the way Miss Jolene told it, he wasn't much, period.

"Jeannie Sue, the daughter, was a sickly child. Frail and quiet, her birth had been real hard on both her and her mother. Maybe it was the memory of almost losing her only daughter—and the fear that she might still lose her—that made Hannah hover over her so. Her mama kept a keen eye on that child.

"Even though Oxbow School was right across the street from the Parker place, Buddy had a hard time getting to school. Besides the fact that he just didn't like book learning," she smiled at the thought, "he couldn't for the life of him understand why he needed to know anything at all about the Louisiana Purchase—or worse—how many times twelve goes into one hundred and forty-four. All Buddy really wanted to do was spend his life in the woods. Tracking deer, studying wild hog, finding all the good bass holes—now that was Buddy's kind of schoolin'. Those were the important things in life. The things a man could really use. That's how Buddy saw it.

"Jeannie Sue, now she was different. The only time the world was really right was when 'she had her nose stuck in a book,' as her Daddy complained time and time again. And she took to writing like she was born with a pencil in her hand. So, for Jeannie Sue, that red brick building just across the way was a haven. My Barbara was a year ahead of Jeannie Sue in school, but they were best friends."

There it was again. Miss Jolene claimed not to remember much about the family, but Barbara was Jeannie Sue's best friend. This Parker family just kept getting more mysterious. What was it that just didn't sit right?

Miss Jolene fell silent again, and I knew my cue.

"So Barbara and Jeannie Sue were good friends." It was a statement rather than a question.

Miss Jolene continued, "Oh my, yes, they saw a lot of each other—at school and at our house. Jeannie Sue used to do chores for us at our house. She'd stay on a while when she was done, and the girls spent some time together. I recall Miss Johnson, the seventh-grade teacher, praising little Jeannie Sue's writing. And she was easily the best reader in the class, Barbara always said. Well, as long as it was silent reading. Jeannie Sue's nerves and shy nature wouldn't allow her to read aloud without choking up every time. I remember one time Jeannie Sue saying that when she read aloud it always made that darn Billy Brownly poke whoever was unlucky enough to be sitting beside him and snicker like he didn't have a brain in his head. Billy Brownly was not one of Jeannie Sue's favorite kids. True 'nuf. As a child he was always such a trial to most folks. He was too loud and too pushy. You could always hear Billy Brownly over the rest."

Miss Jolene shook her head, "Guess he never did really outgrow it. He's still louder 'n anybody else around, but he's got a good heart. Jeannie Sue told me her Mama said best to just ignore Billy and people like him. I still remember her little face when she looked at me and said, 'but it sure is hard sometimes.'"

Wistfully, she continued, "I think Barbara was the only real friend Jeannie Sue had. She didn't have time for havin' fun or just bein' a kid. She had to help Hannah. Even after the worst of the Depression was over, when most folks were gettin' along pretty fair, times were still hard for the Parkers, Milton bein' the sorry excuse for a husband and father that he was."

Miss Jolene's head jerked a tiny bit, and it seemed to end her reverie.

"Sorry, I s'pose I shouldn't talk like that, but it's the God's honest truth." Thinking a little deeper, she said, "Course I guess Milton had his troubles too, and maybe it's not suprisin' that he turned out the way he did. I think losin' his mama when he was so young hit him pretty hard. He was mad at her, you see, because she left him. Cecil was a good man, a hardworking man. He tried to be a good father, but I'm not sure he knew how to raise a child. He was proud, though, and wouldn't accept any help from any of the women in town. Said he could raise his boy just fine by himself. From the time his mama died when we were about eight years old, when Milton wasn't in school he was at work with his daddy. And Cecil put in some long, hard hours. So, I guess that growing up, all he knew was the hole his mother left in his life and working hard with his father."

By this time, Miss Jolene seemed to be caught up in memories from a lifetime ago and couldn't really stop them from tumbling out.

"Milton was a drinker too. Some folks said he drank because he was 4F and couldn't go off to war with the other men. I never thought that was the reason. He was just mean. Always was. Maybe life made him that way. Sometime in the early '40s, I think, the family went back to Georgia. Left in the middle of the night, not a word to anybody," she finished without looking at me.

Before I could ask anything else, she got up and walked into the kitchen, where her daughter, Barbara, was washing up the remaining dishes. She moved a little slower than usual. *Guess the years really are beginning to wear her down a little, after all,* I thought. *What a shame. She's such a sweet lady. What will Oxbow do when she's gone?*

CHAPTER 5

So, Milton Parker was a drunk. Well, so what? There were other townsfolk, some still around, who had a serious and unhealthy fondness for the bottle—and these days, other things too. Mostly, nobody talks about these kinds of troubles. You don't have to. In small towns everybody knows the dirt about local folk. The folks who know that sort of thing just don't talk about it much. It's an open secret to everybody who already knows. So it wasn't a surprise that if Milton Parker had a drinking problem, it was kept quiet even after all these years. What I had such a hard time with was that no one ever talked about the man or his family at all.

What was even more unusual was that the Oxbow Museum didn't have anything on the family. Thanks to Miss Jolene and a handful of the town's "old-timers," the museum had stacks of old photos, newspaper clippings, and writings of all descriptions on just about every man, woman, and child who lived in town in those early days. So where were the Parkers?

The week following the Ladies' Social Club tea, I headed over to the museum again to see whether I had missed anything on the Parker family. It was Thursday because that's the only day of the week the museum was open. Ten till noon, and two to four. Luckily, Mrs. Hendricks was the volunteer on duty that day. She was always early, so when I called her the previous evening she said she'd be glad to let me in when she got there, about eight thirty.

It was also lucky that Mrs. Hendricks had only been in Oxbow for about ten years. If there was a secret about the Parker family, she wouldn't be part of any conspiracy—no matter how well intentioned—to keep it quiet.

For years she and her husband came down from Minnesota on vacation. Like so many others, when they came across Oxbow, with its ancient oaks and graceful river, they fell in love with the town. They found a nice, shady lot, built themselves a cozy little place over the next few winters and, when the time finally came, their retirement home was ready for them. As "snowbirds," the couple had made themselves a part of Oxbow, giving freely of their time and talents in all sorts of local activities. She was a history buff, so naturally she was a major influence in helping to gather all the bits and pieces of life that go into any museum, helping to catalogue and display them.

But, as knowledgeable as Mrs. Hendricks was about old Oxbow, she drew a blank on the Parker family too. After going through every family history catalogued in the museum, we finally gave up. Apparently, I wasn't going to find anything in the Oxbow Museum that would shed any light on this one family.

But how could that be? Virtually every old family was represented in these files. Some had moved away half a century or more before, but their local histories were still there, locked in Oxbow's subconscious forever.

The only things I had to go on were those tantalizing pieces of information Miss Jolene's reverie produced and a couple lines in the Property Appraiser's records at the courthouse. There had been, indeed, a Cecil Parker who owned that corner lot with a house. Milton Parker's birth on April 16, 1909, son of Cecil and Emmy Lou, was recorded in the Florida Bureau of Vital Statistics. Emmy Lou went to be with the Lord eight years later. Cecil followed her in 1929, and Milton inherited the house and lot. He sold them to Anderson St. Claire in 1940 to pay the taxes.

Dead end.

I was headed out over the bridge one Sunday afternoon when I noticed a very large man down in the park with a very small child. Billy Brownly. I had a sudden thought that maybe he could tell me something about the Parkers. After all, he was about the same age as Jeannie Sue (in her class, according to Miss Jolene) and her brother Buddy would have been forty years earlier. According to Miss Jolene, he was a real trial to Jeannie Sue. He had to remember something. I turned around and headed back over the river and pulled up in the park about twenty feet from where the two were obviously having a splendid time.

Billy was a big man, powerfully built. In his midfifties, he still laid claim to a full head of steel-gray hair, with a few dark strands that stubbornly displayed themselves here and there. His substantial mustache showed no signs of gray as yet, though, and it would be hard to find a man who appeared to be more physically robust. His weathered face spoke of a lifetime working on the county's roads in the brutal Florida sun. He had a good six inches on the tallest of men, and his frame had a quickness that belied its size. Looking at Billy Brownly was like looking at a life-size picture of an old-time boxer—solid, massive, powerful. If his mustache had curled into a handlebar on each end, the effect would have been complete.

But for all the strength his build implied, his eyes were playful. Billy's eyes—sky-blue, with their own tiny stars—and his hearty, frequent laugh softened his tough-guy image.

Billy and his wife had been married for—well, a long time. They had two daughters. One was in school in Lakeland, the other worked at the convenience store on the south side of town. Her husband worked at the juice plant. Between their paychecks they just barely managed, so Billy and his wife often kept their granddaughter, Crystal. The child was the light of Billy's life.

I approached the two slowly, watching their delight in each other, a little sheepish about intruding. I needn't have felt that way.

When he saw me coming across the park, Billy's big voice boomed out, "Well, hello there, Molly! Come on over!" Miss Jolene was right. Billy Brownly was louder than just about anybody I knew. "Crystal, say hello to Miss Molly," he told the child.

Crystal looked up at me and then just moved closer to her grandpa, not at all sure about me, but cute as a button in her daisy-splotched top and bright orange shorts with matching Kool-Aid mustache. Her dark hair matched what I imagined her grandpa's was like when he was younger, as did her bright-blue eyes.

"Go on, baby, it's okay. Say hello," he prompted. Still nothing.

"Hello, there, Crystal," I began. "I haven't seen you in a long time! I guess you don't remember me. You were still in diapers the last time I saw you," I teased.

The little girl looked up at her grandpa, almost falling over backward in the process, to verify that information.

"That's a fact!" he told her. She sort of nodded to me then and returned her attention to a raggedy, one-armed doll.

After a little catch-up talk, I turned to the topic I wanted to ask Billy about.

"You know," I began, "I've lived in this town for about twenty years now; worked for the newspaper most of that time. I thought I had heard about everybody that ever lived here."

Billy just sat there, watching Crystal as she investigated a line of ants, their march up a palm tree trunk unrelenting.

"Billy, you've been here all your life. Do you remember a family named Parker?" I asked. It took a few moments for Billy to answer. When he did, his words followed a sigh that seemed to deflate his whole body.

"I was heartsick."

That was all Billy said for a few minutes while he stared at the scuff marks on the toe of his old work boot. "She was such a pretty little thing, Jeannie Sue was. I used to watch the way her curls kind of fell over her face in class when she was working hard on a paper. Jeannie Sue was really smart, you know. She had a habit of twisting one of those curls around her finger when she was thinking hard. Funny how you can still see some things in your head so many years after they're long gone."

"So it was a hopeless romance." I hoped I was commiserating with him.

"Jeannie Sue didn't really like me much," he cast me a rueful glance, "but I truly worshiped that little gal.... I used to torment her something terrible, so I guess she had good reason not to like me. I just didn't know how else to show her how much I liked her, so I did everything I could think of to make her notice me." He trained his sad, jolly eyes on mine and said, "When you're a little boy, all you really want from 'your girl' is some attention, you see, and it don't really matter what kind of attention it is. There's somethin' in a little boy's mind that equates attention with bein' liked. Sad to say, most of the time Jeannie Sue ignored me. Oh, I know now it was my own fault, but at the time I had no idea what to do. I just knew I liked her so much it hurt."

He smiled at the memory of a smitten little boy without a clue how to get the object of his affection to like him back.

"I felt like she'd abandoned me when the family up and left the way they did. Not a word to anybody—just packed up overnight and were gone in the mornin'."

"The family just left?" I asked.

"We all took a bus up to a big war-bond rally in Miami—left early and got back around midnight, I guess. When we got back to town we found that the Parker house had burned down, and the whole family left. Ol' Milton—he was the daddy—took them all up to Georgia. Some farm up there, they said. It was a long time before I forgave Jeannie Sue," he said, shaking his head.

"Put that dirty ol' stick down, baby," Billy said as he got up and gently took the stick from his little granddaughter. Crystal had managed to get really attached to that old stick and started to pitch a fit when he took it away. But Billy just grabbed her up in one massive arm and swung her up to give her a peck on the cheek as he threw the stick away with the other hand. The little girl squirmed and started to protest, but Billy deftly flipped the child around and grabbed one spindly leg in each of his hands, holding her upside down. She tried to muster some anger, but the fun of it was just too much, and she gave in to the booming laughter above her.

I watched the child reflect her grandfather's absolute love and listened to her shrill giggle—the counterpoint to his booming laughter—and smiled to myself, more than a little envious.

I got up to leave, and Billy flipped the laughing child onto his back.

"You know," he said to me, "sometimes I still think about Jeannie Sue. I hope she found as much joy in life as I have."

"So do I," I told him and took my leave.

CHAPTER 6

O VER THE YEARS I had stopped and stared at that pretty little lot just across the street a couple times as I came out of my office—well, more than a couple times, to be honest. But there was always somewhere I had to go. Someone I had to see. Something I had to do. For a long time it wasn't hard to brush off those disembodied eyes. I don't know what it was that finally forced me to look into them. But once I did, I'd never be able to look away again.

It was dusk, and I was coming out of my office. At the front desk Minnie Bruster was still catching up on her paperwork. Funny how, on the one hand, business thrives on all that paperwork, and on the other hand, it just clogs up the wheels. Anyway, I thank my lucky stars almost daily that Minnie handles all that stuff and not me. Frank was gone already—the stroke of five o'clock, and you can count on Frank Logan to be out the door. I think he must have been a union man in another life. But he's a lot of fun around the office, willing to do anything to help out and one of the best graphics guys we've had, so I guess I can't blame him if he's got a life outside the office.

Maria Toros, the only other full-time employee at the *Independent*, was already on her way to take some quick shots at the Lions baseball game. Maria, bless her, was also our in-house translator.

The growth of the Hispanic population in our little town was amazing. Migrant workers had been coming through, following the crops for years. Now, a lot of them were staying, or the men followed the crops, leaving their families here as a home base. They were changing the face of Oxbow, adding another texture to the culture of this area.

It was after five and I was the last one to leave the office. Once again, I automatically avoided looking at the corner lot. It had been a long day. Well, I guess it just seemed like a long one. As I locked the door, I was thinking about driving the few miles home and heating up last night's meatloaf, then maybe getting in a quick bike ride with Dutch—I had been neglecting the poor dog again—and a nice long soak in the tub …

What was that? I was sure something caught my eye. Just a wisp of smoke, a gossamer tendril among the lavender falling stars. And then there they were again. This time, though, was different.

Those familiar, distorted, opaque masks were back, but somehow more vivid. Almost glowing; flickering shards of light and shadow … almost alive? My first thought was that they were a trick of that late predusk sun splashing gold through the treetops.

Again they drew me, pulled me to that place I had been avoiding. It seemed I could no longer resist. No trick of light and shadow, these shapes had depth, feeling. They were, indeed, faces—eyes, noses, mouths, even hair—each distorted yet distinctive. They were real faces, real people. Fascinated and repulsed at the same time, I had apparently temporarily lost the good sense to be afraid.

It was the one I took to be a young girl that really engaged me first. Dark curls, round face, with the saddest expression I've ever encountered. I could feel the depth of that sadness, and it shook me to my core. She looked to be about thirteen or fourteen, with dark, unfathomable eyes and an unfulfilled promise of womanhood about her. There was a young man. Late teens or twenties, maybe. It was hard to tell. But his eyes were light and did not appear to have the depth of the girl's. His hair looked to be fair.

The woman's face was framed in dark curls that looked somehow wilted, like her expression. It was a face that spoke of hardship. Desperate. Longing. Fearful. There was a plea there that clutched at my heart, but I could not comprehend what was wanted of me.

The man—now he was different. He exuded a kind of ghostly

acid. His hair was light, but it was his eyes that held my attention. Almost seeping with venom, they were. There was a raw anger here and a cold, hard hatred so palpable that I involuntarily took a step backward to distance myself a little. He radiated an overpowering, encompassing hatred, and my ability to feel fear suddenly slammed in on me with a vengeance. I began to panic and to fight back—against what I wasn't really sure. But it was a very real attack, almost physical, and it was with unrestrained relief that I greeted expert whistling as it wafted through the air. "Yes, Sir, That's My Baby." *Bless you, Oliver!*

"Hey, there, Mol'!" his voice called out. I never would have believed those words could've sounded so good. In an instant my faces were gone—so quickly that I was left wondering if they had really been there at all.

I almost ran over to the sidewalk, out from under those grand yet now fearsome trees to meet Oliver. As I listened to his prattle, I couldn't keep from continually glancing back into their branches, reassuring myself that those faces were really gone.

Oliver enlightened me on the gossip of the day. He told me about Sally Bigham's boy, Jodie, wiping out on his motorcycle earlier that day. Seems the young rascal took a turn off the highway too tightly and hit a patch of gravel, right over next to Birchwood's grocery. The bike slid, and it could've been bad, but Jodie took a dive, right into a pleasant little grassy patch. *Nice catch, God,* so he just ended up with a quick trip to the hospital to have his broken leg set.

As grateful as I was for the way Oliver saved me from the awful force that was pulling me into those faces, I was even more thankful when he sent me on my way in a few short minutes, saying I looked a tad peaked, and maybe I should go on home.

So there I was. Finally at home. Safe. But peace eluded me no matter what I tried. My brain refused to settle down.

This was not a night to pass with a steaming cup of Earl Grey. I found a bottle of white wine and poured myself a glass. That always mellowed me out. But not this time. Tonight my brain was working overtime; my heart was pounding, as though I had just run the Boston Marathon. And I couldn't rein either one in. Poor Dutch was aware that something was wrong. He kept trying to climb up onto my lap, but he's way too big for that, so I sat down on the floor with him, one arm around him and the other stroking his head. I'm not sure which one of us I was trying to comfort more.

That's when I decided. The pretending was over. I had to find out about "my" faces. If I was ever to find any peace again, I just had to. But I had no idea where to start.

Well, Molly Martindale, now what? I'm no investigative reporter, just a hometown girl who loves to write and got into the local paper fresh from high school. Sure, I've done this a long time, but where do I start? Think, girl! Where do I start?

Another sip of wine. Then another. Steadier now. *Okay. Let's start with the faces. Well, for starters, they're always right there in the trees on that vacant lot. Okay, that's obvious. There has to be a connection between these faces, these people, and that lot. Obvious conclusion: they lived there. Could these be the Parkers?*

But they went back to Georgia, Miss Jolene told me. Billy Brownly told me the same thing. So it must be another family. Who lived there after the Parkers?

Around and around—all questions, no answers. It was late, and there was no one to talk to about it—even Dutch had curled up on his pillow in the corner, his chest rising and falling with his slow, rhythmic breathing. So eventually I decided to give up for the moment. The wine had started taking some effect, and I wasn't going to unravel this thing that night anyway, so I finally took a steaming shower to clear my head and calm my nerves before crawling into bed. Passing the full-length mirror on the bathroom door, I automatically gave my body a quick glance. My eyes flitted over my backside, noting with dissatisfaction the extra padding it carried. *If I could just get rid of those five extra pounds …* Well, I guess my world was still in some kind of focus, after all.

Still, there was no sleep that night. I dozed off a couple times, but my brain was going in circles like a windup doll and just wouldn't quit. It was a very long night.

CHAPTER 7

THE NEXT DAY, SATURDAY, I was driving past the old icehouse, headed to Birchwood's grocery down the highway. Birchwood's has been the "social center" of Oxbow for as long as anyone can remember. If you need to see somebody in Oxbow, just head over to Birchwood's. It won't be long before they show up.

But I was in no hurry, and there was Franklin out in front of the icehouse with those trademark red suspenders draped over his bony shoulders—just like I'd always seen him since I was a kid.

Franklin Brown was the oldest man in Oxbow, as far as anybody knew. His grandparents had been born into slavery on a plantation in Georgia, and he had been born on that same plantation. As a young man, he came to Florida looking for work. Eventually, he found that work—and a home—in Oxbow. I guess Franklin had done a little bit of everything to keep his family fed and clothed. Mostly he worked construction and, later, he got on at the icehouse, delivering ice all around town.

Franklin still spent a lot of time at the old icehouse, even though it was all but shut down.

He had a soft spot for all the kids in town—always had. And all the kids had a soft spot for Franklin. Kids instinctively know who really cares about them. He always kept an eye on them—us, really. After all, I was one of Franklin's "kids" when I was growing up. Guess I still am. He made sure we were safe and kept us on the straight and narrow. Franklin's father had been a preacher and evidently he had a little of the calling himself. He was a deacon, after all, at his church. Anyway, he loved us and we loved him, and that was good enough.

So naturally I stopped to talk. It had been too long since I took a few minutes to do that. As always, when I pulled up, this old black man, so much a part of everything that was good about this town, smiled and nodded and asked me where I'd been.

"'Bout give up on you, Miss Molly," he said. "Thought you was too busy to come by and see dis ol' man anymore." Franklin knew better, but he always said the same thing, with that familiar smile in his rheumy old eyes. And it always felt like coming home.

So, we sat on a couple old boxes out in front of the doorway, talking about little things, mostly. How's the family … where does all the time go … Franklin had a new great-grandbaby that needed spoiling. He and his wife, Martha, were up to the task.

I was about to head over to Birchwood's when I remembered what Miss Jolene told me.

"Guess the view in front of my office is fixin' to be a whole lot different," I said. Franklin just looked up, surprised. It was hard to surprise Franklin—he'd been around too many years.

"Whatchoo mean?" he asked, as much with his keen old eyes as his voice.

"Well, I hear some talk the St. Claires are going to build an office there for some doctor from West Palm who thinks he wants to spend a little time 'in the country,'" I explained.

"How's Dennis gonna feel 'bout dat?" The words just fell out of his mouth.

"Dennis Blankenship?" I asked. "Why would he care?"

"No reason, I guess," Franklin said. "He jus' spends a lot of time aroun' der is all."

"Well, yes, I guess that's true," I agreed. "Guess he'll have to find another nice resting spot. I know I'm going to miss that pretty little lot." I was coming up to shaky ground now, and I wasn't sure how to proceed. *Admit it, this thing's got you, and you're just going to have to see it through. Nothing to do but plow ahead, Molly.*

"I'm not sure how to say this without really sounding weird, Franklin, but lately that lot's been kind of giving me the creeps." I glanced up at that familiar face, but it was a blank. "I can't say just what it is, but there's something strange there for sure. Something unnatural."

Another glance over at Franklin. He looked away; he couldn't meet my eyes. Franklin knew something. I was sure of it. But he was holding back. Now that had never happened before. Franklin was the most straightforward person I ever met. If you could get it straight from anybody, it was Franklin. And there he was, avoiding me.

He abruptly called an end to our little chat by simply saying, "Sorry, Miss Molly, I gots to go now. I done f'got 'bout a special meetin' over to the church."

More than a little rattled, I said, "Okay, Franklin, we'll talk some more later," but I didn't have much real hope of that ever happening. I knew that when Franklin was done talking, that was it. There was no use trying to push him. So I watched one of my favorite people in the whole world walk away from me. He was favoring his left leg as he had been for the past few years, but it didn't slow him down much.

I didn't like the way this little mystery of mine was going. Phantom faces in that old orchid tree; an "orphaned" family the town wouldn't claim; and now my old friend Franklin leaving me to drown in a nightmare that was sucking me in deeper every day.

CHAPTER 8

Still smarting from Franklin's dismissal, I headed over to Birchwood's. *Well, I still had to eat, didn't I?* They were having a sale on pork roasts, and I wanted to have some kind of choice before they were all picked over.

Back home, as I was cutting the roast to freeze half, I thought again about Franklin's odd reaction to the new doctor's office. What did Dennis have to do with anything? Why would he be concerned one way or the other? There were lots of nice, shady lots in town to enjoy. Made no sense to me. So I made up my mind to ask Dennis about it. Not much point in pursuing it with Franklin; when he wanted to talk, he talked. When he didn't, well, he just didn't. Of course, I didn't hold out much hope for Dennis, either. He wasn't exactly the talkative sort.

It didn't take long before I got my chance. I saw Dennis the very next day.

Sunday. I stopped in at the office to drop off the film from Saturday night's beauty queen contest so that our part-time darkroom man could get an early start in the morning. Every small town has a beauty queen contest, and Oxbow is no exception. Every year ten or eleven of the town's finest young ladies compete for the title of Miss Oxbow, the winner of which presides over the annual Oxbow River Fest. This year the Wetzle girl won the judges' fancy with her enthusiastic patriotic presentation. She was a little heftier than your average festival queen, but she could burn up the tap shoes, all right.

As long as I was in the office, I figured I might as well finish up writing my piece on the 4-H/Future Farmers of America hog and steer show coming up at the fair next month. So, after a half hour or so, I was leaving my office—again—when there he was. Dennis Blankenship. Just sitting there, hunkered down by that grand old oak, Li'l Bit lying on his belly at his master's side, face resting on his delicate paws. It occurred to me with a pang that if they really were going to put in a doctor's office there, somebody might just get the big idea to take out that massive tree, along with that spectacular orchid and the locust tree, to make room for a parking lot. What a shame that would be. Still, I couldn't waste time pondering such possibilities. Dennis had a habit of coming and going without notice. I knew I had to seize the moment.

Crossing the street, I kept scanning the branches overhead for misty visages. But those faces that had so terrified me just days before were nowhere to be seen. There was nothing up there but leaves twisting gently in the soft puffs of occasional breezes and a few squirrels chasing each other, chattering on the long, crooked branches. If the feelings those faces engendered hadn't been so overpowering, I would have been tempted to believe they were just in my imagination. Whatever they were, they didn't seem to have any effect on the squirrels.

"Hey, Dennis," I called as I crossed the street. Li'l Bit cocked his head and wagged his stump of a tail but didn't get up to greet me formally.

"Hey, Molly. Working on Sunday again, I see," he called back.

I leaned over to give the dog's head a few quick scratches. "Oh, yeah. Just dropping off the film from the Miss Oxbow contest from last night. Marcy Wetzle was the judges' choice this year," I informed him. "Turned in one helluva tap dance to 'Boogie Woogie Bugle Boy.'" No response. I guess queen pageants just weren't on Dennis's top ten.

"So, what do you think about the new doctor's office coming in?" I asked.

"What doctor's office?" he wanted to know.

"Some West Palm Beach doctor coming up here to open a practice, I hear, right here on this spot," I said, monitoring his reaction.

No explosion. No wild-eyed protests. Dennis just looked up at me like he was seeing me for the first time. Didn't say a word at first. Then, all he had to say was, "Guess it had to happen some time."

Not knowing what to expect, or just how to approach the subject, I decided just to come right out and ask him what it was about that lot that attracted him.

"Dennis, I've always liked this lot. I don't know, but something about it has always kind of captured my fancy, y'know? The trees, especially that orchid tree when it's in bloom—it's all so pretty, so cozy-looking. I've noticed that you spend a lot of time here on this lot. What makes it special for you?"

There, I had finally just asked the question.

Dennis didn't look at me—hardly a surprise. It's more surprising when he actually does look at me. His troubled eyes just swept through the leafy canopy over our heads, lovingly taking in all the colors and shadows, the ripples produced by a passing breeze. He smiled, then. Now that was a surprise!

"I just feel at home here," was all he said.

And then he left, Li'l Bit bringing up the rear, heading back across River Street into the woods.

Hmm. I don't know what I was expecting, but it wasn't that. I had built the whole thing up in my head so much that I guess I really thought Dennis would blow his top. But why? And then, no reaction at all. Why would Franklin be concerned about Dennis's reaction? Franklin's age must be showing. Or more likely, I was just blowing this whole thing out of proportion. Maybe I needed a vacation ...

"Guess it had to happen some time." Odd words. As though for some reason Dennis really didn't want anything to go up on that lot. I'd been thinking. Franklin was right. Dennis did spend a lot of time around there. In fact, the more I thought about it, the more I realized that I seldom saw Dennis anywhere else—except coming out of his camp in the woods and occasionally at the post office or the bank.

For years, this lot had always seemed so ordinary. Then I noticed those faces, and the place began to make me uncomfortable. I was learning about this lot in bits and pieces. Tiny gulps of information, each whetting my appetite for more. I scanned those moss-covered tree limbs one more time before getting off that property. Now it was beginning to feel downright spooky. And nothing made any sense.

CHAPTER 9

B ACK AT BIRCHWOOD'S. THIS time to replenish my supply of tea. A little yogurt, some veggies. *Don't forget the toilet paper. Dishwashing soap, for sure—been stretching the last few drops about as long as I could—more water than soap now.*

At the checkout counter, Barbara's line was the shortest so I fell in at the end. I should know better—the shortest line always seems to take the longest to get through. That's okay. I always like to chat with Barbara anyway.

"Hi, there, Molly! I guess you been pretty busy with the beauty pageant and all," she began.

"Naturally," I answered and then continued, "Didn't see you at the pageant this year. What happened?" A former Miss Oxbow herself, Barbara rarely missed a pageant.

"Oh, I went up to see my boy in Tennessee. Just got back last night," she replied. "He's getting along good. Job's okay, and the kids are growing so fast!" As usual, she didn't mention her daughter-in-law. Barbara didn't like her much, and her tactic was just to leave well enough alone. I knew better than to ask.

She slid my groceries across the scanner one by one, and I paid the bill. She slipped my items into plastic bags. *Man! whatever happened to paper bags—they were so much easier to handle!* I was just about to say my good-byes and make for the automatic doors with plastic bags dangling from each hand when she said, "Oh, Molly, stop by the house some time. I have something I think might interest you." Then, leaning in closer she said, "How about coming over Saturday afternoon. Mom will be over at Grandma's."

Barbara always had something "that might interest me"—a poem she found or a picture. "Any time is fine," she assured me. Great! I had decided it wasn't the time or place to ask Barbara about Jeannie Sue, but she had just opened the door for me! I'd ask her Saturday.

Barbara lived with her mother. She was twenty years older than me, but we had always hit it off somehow. I guess the first time we really got to know each other, besides living in the same small town, was after I went to work for the paper. It was the early '70s. I was right out of high school. I was living with my great aunt—had been since my folks died when I was thirteen.

My plan after high school was to go to Brinkman Community College, some twenty miles away, but the money just wasn't there. I had submitted some articles to the *Independent* while I was still in school, and the editor at that time offered me a part-time job. I took her up on the offer, and that was the beginning of my career in small-town journalism.

Barbara was divorced. When Barbara's husband unceremoniously dumped her flat with no real means of making a living except cashiering at Birchman's, which hardly paid the bills, she moved back in with Miss Jolene. They were a pair—like two proverbial peas in a pod. They looked alike, and where you saw Miss Jolene, you most generally saw Barbara.

Saturday afternoon, two days after our encounter at Birchwood's checkout register, I knocked on Barbara's door. She and her mother just lived on Baines Street, around the corner from the *Independent*. The comfortable home was built sometime in the '70s and stood in the shade of several of Oxbow's massive oaks. Miss Jolene said it would be her last home. She would leave this world within a few blocks of where she had lived her entire life. She was born in her grandparents' home on River Street. She and her sister started Ruby Mae's Café, named after their mother, just down the block and around the corner from where Miss Jolene and Barbara lived. Her sister, Doris, had been married to Oliver St. Claire, and the St. Claires put up the money for the restaurant. Miss Jolene was the only one of the sisters still alive. The St. Claires now owned half of the restaurant, and Oliver managed the whole thing.

Barbara answered the door quickly at my knock. We exchanged easy greetings and went out to the patio. Was that nervousness in Barbara's manner? That wasn't like her—we'd been friends too long for her to be nervous with me. Another quick glance at Barbara. Yes, she was downright jittery. Strange.

Don't push her, I thought. *Whatever it is, she'll get around to it soon enough.*

So we sat, drinking in the beautiful, early-March afternoon along with our iced tea. A soft breeze wafted the sweet smell of orange blossoms over from Miss Jolene's tree. We were going over all the details of the Miss Oxbow contest, among other things. I filled her in on the costumes, the music, the faux pas—the most entertaining of which was when a particularly enthusiastic kick propelled a contestant's clogging shoe into the audience. But it was obvious that, for once, Barbara's heart wasn't in the contest. After about ten minutes, she looked straight at me and said, mostly to herself, "It's time. Past time. I need to give you something."

I watched my friend as she walked away, wondering just what this was all about. This wasn't like Barbara at all. She returned with a book cradled in her hand. Brown leather. Old and worn. The kind of book that immediately gets a journalist's juices flowing.

Reluctantly she handed it to me—so reluctantly, in fact, that I thought for a moment she would change her mind. Then it was in my hands, and I could almost feel the words inside, straining to get out.

But before I could open it, Barbara took a deep breath. The words came haltingly. "Mom told me you were asking about the Parker family." Silence took her away for a moment. She looked away, through and beyond her mother's orange tree dotted with sweet-smelling blossoms and then dragged her eyes and her mind back forty years—to me, sitting across from her. "I've had this since 1943. It was Jeannie Sue's diary. She asked me to keep it for her because she knew what would happen if her daddy found it. So, I kept it at our house, and whenever she got a chance, she'd write in it there. We were living at Grandma's house there on River Street at the time in the apartment over the store.

45

"Grandma was always fond of Jeannie Sue. She knew she had it tough at home and worked out a deal with her father for Jeannie Sue to come over once a week to help her. Both Jeannie Sue and her mama often helped anybody who needed it. Folks tried to pay what they could. We all knew Hannah and the kids needed the money, what with Mr. Parker being the way he was.

"Grandma paid Jeannie Sue twenty-five cents a week, and she gave it all to her mama. But Grandma always gave Jeannie Sue an extra nickel and told her to keep it for herself. Best of all, Jeannie Sue could spend a couple hours at our place, away from her daddy. She'd help out with whatever Grandma wanted and then we could play, or Jeannie Sue would write in her diary.

"I've kept it all these years. Promised—swore—I'd never let another living soul know about it. I never even looked at it myself. Well, that's not true. A couple years after Jeannie Sue left, I read the first couple pages but felt so guilty I had to stop. It was just too hard. Never had the heart to pick it back up again. Then I just forgot about it, I guess–it's been so long, you know? But when I heard you were asking Mom about the Parker family, I thought maybe you'd like to read it. I think it's probably time somebody did. I know I can't."

I was stunned. Could this really be Jeannie Sue Parker's diary in my hand? And Jeannie Sue was dead—I thought. And a grotesque likeness of her and her family was stalking me. Or maybe she was living, fat and happy, somewhere in Georgia. I just didn't know, and it was driving me nuts.

"Barbara, are you sure?" I heard myself say. My journalist head screamed, *What? Are you crazy? Take the damn thing and run! She gave it to you, didn't she?* But my regular-person head was in charge at the moment, and she just couldn't tread on Jeannie Sue's most intimate secrets and her friendship with Barbara. That part of my head had to know, to feel, it was really the right thing to do.

"Yes," Barbara said. "It feels right. I've known you for a long time now, and I know you'll do what's best with it. For a long time I thought maybe she'd come back for it. You know, after we grew up. But, it's like when they just up and went to Georgia, they took every scrap of their lives with them. Even the memories, seems like. Except I still have mine."

I tried to keep my fingers from squeezing the old diary too tightly, waiting for Barbara to finish her fascinating story. Her eyes were closed now, and she was in another Oxbow, not the one I knew. Her fingers twitched a little as she spoke. She opened her eyes—so much like her mother's—and traced a bird's flight across the cloudless, azure sky.

She told me how their teacher gave Jeannie Sue the diary when school let out for the summer of 1943 and how that simple gesture touched her friend.

"Jeannie Sue didn't have much of a life when she was here, but she was ready to live. Wanted to. Ached to. I've prayed for years that she got her chance. Lately, I've been thinking a lot about her. I don't know what's in there," she indicated the diary, "probably just the dreams of a young girl—but Jeannie Sue was my best friend, and it's about time I did right by her. I can't shake the feeling that, wherever she is, she wants someone to know about her. Somebody besides me."

CHAPTER 10

THIS WAS JUST TOO much. After living in this town all these years I'd learned about a whole family that lived here, and nobody ever talked about them. It was an honest-to-goodness mystery. And now I had Jeannie Sue's diary.

There it was. Just lying there on my kitchen table. A nondescript compilation of cheap leather, binding, and paper. The cover was imprinted with "My Diary" in what once must have been shiny gold-colored lettering. All the way home from Barbara's I couldn't wait to open it and empty the contents of Jeannie Sue's head and heart.

But that wouldn't do. Staring at that book, I knew it was sacred. Whatever was in there summed up Jeannie Sue's short, miserable life in Oxbow. I could feel it. It was all that was left. I said a silent prayer, asking God and Jeannie Sue to forgive me if I was violating something I shouldn't, and gently opened the cover.

❦ ❦ ❦

I put Jeannie Sue's thoughts down. It was hours since I had begun, and I was exhausted. I read and reread entry after entry, immersing myself in Jeannie Sue, in the ache for life that only a teenage girl can feel so cuttingly—reliving my own need as a teenager to experience life. For once I put away my own fears and dove headfirst into Jeannie Sue's. That little girl had poured her whole self into her words, and it would take a while for me to shake the deep melancholy they had put me in.

I'd thought I wanted to know about the Parkers. Now I was afraid I might know too much. There was plenty in those haunting words to give me insight into the Parker family and Jeannie Sue especially. But there was nothing so far between those cracked old covers to give me any idea about my faces or what they might want now.

She had gotten the diary from her teacher—probably the same one Miss Jolene said had praised Jeannie Sue's schoolwork. That was June 1943. She had filled those empty pages with her sadness, her longing, her everyday experiences.

I learned from those cracked pages that the family had a boarder, Charlie Weaver, whom Jeannie Sue and Buddy looked up to as a friend. Hannah and the kids took to him right away. He was kind to them and apparently enjoyed being with them. Hannah especially. He told them he was on his way home after being discharged by the Army. He had hurt his back and sometimes walked with a cane. According to Jeannie Sue, he stayed with them off and on, taking off for days at a time, but always coming back. Very mysterious, or so it seemed to this young girl. Charlie Weaver was good to them—way better than Milton had ever been, so I guess it was natural for the kids, and Hannah too, to be very glad he was there. Besides, his rent money helped put food on the table that their father didn't.

The war provided a sense of dread and even fascination. She wrote about the death of Chick St. Claire and how it affected his father, Anderson, the town's most stalwart citizen, leader of the wealthiest family in town and easily the most celebrated pillar of Oxbow society, even to this day. He was never the same after his son's death.

Chick was Oxbow's first young man to fall in the war, but I know he wasn't the last.

Jeannie Sue's words made it clear that her father wasn't just a drunk. He was a mean drunk. This diary was the only release that little girl had as she experienced the fear and pain of what she heard through her parents' bedroom walls.

At thirteen, this young girl was feeling the first stirrings of what it might mean to be a woman. Frightened yet eager, Jeannie Sue had spilled all those feelings out in ink forty years ago.

And I wasn't finished getting acquainted with my little friend yet. Still, the rest would have to wait. My heart couldn't take anymore.

CHAPTER 11

I WAS IN THE office early Monday morning—couldn't sleep anyway. I couldn't turn off Jeannie Sue's voice—yes, by then I was actually hearing her voice, or at least my brain was hearing the words as much as reading them. I had some feeble hope that maybe I could take some of that mental energy I'd been wrestling with all night and put it toward something useful. God knows I wasn't getting anywhere going over and over those lonely words written by an adolescent girl forty years gone.

It was a typical Monday. Harry, our darkroom guy, came in around eight and started working on the big pile of film Maria and I had stacked up for him. A little guy—wiry, as they say—Harry is one of those people everybody likes. A WWII Navy veteran, he had been a still photographer, mainly on ships throughout the Pacific. That's where he learned his photography and darkroom skills. From Maryland, Harry had been in Florida about fifteen years and in Oxbow for five. A widower whose grown kids live somewhere around Tampa, I think, he always had a story to tell. And he made a really great apple pie.

While Harry was holed up in the darkroom, I forced my mind to stay on task. It worked pretty well too. Before I knew it, Minnie was at her desk, answering the phone and getting last-minute classified ad buyers lined up. It was amazing how every Monday people lined up to get classified ads. You'd think they'd know by now that noon was the deadline for that week's issue. How is it that nobody knows they have something to sell or are looking for something to buy or need somebody to clean out their gutters until right before deadline on Monday?

For that matter, they do the same thing with news. Nobody ever calls and says, "When's the earliest I can bring in something for the paper?" It's always, "When's the latest I can bring something in?"

By noon things were humming along. I was proud of the way I'd mastered my brain, forced it to do my will and concentrate on the newspaper. Still, I was well aware, even as I successfully managed to keep up the mental fence that kept Jeannie Sue safely tucked away in 1943, that if I blinked even once it would all be over. Jeannie Sue would take over again, and my deadline would be shot.

And that's the way the day passed.

Coming out of the office that afternoon, I allowed myself to be drawn across the street. After that experience of a couple weeks ago, feeling an almost physical attack, I promised myself I wouldn't set foot on that place again till it was a doctor's office. But reading Jeannie Sue's diary made the whole place seem more homey. It had always held a kind of fascination for me. Even Hazel Bartlett, my old friend and editor, told me once that she used to sit and stare at that orchid tree, wondering about who had lived there and what kind of people they were.

And now it was becoming more real. In fact, by this time it was uncomfortably real. The light was just about gone now. *That's what I hate about winter—it gets dark so darn early. It feels so good when the time goes back to normal again, and there's actually an evening to enjoy.*

Funny. No creepy feelings this time. No faint, peek-a-boo personalities caught like spiderwebs strung through the branches, just the encroaching darkness, rapidly swallowing up the moss-hung branches, the tang of musty earth cooling after the sun went down.

Maybe reading Jeannie Sue's words was a key. Maybe she needed to be heard. Any doubt that these fragile-looking visages were shadows of the Parker family was fading. It had to be them. But then, why the big mystery? Why didn't anybody just come right out and say the family was dead? And how did they die? The death of an entire family surely would be so traumatic that it would burn itself into the town's memory. And where was the newspaper coverage? I had checked the bound volumes of the *Oxbow Independent* for 1943. There was the loss of Chick St. Claire, a hometown hero felled by the enemy while in service to his country, just as Jeannie Sue had said.

I even extended my search and found Chick's girlfriend, Jenny Patterson's engagement announcement to a George Brenner from Okeechobee later in the year. Now that was a surprise. According to Jeannie Sue's diary, Chick and Jenny were inseparable. Still, it didn't take ol' Jenny long to find a new beau.

But I couldn't find a word about the Parker family leaving town or what had happened to them. Standing under that orchid tree, I knew that was just too curious, so I made up my mind to go through the bound volume for 1943 one more time. The office was empty by now. Even Minnie, who always seemed to stay late, was gone. So I turned around and recrossed the street, unlocked the front door, and let myself back in. I headed to the morgue in the back, where I picked up "1943" and laid it out on Maria's open desk because mine was always too loaded down with papers. *Maybe someday I'll learn to be neater.* Beginning with January, I carefully went through the stories that, by now, were quite familiar to me.

The bound volume of a community newspaper is a kind of living history capturing and preserving forever individual moments in the town's collective life. And here was Oxbow 1943, right in my hands. The echoes of real people's lives. Not fancy or even very special, most of them. Just real. Births and deaths, weddings and engagements. The story of the community and how it evolved into the present.

I read every word. The problem with getting into old newspapers is that they're hard to get back out of. They're captivating. They suck you in. The things you find in an old issue of the paper! So many stories, so much that went on. So many people—some I had read or heard about before. Some I even knew. There were Miss Jolene and her sister—young and fresh and full of possibilities.

A smiling, middle-aged Anderson St. Claire himself stood outside the courthouse, which was only about twenty years old then, buying a war bond. "We must all do our part to support our fighting boys," said Oxbow Mayor Anderson St. Claire. "Buying bonds keeps America strong" was the caption under the picture. I wondered how Anderson felt after he got the telegram about his only son. Did he continue to buy war bonds?

Old *Independent* issues were unique in having quite a few local pictures in them. It was really expensive to do that back then, but the St. Claires liked having local photos in the paper so they bought the *Independent* and published it themselves up through the '40s and part of the '50s, I'm told.

Head over heels into it by this time, I was living 1943 in Oxbow, Florida. Turning to page eight, I started to scan the society page. In the '40s, community newspapers ran whole pages on the comings and goings of townsfolk: such-and-such family entertained friends from Atlanta last weekend; Mr. and Mrs. So-and-So were feted at their twenty-fifth anniversary ...

In an odd way these little tidbits of life are, in themselves, interesting. A trip to the coast or a children's birthday party were real events in the days when there wasn't so much outside home and hearth, pulling people in so many directions. I was halfway down the column: "Mr. and Mrs. R. J. Simmons enjoyed a trip to Arcadia last Sunday visiting family" when there it was. It was so much a part of the entire feeling of the page that, as many times as I had searched before, I had completely missed it.

"Mr. and Mrs. Milton Parker, their son and daughter, moved to Hayworth, Georgia, this past week to take over running the family farm there. Shortly after the family left, an accidental fire broke out, gutting the home."

There it was. A handful of lines that corroborated what Miss Jolene had told me. The family had, indeed, moved to someplace called Hayworth, Georgia, where they were to take over Mr. Parker's old family farm.

It was kind of a letdown.

Well, What did you expect, Molly old girl? I admonished myself. *Have you been looking for a mystery so hard, the truth is too ordinary for you?*

Somewhat deflated, I read through the rest of the year and found nothing more. So I pulled out 1944 and began—I was too hooked not to go just a little further. There had to be more, I thought, knowing how futile it was. If the family was gone, why expect to find anything more in the newspaper about them? But it was an obsession now, and

I kept searching. It was getting later, and I knew that I'd be sorry in the morning—Tuesday was always "crunch day"; putting the paper to bed meant a late night for everybody. But I kept reading. Then, about ten o'clock, I got my reward. A two-inch story at the bottom of page three in the February 20, 1944, edition:

"The Oxbow Fire Department burned down the old Parker house on St. Claire Ave. as a training exercise last Saturday. Mr. Anderson St. Claire, owner of the lot, asked the Fire Chief to burn down the house. An accidental fire that broke out just hours after the renters left the place to move to Georgia had rendered the structure unsafe. Officials said the original fire was probably caused by an oil lamp left burning."

So, there you are. The family moved, a fire gutted the place, and the fire department finished the job. It was as simple as that. And the whole story was so mundane, even in the '40s, that it only rated a total of about three and a half inches in the local paper between the two stories.

At least, that's what my head was telling me. My gut—and my reporter's instincts—were rebelling. They just weren't buying it. The words all made perfect sense, but if the family moved to Georgia, what were my faces? I had come to believe that they represented the Parker family. Who else could they be? Nobody ever lived there before or after them—that much I had gleaned from Miss Jolene.

My faces were too real, too strong. Either I was losing it totally, or there was more to this story. A lot more.

I wouldn't have thought it possible, but while I was scouring the bound volumes, I actually forgot about Jeannie Sue's diary. I guess that's why I'd missed the story before. I finally pulled myself away, and, driving home, I realized that I was famished. And exhausted. I knew I had to give Dutch a little TLC when I got back, but as soon as I walked in my kitchen that night she filled my head. *Jeannie Sue, I thought, did you know they burned down your house? Were you glad to leave Oxbow? Did you find a better life in Hayworth? Or is it all a lie?*

God help me, I just couldn't bring myself to believe that Miss Jolene had ever lied about anything in her whole life. So how could that lady possibly be a party to … to exactly what? I still didn't know that there was even anything to be a party to.

As wired as I was, I knew Jeannie Sue would have to wait a while longer. *I'm coming, Jeannie Sue. It's been forty years. Wait just a little longer, please. I've got to get some food and some sleep. Then I promise I'll start looking for your truth again.*

CHAPTER 12

I F I WASN'T QUITE refreshed the next morning, at least I could function. It was Tuesday—crunch day—and we had to get the paper out. It had to be at the printers at six a.m. Wednesday, so we all just worked till every last picture, every ad, and every story was on its appropriate page. Computers were coming in to make things easier or faster or … something … but we were still stripping in galleys by hand then, long strips of typed stories, waxed on the opposite side, cut and pieced onto grid sheets. The ads were all placed first at the bottoms of the pages, and all the editorial copy wrapped around them. Photos went on the same way. It could be tedious, but the work usually went pretty well.

Most Tuesday nights were full of good-natured jibes. We stopped to eat about ten p.m.—fried chicken; some of the best tasting, crunchiest chicken ever to find its way into a human mouth, grease and all—and banana puddin' from Brown's Fried Chicken down on Baines Street, most Tuesday nights. With luck, we'd be done by midnight.

By the end of the night, I was again surprised to realize that Jeannie Sue had taken a backseat to my immediate needs. Though I was still wound up by the time I got home, I knew better than to get involved in Jeannie Sue's diary—I needed some sleep and that surely wouldn't come if I started another dialogue with her. So I resolved to steep myself in her life again in the morning. We usually took Wednesday morning off anyway; only Minnie was in early to answer the phone and take care of customers, but then she always left early Tuesday evening.

Poor Dutch must have felt like an orphan! He hadn't gotten much attention for days, and I was really feeling guilty. Of course, he had a way of pinning me with those expressive eyes of his, letting me know how hurt he was. *Sorry, boy, I'm afraid you'll have to settle for your supper and a belly rub tonight. I promise I'll do better. Soon. Once I can find my way back from Jeannie Sue and 1943.*

My brain was working long before I became aware of the murky daylight all around me. It was Dutch's low, snarling growl that I think really brought me back. I don't usually dream, or at least I don't usually remember dreaming, but that night something changed.

Faces. So close I could have touched them. But different from my orchid-tree faces—not the smoky, spun-cotton visages tangled among the leaves and orchid blossoms. These were practically flesh and blood faces, so real you could touch them. Achingly real with color and texture, but still not quite clear, slowly moving, changing, their expressions unfathomable. But real though they seemed, there was a coldness about them that plunged me into a frozen hell. I remember trying to speak to them. Knowing I was in a dream, I could hear myself speaking to them, begging for answers. "You are the Parker family. I know that. Milton. Hannah. Buddy. Jeannie Sue. What happened to you? What do want of me?"

It's a good thing I live alone. If there had been anyone else there that morning, they would have had me committed. I came out of the bed not exactly screaming, but for sure not in what anybody would have mistaken for my right state of mind. And cold. So cold. It was a perfectly lovely, mid-March morning in southwest Florida, probably in the seventies, but I bolted upright, clutching my blanket so tightly around me there was a real danger of it ripping.

Dutch finally came out of the corner and jumped up on the bed. For once, I didn't complain. He laid his sixty-pound frame down next to me and put his head in my lap. I half-remember stroking his back and holding on tight as he lay there whining. I don't know how long

I sat there, gulping greedily for every breath of air I could force into my lungs. But I know it was a long time before I could swing my feet to the cold wooden floor and still longer before I could stand. I'd been caught up in Jeannie Sue for weeks, wondering about that innocent child's life, trying to fathom why her spirit was still here after forty years—if, indeed, that's what I had been seeing; searching for some understanding of what happened to her. But it was Milton's face that I couldn't get out of my head that morning. As a spidery wisp clinging to a shadowy limb just a few feet from me, its unspeakable malevolence unnerved me. In the fleshy reality of my dream, its ghastly presence absolutely terrified me.

My feet found my fuzzy pink slippers, but even their familiar warmth didn't begin to staunch the unearthly chill that had taken over my bones. I found my feet unsteady, so I held onto the bed and then the dresser for support, dropped the blanket, and slid my arms through the sleeves of my ratty, old, floor-length robe, tying it tightly around my waist. Then I pulled the comforter off my bed and wrapped myself in it, heading for the living room. Locked in a fetal position, swaddled in my friendly old robe and comforter, I sat on my couch and tried to think clearly.

Okay, Molly, it was a dream. Just a dream, I repeated. "Don't be stupid. That was not just a dream!" I almost cried aloud. So what was it? A warning—"Back off and stay in your own life, you're not wanted here"? A plea? If so, then a plea for what?

Of course, the simple answer was just that I was losing my mind.

My normal head said the latter—and it should be advice well taken, I told myself. Just who do you think you are, meddling in some forty-year-old mystery, anyway? Truth be told, it was all probably easily explained anyway … you're just not smart enough to see it.

But then my reporter's brain would kick in—*okay, Molly, lay it out. First of all, you're either seeing faces up in trees or you're a certified nutcase. So, I guess that's the first thing we have to decide here, old girl. Are those things real? Or do we head for the mental health department this afternoon?*

Couldn't think. Couldn't get warm. So I went out to the kitchen, still wrapped in my comforter, trying to keep my hands steady while I poured water from the purifying pitcher into a nice, big cup. Good. The cup was in the microwave, and I only spilled a sip or two. While it spun around being bombarded with whatever things are bombarded with in a microwave oven, I ignored the spill and pulled a tea bag from the box in the cupboard. English Breakfast Tea—strong and hot. I stirred two teaspoons of sugar into the hot brew and grabbed the biggest caramel roll from the box. Those five pounds I'd been trying so hard to lose be damned—I needed all the comfort food I could get. I stuffed half a roll into my mouth and shuffled out onto my back porch. That was always the place where I could do my best thinking. Wrapped in my comforter, sipping my tea, and chewing away on mouthfuls of roll, I watched a million dollars' worth of sailboat slowly materialize out of the mist rising from the water and silently steal up the river toward Lake Okeechobee. From there its captain would guide her through the Intercoastal Waterway, maybe out to the Atlantic Ocean. The passengers waved—obviously Yankees lounging on deck in their cute little shorts and tank tops. Yes, it was warm out, but not quite that warm. It would be a few weeks before any locals broke out their Bermudas.

I'm sure they thought there was something wrong with me, wrapped up as I was like a mummy sitting in the bright sunshine and mild morning air. And truthfully, I was ready to believe they were right.

I was scared. I didn't know what the devil I was dealing with—or what devil I was dealing with—didn't know how to proceed. I was not, after all, an investigative reporter. Small-town news was my thing. Now here I was, trying to wade through some sort of mystery, the diary of a long-dead teenager my only real guide. *At least, I think she's dead. I believe the whole Parker family is dead. But I don't know that for sure. There are no death records for any of them in Florida; I checked. The family moved to Georgia, so maybe I need to look for death certificates there. But that wouldn't explain those ghastly, contorted faces stalking me from between leaves and orchid blossoms—and now even in my own bed.*

I got up, still swaddled in my cozy little cocoon, brushed the caramel roll crumbs from the table, picked up my teacup, and moved back inside.

Well, I told myself, *for now I know what I need to do.* Building up the courage to open the pages of Jeannie Sue's diary, I busied myself making a whole pot of tea. As it steeped, I watched another craft through my kitchen window, a small cabin cruiser making good speed downriver, this one headed toward the Gulf of Mexico. When the tea was ready, I wrapped a cozy around the pot and placed it, another roll, my cup and spoon, and a bowl of sugar on a tray. I picked the whole thing up and shuffled back out onto the porch, placing the tray and its contents on the table. Then I headed back into the bedroom where I had left the diary and made my way back to the porch with the diary burning my hand.

Ol' Dutch had been following my every step and finally chose a spot next to me on the porch.

Maybe I shouldn't have been reading it in bed, before falling asleep. Perhaps that was it—I had been exhausted and my overworked mind took control, twisting the scant pieces of the puzzle into something grotesque and over-the-top.

Finally, something made sense.

So I sat on my porch a while longer and let the calm return. Dutch busied himself chasing some little critter over by the shed. Listening to the buzz of insects and watching the water flow gently by, I gradually became aware that I was being watched. Not an ominous, unsettling feeling this time—just the unmistakable feel of two eyes trained on my every move.

"Well, Irving! Long time no see!" I said.

Two beady little black eyes remained focused on me while four sets of slender toes tenuously grasped the gently swaying hibiscus branch next to my porch swing.

Irving the chameleon and I were old friends. He lived on my back porch and, as rent, helped keep it clear of less welcome critters— Florida folks understand. I had long since given up wondering if I looked as ugly to him as he did to me, and we had some very lively one-sided conversations.

"So, Irving, what do you think? Have I finally gone round the bend?"

He just stared with his clear, round, onyx eyes. He bobbed his head sagely and expanded the red pouch on his throat several times.

Scientists call this pouch a "dewlap." By expanding it this way, the little critter was either advertising for a girlfriend or warning off an interloper. I wondered which one Irving considered me.

Just then he skittered off after some unseen breakfast item— unseen by humans, anyway. He reappeared, opening and closing his mouth convulsively in what I can only describe as the chameleon version of licking his chops.

Dutch loped back over to me, and we sat there a while longer— Irving, Dutch, and I—congenially enjoying the morning. Then, fortified with pure sugar, strong tea, a pleasant visit with my buddy Irving, and a plausible reason for my hysteria of the morning, I moved inside. I called the office to tell them I wouldn't be in that afternoon and settled onto the living room couch for my date with Jeannie Sue, legs curled under me.

I promised myself not to read too late this time.

Restless. That's what I was. I had spent the day with the Parkers, reading and rereading Jeannie Sue's words. I couldn't read anymore, but I couldn't put Jeannie Sue's diary down, either, so, diary in hand, I walked back outside and stared at the endless water a while longer, as it flowed down the river to the Gulf of Mexico.

Fleetingly I thought about the pile of background material sitting on my desk for a story on drugs. The big-city scourge was creeping into small towns like Oxbow. For days I just kept picking it up and putting it back down again. Couldn't even pretend to get into it. Had to get to it soon, though. Promised myself I'd get a story written about it for the next week. Maybe the week after. Problem was, I just couldn't get the Parkers out of my head. I tried to eat something, but that was a waste, so I just fixed another cup of tea in the kitchen and headed out to the back porch, Dutch at my heels.

A day lavished with the kind of incredible weather folks come to Florida for began to give way to cool darkness. I was actually distracted for a while, watching the sun melt into the river, allowing the gray shadows to take over the world. Like in Hannah's world. But this wasn't the end of beauty; it was just the entrance of a different kind. Soon I was enveloped in the starry painting above me. For a moment—for an hour—I was lost.

Shadows lengthened as darkness took over. The moon was already up, bouncing diamonds off the slow-moving water. Dutch chased something at the river's edge and answered a buddy of his calling from the other side. A gator grunted; a cool breeze wafted orange-blossom perfume my way and kept any pesky mosquitoes at bay. Yes, it was a chamber of commerce night, all right. But my mind was on far less inviting things that were taking over my life.

I was still stunned by what Jeannie Sue had told me. There was so much pain in those yellowed pages. Unwittingly, I had learned about a young girl's ruthless and premature entry into womanhood. This was Hannah's bitter secret—and it was not unlike my own.

Once again, Jeannie Sue's words had been a revelation. *Is everything twisted?* Jeannie Sue had let her feelings and her fears go, bleeding onto those now yellowed pages. This young girl clearly described how her mother desperately tried to protect her from her drunken father and worse; told me about Hannah's family—people Jeannie Sue never knew but who had a huge impact on her young life, which she was just beginning to understand. Hannah's parents—Reverend Samuel Fletcher and his wife Bernice—lived in Georgia. They were fire-and-brimstone, wrath-of-God preachers. They were hard people, and Hannah never talked about them much. When she did, it was clear to that little girl how much it still hurt.

Hannah was an only child, and she used to be deposited at her Uncle Clem and Aunt Sarah's farm in the summer when her folks went out on the road "preachin' the Word."

Jeannie Sue's tight, tentative script seemed emblazoned inside my eyelids. When I closed my eyes I could still see clearly her description of Hannah and her Uncle Clem ...

> His eyes were squeezed and watery and he was gaspin' like a fish outta water. And there was that awful smell ... he held both her hands down with just one of his and ripped her nightgown ... almost gagged when his mouth covered hers then trailed down to her most private parts ... She told me a lot of

other things about what happened, things I don't dare write here. Things that scare me so bad I don't even want to think about them ... Uncle Clem finally got real still—his body weighin' hers down till she could hardly breathe ... the last thing she remembered was the sound of Aunt Sarah's little pink ballerina music box smashin' on the floor ...

Her Aunt Sarah's music box—a gift from Clem while they were courting—had played a tinkling version of "Bicycle Built for Two." It had been one of Aunt Sarah's treasured mementos. Painfully pure and innocent. It was one of the things Hannah looked forward to seeing when she came to stay at the farm.

Jeannie Sue's diary explained even more, unraveling Milton's role in all this. When Hannah came up pregnant, Uncle Clem disavowed any knowledge of what might have happened. Her parents disowned her and virtually sold her off to Milton when he took his father home to Georgia to be buried. Milton married Hannah—took the "sinner" off the hands of her "godly" parents—and the couple returned to Oxbow. Jeannie Sue's words ...

That was how I came to be. It was how Mama and Papa got married. It was how Buddy and me became brother and sister and it was why Mama "owed" Papa. He had made her "respectable" even though he knew she wasn't ...

What kind of woman were you, Hannah, that you could survive the kind of life you had? Pushed aside by parents serving an unfeeling, vengeful god. Raped by an uncle you trusted more than your own father. Given—sold, really—to a man with a soul as cold and hard as your parents?

Jeannie Sue wrote it all down, just the way you told her. Hannah, you lived alone with your secret until you felt your own daughter needed to be protected from the Uncle Clems of this world. I know the toll keeping that kind of secret requires, but telling Jeannie Sue must have been even harder than living with it. What was it you told her? "Jeannie Sue, I've seen the way your papa looks at you sometimes when he's drunk. He's noticin' that you're becomin' a woman. I know you've seen it too. Don't you ever stay in the house alone with him when he's that way. Go to Miss Jolene's—go anywhere—but don't you stay with him!"

Hannah, could I handle your life? I wondered. *How many of us could? Did you keep all that strength when you left this world? Is that you that keeps pushing into my consciousness? If it is, could what your Uncle Clem did to you be the reason you can't cross over the Styx and live happily ever after in a world where you should belong now? Does what happened to you have some connection to me? To Mr. Templeman?*

Uncle Clem. Mr. Templeman. God help me.

I knew this was an avenue I had to go down, though I surely didn't want to. It had been a long time since I thought about Mr. Templeman, and that suited me just fine. I had locked him away for good. Well, that's what I thought, anyway. But Hannah's Uncle Clem had unlocked that door, it seemed, and there he was again. Big as life. Maybe bigger.

Nothing to do but get on with it. This had to run its course, I knew, and so I enjoyed the innocence of the evening for a few more minutes, preparing to live the loss of my own again.

I started where I always did, on the bus trip to Florida after my parents' death …

I had only been gone for about an hour, and I was missing my big brother more than I ever thought I could. Just the day before we had stood in the old cemetery and said good-bye to our parents. It was a small group. Clouds gathered in the western Pennsylvania sky but wouldn't give up their watery drops. The day matched my mood exactly, but my own watery drops spilled quietly down my cheeks. In true brotherly fashion, Paul stayed close to me while a stiff wind whipped around us. Later he helped me pack. We started to talk about what to do with the house but found we couldn't, so we ended up spending our last night in our home playing a halfhearted game of Monopoly. Neither of us could talk about anything we really needed to say. Maybe we didn't really need to say anything, after all. We just played and ignored the fact that life would never be the same again.

Paul had to get back to school in a couple weeks, and I had to get down to Aunt Nell's. Life would go on.

The next morning Paul took me to the bus station and wrestled with Mom's two old suitcases crammed with my stuff. I was scared out of my wits, and I think he was too, but neither of us would say so.

"I love you, Sis," he whispered to me. It was the first time Paul ever told me that.

"I love you, too, Paul." It just felt natural. I could tell he was trying to think of important things to tell me, but either there weren't any, or he just couldn't think of them because neither of us said much.

Finally, the bus driver climbed into his seat and said it was time to go. "It'll all be okay," Paul assured me. "We'll keep in touch, and Aunt Nell will be good to you. Let me know as soon as you get there. You have the number at my dorm."

I just nodded. My voice failed me. One more quick hug, and I clambered aboard my exhaust-belching chariot, finding a window seat next to where Paul was standing on the wet pavement. The bus started moving, and I felt a sudden panic. This was really it! I was leaving my home and my family—which was just Paul now. I knew I had to do it … there just wasn't any other way. But I was quickly learning just what a big baby I really was. I was scared stiff and feeling a little ashamed of it.

As the driver cranked up the bus, Paul evidently thought of one of those important things big brothers are supposed to tell their little sisters, because I heard him shout, "Be good—and don't talk to strangers, Pipsqueak!"

I rolled my eyes but nodded that I understood, just as the bus started to pull away. Sitting on that hard bus seat, I willed myself to feel again the warmth in his arms when he hugged me. I think I was more scared of losing that touch than anything else.

And there I was. Hours later, stunned and too numb to think about how scared I was anymore. I tried to read a magazine Paul bought me before I left but couldn't focus. Tried getting interested in the world outside my window. That didn't work, either, but I kept trying because I just didn't want to think anymore.

I had been sitting alone, but a pleasant-looking, crew-cut man in a blue shirt with button-down collar and dress slacks got on earlier that afternoon and took the seat next to me. I pretended to be asleep for a while, but how long can you do that? Eventually, one of us had to speak, even if I wasn't in the mood for it. He went first. His name was Mr. Templeman, and he was headed all the way down to North Carolina for a job. Minding my manners, I told him my story. Well, just that I was going to Florida to see my aunt. He chatted for a while, and I tried to be polite, but that was all. I went back to the blurred pages in my magazine.

By and by the bus stopped at a station, and most of the passengers got out to stretch. Some got a sandwich out of a not-too-clean-looking vending machine, but I wasn't very hungry. Mostly for something to do, I went over to one of the machines to get a candy bar. I dropped my coins in the slot and made my selection, then waited for my Snickers to drop down to the opening. The coins clattered down, and the candy bar teetered but wouldn't quite fall. It just hung there, defying gravity. Mr. Templeman came by and saw my difficulty. He just winked at me and gave the machine a well-placed kick, sending the candy bar down to the opening. I thanked him and stuck the candy in my pocket for later.

Not long after that, back in the bus, Mr. Templeman and I struck up a conversation. He told me he did magic tricks, and I'm sure I gave him an "oh, yeah?" kind of look—the kind adolescent girls are so good at. He proceeded to pull a quarter from behind my ear, and, for some reason, it struck me funny. I laughed long and hard—mostly a release of nerves, probably. Of course, he laughed too, because, well, when somebody else is laughing, you just can't help but join in.

So he showed me some more dumb tricks, and I was grateful. It was better than staring out the window and trying not to think.

Hours later we pulled up to a grungy old building in a town that seemed to be a carbon copy of all the others we'd been through that day. Another bus station. Out in the street, stark, white lights bathed the dirty sidewalks in a harsh glare. It was late, and we'd have to wait hours for the next bus. Mr. Templeton and I sat on a drab, green, vinyl-covered bench in the equally drab bus station. Just sat there. Neither of us spoke. When I looked around, all the other passengers were gone. The attendant put up a sign saying "Back in 15 Minutes," and we were alone.

A couple minutes passed, and Mr. Templeman got up and went around a corner where a sign over the door indicated where the restrooms and a bank of pay telephones were. After a few minutes I heard him call, "Come over here, Molly. You've got to see this!"

So I went around the corner and through the swinging double doors to see what was so interesting. Immediately hands were grabbing at me, pulling at my clothes. Probing. Slimy lips sucking on mine. My stomach was churning, and my mind froze. What was happening?

I sat on my safe, comfortable back porch and forced myself to remember it all. The black sickness that overcame me. The inability to scream. The knowledge that there was no one there to hear me if I did. The blind confusion and all through it the ugly feeling of my body not belonging to me anymore. The stark coldness of the tile wall seeping into my back. Ripping pain. Mr. Templeman's ragged, rasping breath in my face. His sweat trickling in my hair.

When it was over, Mr. Templeman barely looked at me when he warned me not to tell anyone.

"No tears, now. Don't you try to act like you didn't want this. It's your fault, anyway," he told me in the same tone he might have asked me to pass the salt. "You know it is, so don't be a baby. I'll be gone in a minute, and nobody will ever find me. If you say anything, nobody will believe you anyway. Besides, it was time you learned a few things. You're not a little girl anymore."

Bruised and sick, I sank down to the floor as a cockroach scurried around the corner. When I finally worked up the nerve to look up, Mr. Templeman was gone. All that was left of his presence were the doors swinging back and forth and a blossoming pain inside of me. But the air had an evil, oppressive quality that I hadn't noticed before.

I looked around and the night looked every bit as beautiful as it had before. It just didn't feel that way anymore. I was exhausted. I needed sleep—more than that, I needed rest, the kind that comes when your mind is at peace. *Where was your peace, Hannah? Where is mine?*

I can't keep thinking in circles like this. I have to work in the morning.

I can't let Hannah and Jeannie Sue take over my whole life. Rest. That's what I need, starting right now.

I stood up and took one more long look at the sparkling water drifting past, headed out to the Gulf. "Come on, Dutch!" I hollered, and my good old friend came loping up to me, quite pleased with himself about something. Sometimes I wish that dog could talk.

So I dumped the cold dregs of my tea, left my cup in the sink, and headed for bed. Dutch settled down in his customary spot on the floor at the foot of my bed. I said a silent prayer for an eventless, restful night. If ever there was an evening conducive to it, this was it. The soft, cool breeze breathing jasmine through my window promised it. And I wanted to believe as I drifted off, unprepared for the dream that was forming in my unconscious ...

ぎ   ぎ   ぎ

Soft blues and greens surrounded me. Lighter than air, I was. Floating. Floating. So nice. Such a lovely cool breeze tickling my nose. What's that? Music—soft and lilting notes, melting into one another. Old fashioned. Sweet, innocent, corny. And nice. "Bicycle Built for Two" tinkling all around me. Pretty ballerina floating with me. Gliding together through the soft, mellow tones. "Daisy, Daisy, give me your answer, do ..."

What? What is that? What's happening?

Falling ... slow and easy ... falling ... faster now. No, wait! Explosion in red and orange. Then black. Far away, coming closer ... Red suspenders hanging limp. Pressure ... a face. Contorted and smelling sour. Can't move. Uncle Clem! What are you doing? No!

Hot breath on my face. Mr. Templeman! No, stop!

"I'm half crazy all for the love of you ..."

Another face hovering around me ... hazy, misty. Milky white, lifeless. No, not lifeless ... she moves! Crystal tears flowing from sad, cold eyes. Her eyes ... so bright ... so empty. But how can that be? Hannah? I know that's you. What do you want? I can't hear you! Oh, please, God, I need to understand.

The tile is so cold. The air is so thick. The pain ... it's inside. It's swirling all around. Swirling through me. I can't stay here. I can't get away.

There's something on the ground … You'll Look Sweet Upon the Seat … Delicate pieces. Innocent pieces. Smashed. Oh, no. Oh, God, no. Tiny pink ballerina, what have they done to you?

I woke up with beads of sweat sprinkled on my face. *My God! Let this be over soon!*

I sat up in my bed, hot tears flowing, pushing down the fear and the ache inside. I needed to be with someone. I could only think of Jeannie Sue. Would her innocence save me tonight? Reluctantly, I reached over to my bedside table and picked up her words once again, reaching for the people who had become more real to me than flesh and blood.

CHAPTER 13

I KNEW I WAS going to have a really hard time keeping my mind on newspaper business when I unlocked the front door and found an envelope on the floor. Someone had pushed it through the mail slot. Scooping it up, I walked back to my office where I threw the envelope and my camera bag on the desk and went back to make the coffee—always the primary order of business for the first one to walk in the door.

A few minutes later, settling down to begin the day, I opened the unmarked envelope and pulled out a single sheet of paper revealing a short typed message:

"If you're really interested in the Parkers, come to the park—the path by the river—tonight at eight o'clock."

Hands shaking and heart racing, I read and reread the message. No signature. No way even to guess where it came from, but the implication was clear. Somebody knew what had happened to the Parkers and was willing to talk to me—and whatever it was, it wasn't good. Instinctively, my eyes focused on the lot across the street. A tiny breeze ruffled the leaves on "my" orchid tree, and I scanned the green canopy, searching for ghostly faces. No traces of evil reached out to me, just a pleasant, tree-covered lot that promised nothing more than a cool place to rest.

I felt like the evil that held me hostage was inside of me, teasing me, laughing at me. I gave up my consciousness to it, letting my

71

thoughts run wild. Who could want to talk to me now? And why not talk here? Why did everything involving the Parkers have to be wrapped in secrecy, hidden from the light?

The day was a waste. Even Minnie and Frank kept their distance. By five o'clock I was alone with my dark thoughts. I knew I should eat something—I hadn't touched anything solid since breakfast—but the thought turned my stomach. My mind raced over each member of the Parker family and any connections each might have had with the folks still in town.

Nobody liked Milton. Did somebody want to implicate him in his family's disappearance? That wasn't hard to imagine at all. But why would it be a big secret after all these years? He didn't even have any kin in Oxbow.

Everybody liked Hannah. Did somebody want to give her delayed justice?

Buddy and Jeannie Sue. They were just kids. Could they possibly be responsible for anything?

Then there was the boarder—Charlie Weaver. Now there was a possibility. According to Jeannie Sue, he just showed up at the sawmill one day—one of the few days Milton actually decided to go to work—and came home with Milton. Her diary told me he had been in the Army but was discharged when he hurt his back. He was supposedly on his way back home to "Indiana or Illinois" but apparently wasn't in any hurry.

Quite the mystery man, Charlie was. Other than "Indiana or Illinois," no one seemed to know where he was from or what was keeping him in Florida. He'd pay his rent but go off for days at a time and then come back and remain with the Parkers for weeks.

Strange one, that man. Naturally, Hannah wouldn't let the kids pepper him with personal questions. Perhaps she was just happy to have a nice person in the house who brought in cash regularly.

Having him around must have been a big contrast to living with Milton. How did Jeannie Sue put it?

> I know he knows how Papa treats us all. But he doesn't
> say anything about it. Doesn't even seem to take any
> notice. Maybe he's used to it. Guess he figures it's

none of his business. But he seems to like Mama and us kids. He's nice to us. Even bought Buddy and me a candy bar when he got paid. Papa bought another bottle.

It must have been a revelation to that little girl—a man who could treat her family well. I could read it in her words. She just about worshipped him. The things he did for them were so small, but the contrast to what she was used to amazed her. Her diary laid it out clearly:

> Yesterday Buddy had a birthday—a real birthday! With a present and everything! Imagine that! It was Mr. Weaver who started it, I know. Must have. Mama always bakes us a cake and is extra special nice to us on our birthdays, but this! It had a candle and everything! Buddy and me just stared at each other when we saw it.

Charlie Weaver had given Buddy a radio for his birthday. He brought an old radio to the house and spent weeks with Buddy, teaching him about radios and showing him how to fix it. He even managed to find some vacuum tubes in the middle of the war to get it playing. What a surprise that must have been for Buddy!

The kicker is that Charlie Weaver and Hannah really hit it off, according to Jeannie Sue. What a cruel twist—finally meeting such a nice guy and being stuck with someone like Milton Parker. Could Charlie Weaver have been the instigator of whatever happened?

Captivated as I was with Hannah and Jeannie Sue's secrets, my head still turned to the mystery that had led me to these people. What had happened to the Parker family? Jeannie Sue had opened the door to a lot more than I ever dreamed she could have. I would probably always be choked by our common pain, but her diary did provide one answer—or at least pointed to it.

The *Oxbow Independent* said the Parker family went to Georgia to take up working the family farm. Jeannie Sue herself intimated otherwise. Her father had no interest in the farm and intended to sell it. Surely he didn't suddenly have a change of heart when he went up there—decided he loved the farm life after all. By all accounts the only thing Milton Parker truly loved was his drink. Not the kind of man who heads to the farm to make his living. No, I couldn't believe Milton Parker would take his family to live on any farm anywhere. The end of the story remained a mystery, but apparently somebody knew something. The note proved that.

By seven o'clock I could pace in the office no longer, nor could I pretend actually to be getting any work done. I locked up and walked over to the park.

The path by the river is a lonely place, especially after dark. I watched the molten sun bleed into the river, sending pink and orange ribbons skyward. As the colors faded into gold and gray and then black, small noises crept into my consciousness. Rustling leaves. Tiny feet skittering through the underbrush. A dog howling in the distance. As beautiful as this place was at sunset, the spook factor began to take over after dark. I knew there was nothing to fear, but some primal instinct inside wasn't so sure. Small noises became big reasons for alarm. Silence even more so. Why didn't I think to go home and get Dutch? That would have been the smart thing to do. As usual, the smart thing was the last to occur to me.

Easy, Molly. When was the last time you heard of anything bad happening in this park? Never, right? You're letting your fears run wild. Think, girl! There's nothing here to be afraid of.

A sudden splash in the water just a few feet from me pulled a small cry from my lips, but the sound of my own foolishness called common sense back to the fore. I smiled at my own absurdity, just as an iron arm wrapped around my waist from behind, pulling me against a hard, male body. Another arm came from behind and held mine uselessly at my sides. A familiar whisper in my ear froze my soul.

"Still scared of the bogeyman, Molly? You should be!"

Oh, God, no! Not him! Not now!

"No mangy mutt between us now, is there, Molly?" Greg Richards smirked.

Something perverse in me searched for a quick comeback, but I couldn't even breathe, must less talk. Questions bombarded my brain. What was Greg doing here? What did he want? And most important, how could I get away from him?

"What do you want?" In mortal fear of my life, I was still embarrassed at the pathetic little squeak I managed to force out of my mouth.

Greg chuckled as he twirled me around and pinned me up against the trunk of an ancient oak, its rough bark scratching my skin.

Something in Greg's eyes warned me, but I wasn't fast enough to turn my face away as he crushed his lips down on mine. When he pulled back, his eyes were hard and flushed with perverse hunger. As I struggled, my stomach churned, and my brain went numb, but then he seemed to push any savage desires aside.

"Lucky for you I've got business to attend to." It was more a threat than a reprieve.

"What do you want?" I repeated, trying to keep the panic at bay.

"I understand you're asking about the Parkers."

His answer confused me. Greg's sudden reappearance had sent the entire Parker business totally out of my consciousness. Just seconds before I would never have believed anything could do that.

A groggy "What?" was the best answer I had.

Smiling at the effect his presence had on me, Greg's natural cockiness asserted itself. "Come on, sweet cheeks, concentrate. You've been asking about the Parker family, remember?"

I couldn't get past my confusion, and I knew Greg was loving it. But at that moment, the fear outweighed my frustration. I thought fleetingly about asking him to let me go, but I knew that was useless—and just what he wanted—so I kept my mouth shut. If I just let him talk, maybe he'd give me some information I needed.

"So, what have you found out?" He crushed me a little harder into the tree trunk, and I think I cried out.

Now I was really confused. Greg wanted to know what I knew about the Parkers? I thought I was there to get some answers, not give them.

"I thought … don't you know what happened to them?" I stuttered.

"Some people are a little unhappy about all these questions," Greg said. "You know, you seem to have a real knack for pissing people off, Molly. You really need to get over that, sweet cheeks. It'll be the death of you, yet."

Was that really a threat? Or just more of Greg's posturing? He'd shown me he could be very dangerous, and I wasn't stupid enough to cross him when he was mad. Still, what I needed to know was, how could he be involved in something that had happened forty years ago?

"Of course, your nosiness might just get somebody else hurt," he continued, teasing my neck with the tip of his foul tongue. "By the way, have you seen Franklin lately?"

Franklin? Was he threatening him now?

"Greg, stop that!" I demanded, twisting my head around. "I don't know what you're talking about. I've asked some of the old-timers about the Parkers, yes. Nobody knows anything. Except they were here one day and the next they were gone. The house burned down that night because somebody left an oil lamp burning when they left town. That's it. What business is it of yours, anyway? What do you care?"

"You'd be surprised what I care about, Molly," was his cryptic retort. "Just remember, the Parkers are gone, and some things are best left alone."

A twig snapped a few feet away.

One more grotesque kiss, and he was gone, melted into the blackness.

That was fine with me. I slid down to the ground right there in front of that oak tree, bark scraping my back. I was too relieved to care. He was gone!

And for the time being, that was enough.

I managed to push back any thoughts about Greg till I got home. When Dutch came to greet me, I sank down beside him. Picking up on my emotions, he toned down his usual boisterous welcome and licked my face, placing his big paws on my shoulders. He whined a little, commiserating with me. After his regular patrol around the perimeter of my property, he remained by my side for the rest of the evening, foregoing his usual romp outside.

This Parker mystery had to end. My whole life was being affected—and now Greg was back. For the next week I looked for him everywhere. I even asked Franklin whether he had seen him. Franklin knew everything that went on in Oxbow. I just wished he could tell me about the Parkers, but when I asked he just shut down and wouldn't say anymore than anyone else. Still, if Greg was still around, he'd know about it. I was certain he'd let me know. Franklin had no use for Greg Richards at all.

I couldn't go home without seeing Franklin. He had to know if there was any danger to him. I knew Franklin would be at the church, so I headed over to Oak Park. When I told Franklin about Greg's intimation that something could happen to him, he assured me that there was no danger. Even Franklin said the Parkers were gone … leave it alone … there wasn't anymore to it. Greg was no threat to him, he said, but he warned me to be careful. Franklin was well aware of my history with Greg. He'd always warned me about him; I had been too foolish to listen.

But with everything that was happening—the faces, the dreams, Jeannie Sue's diary, Greg's warnings—I knew I couldn't let go. I had to have a more satisfying answer.

I'd been fighting the idea, but my little reunion with Greg convinced me that the only way I could figure this thing out was to head up to Georgia myself. Check out what had happened to the Parker family farm. See if I could find anybody who knew Hannah or her family.

I surely had time off coming to me. It was late March, and not a lot would be happening until graduation in early June. So I should be able to take a little time off and head up to Georgia. Minnie and Frank and Maria could take care of things till I got back. I was tired of playing peek-a-boo with four filmy strangers. Jeannie Sue's diary held no real answers, and I couldn't have another go-round with Greg. Something about this was very wrong. I needed some answers.

Yep, Molly, old girl, you've got to get yourself up to Georgia.

So, I told everybody at the paper I was going to take a week and head over to the beach, check out the snowbirds and the Gulf. I wasn't ready to tell anybody about my mystery, and I had no other reason to go to Georgia, so the beach was my best cover story. Before leaving I scrambled to get a couple extra stories done; it makes me feel better to know they've got some extra copy to use while I'm away in case things get slow. Anyway, I had the mechanic at the gas station check over my aging Olds; she was good enough for driving around town, but I didn't really trust her on a long trip. When the day came, I threw some clothes in a bag, filled up with a tankful of regular, and headed north out of town to US 27.

CHAPTER 14

I AVOID LONG-DISTANCE DRIVING. It brings back too many bad memories, but this trip was not optional. I had no one to spell me, so I stopped every couple hours or so to work the kink out of my neck and make sure my legs still worked. Consuming large amounts of junk food—mainly in the form of chocolate—and lots of caffeine helped keep me focused on the road, too.

I watched the familiar countryside go by for the first couple hours. Tall pines, oak hammocks, and mounds of palmettos with their spiked fronds—splayed out like green bayonets—sprouting out in all directions, all seemed to glide past my window. Cows meandered through pastures, lazily chewing grass, and the weathered boards of worn but still serviceable cow pens stood waiting till they were needed again. A sprinkling of snow-white egrets—cow birds—flitted among the black Angus cows.

Clean clothes hung on lines, and out of virtually every window at the labor camp near Craven's Point where migrant men lived while they picked the local oranges, tomatoes, and peppers or worked in the cane fields before moving northward to follow the crops.

I could just barely detect the land rising under me through Highlands County—the remnants of ancient Florida's seacoast climbed higher above twentieth-century sea level. Passing over these ancient coastal delineations, I was following the black rubber trails left on the pavement by the braking of countless truckers on the same land that formed the floor over which fantastic creatures of the ancient waters lived out their lives. I always find myself imagining these original Florida natives as I drive up this way. Something about them, and this ancient seashore, seems to stimulate my imagination—or maybe it's my primal memory. *Okay, enough of that, Molly. Another one-sided conversation that's getting way out of control!*

I followed the road northward, past citrus groves and vegetable stands with gaudy signs tempting locals and tourists alike to stop for a refreshing taste of Florida Sunshine—and "take a bag of it home with you," too. From the tank high above the juice plant, Donald Duck waved to passing motorists near Haines City.

And so it continued, past shopping malls and homes, cattle ranges and Florida scrub forests.

I stopped early at a pleasant-looking little mom and pop motel—couldn't tell you just where it was—but the place was clean and the owners pleasant. Next morning I was on the road about seven o'clock. Day Two, and my senses were beginning to get a little dull. Driving and thinking, thinking and driving. Spells of trying hard not to think at all.

CHAPTER 15

EARLY SUNDAY AFTERNOON I pulled into Hayworth. It looked just like every other small Southern town in the '80s—which was pretty much like every small Southern town in the '50s. The world just turns more slowly in small towns.

With no real clue where to start, I spent Sunday driving around awhile, soaking up Hayworth and the surrounding area. I stopped at a little diner for lunch in the middle of town. The Hayworth Diner looked like it had been there since Day One. A worn, gray-green Formica-topped counter fronted by cracked, mismatched vinyl-topped stools lined the front wall with booths along the other walls and tables in the center. Each table had a sugar dispenser, ketchup bottle, salt and pepper shakers, along with a bottle of pepper sauce and a black, two-sided napkin dispenser. A small glass vase with either a yellow or pink plastic tulip was more or less centered on each. A silent jukebox stood in one corner of the room. I could imagine Milton Parker walking through the door and claiming a stool up at the counter. I could even see him flirting with a pretty little waitress—bored to tears and hair all tucked up in a hairnet—telling her all kinds of stories to get her interested. "Come on now, honey, it won't do ya no harm to step out with me a while after ya get off!"

Yup, I could almost hear old Milton laying it on.

That's it. I've got to get this thing figured out and soon. It's beginning to affect my thought processes.

I sat at the counter, ate my hamburger, and chatted with the waitress. Mazie was just seventeen, a cute little light-skinned black girl with her hair neatly twisted up into cornrows. She was pleasant and efficient, deft at handling customers and food-laden plates.

After lunch I opted for a little walk around the town. I knew I had to get serious about my search, but you never know what you might find just looking around. Besides, there wasn't anything else to do. It was Sunday.

I guess I was still dragging a little from my drive. Well, I told you I wasn't much of a long-distance driver, and it was after nine Monday morning by the time I started down to the diner for a little breakfast. The chilly March morning told me I definitely wasn't in Florida anymore. Passing a department store, which I was pleased to see open, I went in to buy a sweater; it was a lot colder here than in Oxbow. I was a lot more comfortable when I went back out to the street and turned into the diner.

Mazie was there again, and I teased her about having slept there. She said no, it just felt like it. She took my order—an English muffin and hot tea—and went on to take care of her other customers. Finishing up, I nodded to Mazie and went through the door, the chilly morning greeting me on the other side.

First stop was the county courthouse, a three-story antebellum affair right on the main thoroughfare. It was just what you'd expect in an old Southern town. Hayworth was chock full of lovely old buildings, including the courthouse.

I had scoped it out when I got to town. A plaque in front announced that it had proudly served the local citizens since before the Civil War. Inside I asked a middle-aged man with sparse red hair and a gangly frame where I might find the real estate records. He fixed me with keen gray eyes, at once pleasant and a little suspicious of this stranger. He was obviously on his way to deliver a stack of papers somewhere, but he stopped and led me to a dusty room on the second floor.

He didn't wait for an answer as he deposited me in front of a tiny, wrinkled lady behind the counter. Already headed back toward the door, he said to the grandmotherly figure, "Miss Mary, could you help this young lady?"

Miss Mary looked up over the top of pearl-rimmed glasses she had surely worn since the '60s and smiled. "What can ah do for you, young lady?" she asked.

"Well, I'm looking for real estate records from 1943. I understand the Parker farm was sold then, but I really don't know anymore than that."

Her brows knitted over lively, blue-gray eyes as she thought for a moment.

"Parker farm?" She was clearly perplexed. "Well, my lands, miss, ah've been here all my life and ah don't recall any Parker farm atall! Are you sure of this?"

I felt my heart practically hit the floor. Could I have driven all this way for nothing? How could she not know about the Parkers? Maybe this perfectly lovely old lady had memory lapses.

"Well, ma'am, I'm not really sure of anything. You see, I'm just driving through here from Florida and a friend of mine asked me to stop and check out a few facts about her family." It was a story I'd been rehearsing on the way up. "You see, the farm had been in her family for years, and she was curious about whatever happened to it."

More than a little unsure of this whole business, Miss Mary led me to a musty room off the main office. It was lined with shelves that were loaded with huge, bound books, each marked with the year its contents covered. Tiny as she was, she deftly stepped up on a small ladder and scoured the shelf.

"Well, ah'm truly sorry, miss, but ah just don't see anything atall for 1943 nor 1944 neither! Let me go check with Mr. Blair. He's the supervisor."

She left me back in the main office and disappeared behind a door marked "Mr. Blair." I didn't even have time to check out the lovely old tile on the wall before she was back.

"Why, miss, ah'm so sorry. Ah just don't know where mah head is these days! Those records used to be kept in the basement, and there was a flood back a few years ago. Some of the records were ruined."

I know the disappointment showed on my face, and Miss Mary seemed genuinely distressed on my behalf.

"These things happen, you know," she commiserated as she patted my hand. "Is there anything else ah can do for you?"

"No, ma'am," I stammered. "I had hoped I could get some information for my friend, that's all. Maybe I can find out somewhere else."

The look on Miss Mary's face told me she doubted it very much, but her lips said, "I hope so" and wished me luck. I packed up my disappointment, and I took my leave.

A short walk took me over to city hall—the next logical starting point, I thought, to ask a few questions. The only person I could find was a young girl, eighteen, maybe twenty, filing her nails. I know it's the classic cliché, but I swear it's the truth—big hair and all. Okay, so there may have been the tiniest bit of jealousy in my attitude. She finally looked up when I spoke.

Hopefully, I launched into my quest. "Morning. I just got into town, and I'm looking for some information about some folks that used to live here. The Parker family had a peanut farm in these parts in the '20s and '30s, and there was a preacher named Sam Fletcher. He was a pastor at a small church. His wife's name was Bernice."

In spite of the caricature I saw when I first walked in, the girl was actually very pleasant. Good Southern upbringing always comes through, though I doubted she could be of much help to me. At least she didn't crack her chewing gum.

"Well, ma'am, ah'm afraid ah don't know nobody that old. Ah wasn't born here, ya know. But ya might wanna talk to somebody at the old folks home. Miss Patrice is real nice—she runs the place—and she might know somebody that can help ya."

So, I thanked the nice girl while she went back to her meticulous nail inspection. I glanced down and tried to hide my own raggedy nails, gnawed down almost to the quick. I had to admit, her nails really did look great.

Following her directions (another point for Nail Girl—she gave great directions), I pulled up in front of an aging but well-kept two-story brick building with a massive magnolia on either side of the walkway. The sign read Belle Wood Nursing Home. It was about eleven a.m. Double doors opened to a spacious waiting area with comfortable chairs and tables arranged for pleasant visiting. Several were occupied by residents and, I presumed, family members. No one was watching the soap opera on the TV in the corner. I was only there long enough to get a quick look around at what seemed to be a nice enough place for senior citizens to live out their days with folks their own age, before a nice-looking, middle-aged woman with bifocals approached. She was wearing a pair of light-blue slacks and printed blouse.

"Hello, I'm the director of Belle Wood. Can ah be of some help to ya?" she smiled. Her accent told me that, if she wasn't a native of Hayworth, she hadn't come from very far. I was encouraged—I needed someone with a long local memory.

Using information Jeannie Sue had supplied, I explained that I was looking for information on the old Parker farm and also on a man and woman who pastored a church there forty years ago. *I might as well go for broke—find out everything I can about Jeannie Sue's and Hannah's world.* She gave me a quizzical look, obviously trying to figure me out, but she kept her curiosity to herself.

"Well," she said, "ah don't know anything about a Parker farm, and there've been a whole lot of churches in this town since the '20s. Most are long gone, though. They were mostly small congregations that died off over the years."

"The pastor's name was Sam Fletcher. His wife's was Bernice," I offered.

"Ah'm sorry, but those names just don't mean a thang to me," she said, managing to look genuinely sorry.

"Do you have any residents who might remember them?" I ventured. After all, they were the ones I really needed to talk to.

"Well, let's see. There's Mr. Harding, but he's not able to communicate very well. Then there's Miss Baldwin. She's eighty-six, bless her heart. A little hard of hearing, but her mind's almost as good as it ever was, 'cept for having a little memory lapse now and again, but then don't we all?" she said, smiling at me. "She's usually in her room taking a nap about now, though, and we always have lunch promptly at noon. We have to keep on a rigid schedule, you see, or these old folks get so confused. Let me just take a look."

When she returned, she said Miss Baldwin was napping after all and asked whether I could come back after lunch. I assured her it was no problem at all.

🍒 🍒 🍒

Okay, more time on my hands. So I headed to the diner and got a ham and cheese sandwich and a Coke to go. *That English muffin didn't stay with me very long.* I found a nice bench in a lovely little park I had seen earlier just down the road from my hotel, across from city hall. I ate my lunch at a little picnic table. With the air still so chilly, I was taking advantage of all the sunshine I could. Then I wandered over to a bench that looked out over a little pond where there must have been fifty ducks quacking and bobbing in the water and, on the ground, waddling from place to place. I watched them scuttle around, mulling over what I should do next. I had saved the crust from my sandwich for the ducks, and once they found out I had lunch, the tussle was on. They scrambled over each other to fight for the crumbs.

When the last of the bread was gone, they hung around—quacking and nibbling—looking for more. I'd never seen ducks do that before; usually, once the food stops, they just turn and waddle their way back to the water.

"I like to watch them too." I turned to see a young man, about thirtyish, pulling up beside me in a wheelchair. He parked the chair and pulled out a bag of popcorn.

"Ah, the hero arrives just in the nick of time!" I laughed. "I just ran out of bread!"

"Well, me and the ducks have a standing date this time of day," the young man said. "That's why they didn't leave you alone once the bread was gone."

Throwing out popcorn, he turned to me and said, "I'm Glenn."

"And I'm Molly," I answered. We left it at that for a while. He offered me some popcorn to throw out to the ducks, and I stayed till the last duck downed the last yellowish puff, talking and laughing with Glenn.

"That was fun," I said. "I haven't done that in years! So, you're here every day at lunchtime?"

"Yes, ma'am. I work just down the street there, at my dad's hardware store during the daytime. At night I'm taking courses at the college. Just two more years, and I'll be an honest-to-goodness lawyer," he said.

"Sounds like a plan!" I said approvingly.

86

Finally convinced that the free lunch was over, the ducks reluctantly waddled back to the pond, and the two of us just watched for a while. A group of them turned on some kind of cue and came straight back to us before changing directions again. Could it be they refused to believe that the goodies were all gone?

Turning his chair around to head back to work, Glenn said, "I'll be here again tomorrow about the same time. Maybe I'll see you then."

"Could be," I said. "My time's pretty flexible, but I'm not sure just where I'll be yet." I stayed a while longer, thinking about this guy Glenn and this little diversion from my quest. I watched the ducks go through their raucous gyrations till it was time to start back over to the Belle Wood Nursing Home and my date with Miss Clara Baldwin.

When I arrived at Belle Wood about two o'clock, I learned that Miss Baldwin was awake. *Yes!* I finally felt as though I might get somewhere with this weird odyssey.

I followed Miss Patrice through the halls, beginning to pick up a little of that chemical odor that always seems to permeate old folks' homes, no matter how nice they are. We stopped at Number 22 on the left, and Miss Patrice preceded me through the door. The room was small but clean and very homey. I had a quick thought that, if I ever got this old, it was the kind of room I'd like to have. *Whoa, now, Molly—let's get a handle on this! It's way too early to be thinking like that!* Silk flowers were on a tiny table next to the bed, and a lively pot of deep-purple and white African violets cheered up the only windowsill in the room. Hand-crocheted doilies and afghans decorated almost every flat surface or chair, and a small radio softly played. I'm a little rusty on my Big Band, but it was a Glenn Miller tune, I think. Yes, it was nice and cozy.

A shriveled, frail-looking elderly woman lay in the bed with her eyes closed. I was afraid she was taking a nap after all, but then she opened her watery, sky-blue eyes and snapped, "Cain't a body get any peace here? My land, I was just tryin' to listen to my music without no interruptions, but I guess nobody cares much what an ol' lady wants. Glenn Miller's my favorite too." *Bingo—nailed that one!*

Miss Patrice patiently introduced me and said I had some questions she "might could answer." So, Miss Baldwin turned her hawkish eyes in my direction—not without some hostility, I thought—and dared me to make the first move.

"Afternoon, Miss Baldwin. I'm sorry to bother you this way, but I've come a long way and hope you can help me with some answers," I said, more than a little flustered at her blatant challenge.

No response. Just a steely glare right through me.

"I'm looking for information about the Parker family. They used to have a peanut farm around here."

There was no response. Apparently, she didn't recognize the Parker family at all.

"You lookin' for information on the Parker farm?" It was almost an accusation.

"Yes, ma'am," I said and filled in a few more details Jeannie Sue had given me in her diary. "Milton Parker had a cousin Junior who worked the farm for a long time. I understand that when Junior died in the '40s, Milton inherited it and brought his family up here from Florida." I finished up with Oxbow's version of the ending.

"Well, missy, ah don' know where yore gettin' your information, but somebody's shore got you mixed up! 'Tweren't no Parker farm round these parts."

So, Molly, what did you expect? You are asking for information from a very old lady in a nursing home.

I plowed ahead anyway.

"Well, ma'am, it was way back in the '40s," I explained. "The Parkers had the farm going way back and ..."

Ms. Baldwin cut me off with steel-like precision.

"What's wrong with yore ears, Missy?" she demanded. "Didn't you hear me? Why are all young people so disrespec'ful these days? Ah said there weren't no Parker farm round here. You think ah'm teched in the haid or somethin'?"

I tried to assure her I thought no such thing, but she cut me off again.

"Look here, girlie, it was never the Parker farm. It was the Whitfield place. Yes, that sorry buzzard Milton Parker inherited the place, but it came down to him through his mama's family, not his daddy's."

I let that information sink in. I was ashamed to say I had just assumed it was the Parker farm. *Molly, you know better than to assume anything. You need to get your head back on your shoulders. This thing's got you all off-kilter.*

I tried to get more on what I now knew was the old Whitfield place but it seemed Clara Baldwin was finished on that subject. I had proved to her I didn't know what I was talking about, and she washed her hands of the whole thing.

But there was still information I craved, so I tried the other angle.

"How about the preacher at a small church here in the late '20s and '30s? I'm not sure what denomination it was, but his name was Sam Fletcher, and his wife's name was Bernice."

Whoa! That was recognition on the old lady's face. I was sure of it.

"Hmph," she said, closing those sky-blue eyes again. "What would a decent body want with them folks? Are you one of them overbearin' holy rollers, too?" There was that accusatory tone again.

"No, ma'am," I quickly answered. "I just have an old friend who is really anxious to know whatever happened to them." Well, it was a very long stretch of the truth, not a real lie, I consoled myself.

"There was somethin' wrong with them folks, I always said. Cain't see how treatin' folks like they did—well, leastways folks who didn't believe same as them—cain't see how they could rightly call themselves Christian. Yes, ah knew them, but ah for shore held no truck with them nor their kind. But my cousin, Grace, she bought the whole story. A real Bible thumper, she was. Still is. Lives with her great-nephew and his wife out on her family farm."

I thought for a moment she fell asleep, then, because she didn't say anymore. I hesitated to wake the old lady, but I was getting closer now, and I could feel it. I sheepishly asked, "Can you tell me the great-nephew's name and where he lives, please?"

"'Course ah can!" she snapped. "Do ya think ah'm senile or somethin'? It's David Livingston. Lives with his wife—can't remember her name, foul little creature, watches David like he was made o' gold or somethin', out on the ol' highway. 'Bout five miles out of town. But if you're thinkin' 'bout headin' over there, don't. It's Monday, and Grace will be at her prayer group."

Heading back out of the Belle Wood Nursing Home, my feet were floating, and my mind was racing. I was finally getting somewhere. Yes, Miss Clara Baldwin was still sharp as a tack, bless 'er heart. I was just hoping her long, clear memory ran in the family and that Cousin Grace shared it.

CHAPTER 16

IT WAS ABOUT THREE o'clock when I left the old folks home. I was hungry, so I picked up a snack at the grocery and an extra in case I got hungry later and headed back to my little hotel room.

While making my tour of the area, I had made a list of the bars in and around Hayworth that looked like they might have been in business in the '40s Well, let's see. By all accounts, Milton spent a lot of time in bars. No doubt that didn't change just because he was up here. So, I wondered if there might be somebody still around from those days, a drinking buddy.

Well, Molly old girl, that's got to be a real long shot. All I have to do is find some old guy who was hell bent on drinking himself half to death forty years ago but hasn't quite made a success of it yet. Shouldn't be any problem a tall. Must be lots of men around here who fit that description. Nothin' to it.

So, naturally the best place to look would be at the bars. Great. My all-time favorite places! Can't think of anything I like better than the smell of beer and the blaring of honky-tonk music.

I decided to take a nap, knowing that I'd have to force myself to go barhopping that night if I wanted to look for someone who might recall Milton Parker, or at least something about his story.

Well, there's no help for it. A girl's gotta do what a girl's gotta do.

That night, I went honky-tonkin'!

91

Tuesday.

My second full day in Hayworth, and it was already encouraging. I started the morning by taking stock of what I'd learned the day before. Nothing on the Parker Farm, except I did know now that it was the old Whitfield place. That had to be a big plus. At least I could ask about the right property! I had more success finding out about Sam and Bernice Fletcher. It wasn't strictly speaking what I came to find out, but who knows what it might have to do with why my faces were so belligerent?

I was still having barroom fatigue, so I decided to walk around town again and see if I could find any local establishments I'd missed on my Sunday walk. Then I'd head back over to the Livingston's farm to talk to Grace in the afternoon. Maybe in the meantime I'd have a revelation. I knew I was procrastinating, but I just couldn't help myself.

Hayworth had the kind of charm that makes people feel at home. I wandered around for a while and then on my way back from admiring the old courthouse, I decided to stop at the Bull's Eye, a decent-looking blue-collar bar just down the street from my hotel. It was a whim, but I thought it might be easier to find and talk to somebody about Milton Parker when the music was a little lower and the drinking a bit slower. Besides, I wasn't really keen on sitting in a strange bar in a strange place all evening again, ducking drunks with stale beer breath and even staler pickup lines.

It was a pleasant enough place inside. The wood floor was swept clean. The wooden tabletops had a high-gloss veneer covering pictures of locals, I assumed, holding up nice catches of fish or wild game they had shot. A glossy-wood bar ran the whole length of one wall, and there were three booths in the back corner. Colorful neon signs did double duty as wall decorations and advertisements. As in most bars, the light was dim. It was just the bartender and me at that time of day, so at least I didn't have to choke on cigarette smoke.

The bartender was a clean-cut man who looked to be in his midthirties. We chatted—probably as much from boredom on his part as the necessity to find information on mine. He had a rural mail route that started early in the mornings and was at the Bull's

Eye in the afternoon to pick up some extra money. I told him my story—the abbreviated version everyone in Hayworth was getting. I was looking for anyone who might remember Milton Parker and gave him a quick rundown: he inherited the family farm that his cousin Edward Whitfield worked till he died in the '40s.

He wasn't sure, but he thought "old man Martin" had bought the place in the '40s. He knew the Martins real well and offered to call out there for me. I was pleasantly surprised that anyone was so ready to help me. I had been afraid that they would clam up when a stranger came in asking foolish questions about long-gone locals.

Hanging up the phone, he said, "Yes, ma'am, the ol' man bought up that farm some time 'round 1943 from a man named Milton Parker, Mrs. Martin said. It was right next to their farm, and Parker was anxious to sell. 'Parently he didn't have much taste for farmin', and he wanted to get what he could fast. She said she'd be glad to talk to ya if ya want to head over there. It's just a few miles out of town."

My heart jumped. In fact, it was racing. Ohmygod! For the second time in two days, I actually hit pay dirt! So I paid for my Coke, got my directions, and thanked the man for all his help.

I drove for what seemed like miles past tractors on either side of the road, moving to and fro along rows of peanuts. After a few wrong turns—my sense of direction never was very good—I headed up the drive to one of those big, old farmhouses that seem to look much the same from one ocean to the other. The house was probably about a hundred years old, I guessed, recently painted, and looked to be very well kept. It was exactly what you'd expect—Norman Rockwell, Georgia-style.

Jean Martin greeted me at the door, her dark-brown hair streaked with gray and tied up neatly in a tight bun at the back of her head, and she didn't hesitate a second to invite me in. The big, old kitchen was sunny and cheerful, with large windows trimmed with yellow daisy-patterned curtains. The coffee pot was on, and the large kitchen table was strewn with papers.

"Sorry 'bout the mess," she apologized. "Ah got to get this church newsletter out by tomorra. Been in charge of it for twenty years now. Never been late once—not even when ah went into the hospital for gall bladder surgery. Help yourself to a cuppa coffee while I sort this stuff," she added.

It was the kind of kitchen you immediately feel at home in. Cozy. Comfortable. A kitchen made so by living.

I found out as we visited that Jean Martin had spent her whole life on a farm. She grew up just on the other side of the county on her parents' place. She milked and fed and tended to the animals, although she didn't go out with the men to tend the fields. When she married Randall Martin, she knew what she was getting into, and she relished it. It was a good match, and the family—and the farm— thrived. The couple had four boys, all strong and healthy and all good farmers. That's why they wanted to buy the old Whitfield place when it was up for sale. With four boys and only one farm—well, it just wasn't going to work, that's all there was to it. They knew they'd need more land some day, so the boys could each have a place. Jean and Randall put up everything they had as collateral. They scrimped and saved for years till they could finally pay off the loan. Now the old Whitfield place was part of the old Martin place.

As it turned out, only three of the Martin boys ever got their own farm. The oldest was killed in Korea. Jean would live out her days on the farm she and Randall had made profitable. When she was gone, the two older boys would split the "big farm." The youngest boy, Sammy, got the old Whitfield place, the smaller of the two farms.

As I settled in with my coffee, and Mrs. Martin sorted her papers, she glanced over at me. Between shuffling papers and licking envelopes, she asked, "Anyways, what was it you wanted to know?"

"Well, ma'am, as I said, I'm just coming through from Florida, and I'd like to find out some information about the old farm for a friend," I told her. *Hope that stuff about weaving tangled webs doesn't apply to little white lies too.* "You see, it used to be in her family and she was just wondering whatever happened to it. She was kin to Milton Parker somehow, and the family lost track of that part of its history."

Her eyes flared a little. "Ought to be dang grateful for it too!" A quick glance at me. "Sorry," she recanted a little, "ah should be more

Christian in my attitude, ah guess, but ah'm afraid ah ain't got nothin' nice to say about Milton Parker. Didn't know him very well myself, y'see, but ah sure remember that scoundrel. We was about the same age, but he lived down in Florida, as you say.

"Anyway, he was a drinker, shore. Come from a right good family, though. His people built up a nice peanut farm just east of this'n here. My granddaddy and his granddaddy started out about the same time, ah reckon. My daddy kep' this here farm agoin', then me and my husband took over and kep' it up. Milton's granddaddy made a good start, my daddy always said. Far as the farm was concerned, that was the Whitfield farm—Milton's mama's fam'ly.

"There was a lotta fam'ly history that you prob'ly don't care about, but eventually when ol' man Whitfield passed on, Milton's Uncle Edward took over the farm and Milton's mother and daddy went on down to Florida. Ah was just a kid, but I remember my daddy talkin' 'bout it. Cecil—Milton's daddy—always had a way with wood. He could build anythin', from a whole house down to a picher frame. That's what he wanted to do, and that's what he was good at, so he went and moved on. Edward's son, Junior—Milton's cousin—took it over after his daddy passed on, but Junior never had no younguns, nobody to pass the farm on to, so Milton ended up with it.

"'Course, Milton had no use for a farm! No, sir. It was plain when he come up here for his inheritance that he had no interest in farmin'. In fact, from what anybody 'round these parts saw, the only thing he was interested in was drinkin'. Ever'body knows he jumped around from one bar to another, tellin' anybody who'd listen what they could do with that there farm. All he wanted to do was sell it and git outta here.

"So, when my Randall heard he wanted to sell—Randall didn't hold with bars and such, but it don't take long for news to get around in a small town—well, there just wasn't no decidin' to it, really. It weren't no secret that we wanted the place. Even talked to Edward an' Junior both about buyin' it once or twice before they passed on."

She kept talking as she collated the newsletter, hand-addressed envelopes, and licked stamps. Jean declined my offer to help, so I just sipped my coffee and listened.

"Anytime you need a refill on that coffee, honey, jus' jump on up and get ya some," Jean invited. "So, as ah was sayin', when Randall come home and tol' me the place was for sale, we started figgerin' on how we could buy it. The war was on, a'course, and things was tight, but we got together with the First Hayworth Bank and worked it all out.

"That's about all there is to tell. We've ran the place ever since and now our boy Sammy's doin' a good job of it, too, even though times is tough." Reflecting for a second, she added wearily, "Seems like times is always tough."

By the time she finished her story, she had a pile of envelopes ready for the mail.

I thanked her for the coffee and the information as I got up to go. She smiled, wiping her hands on her apron and said she'd enjoyed the visit. As I was about to leave, she said in an offhand way, "would you like to see the old Whitfield place?"

"Why, yes, I would," I answered, not knowing exactly what that would accomplish, but feeling that it might at least satisfy my curiosity. "Then I can tell my friend what it looks like now." *It's surprising how easily those little white lies slip out once you get started!*

"Well, honey," she said, "just drive on back out the way you come in and turn right onto the highway, then left when you see a big red barn—it's just a short ways down the road, first barn you come to. Turn in right there. My boy Sammy or his hired man, Luke, one, is usually there this time a' day. If not, they won't be long." She waved from the porch and turned back into her sun-yellow kitchen to finish her newsletters.

As I pulled up, a man with what appeared to be a seventy-year-old face on a forty-year-old body was tinkering with some machinery in the barn. I could see him clearly through the open double doors. I marveled at the disparity between his face and his physique and could only attribute the difference to a lifetime full of healthy outdoor work in all kinds of weather.

When he realized I was there, he got up and walked over to the double barn door where I was standing, wiping his greasy hands on an equally greasy rag.

"Hello, there," he said. "Reckon ah won't shake hands for reasons you can shorely see." A friendly voice went with the friendly smile on his face. "Can ah do somethin' for ya, miss?" he asked.

The scent of grease and hay permeated the air. I introduced myself and told him that Mrs. Martin had sent me over, giving him the same explanation I had given her.

"Well, ah'll be," Luke Bolton said, shaking his head. "Been a long time since ah thought about that man! Come on over thisaway and let's set a spell," he said, opening the door to a small room just off the garage area. The room contained two old easy chairs, a couple small tables, an old refrigerator, an electric box fan, and a heater.

Heading across the room, he flipped a couple "girlie" magazines face down on one of the tables and pulled a beer out of the refrigerator for himself, asking if I'd rather have a "co-cola." Noticing my glance over at the wall, he apologized for the calendar—it went with the magazines. I assured him I wasn't offended; this was, after all, usually the domain of men; who was I to walk in and tell him what kind of reading matter he should have? I accepted the cold drink as he pointed me to the least greasy easy chair.

He tossed his head back and took a long sip before beginning. "Milton Parker. What a piece of work that one was!" He slid his old ball cap back on his head and scratched just above his receding hairline as he spoke. His tone was thoroughly disgusted, but he immediately softened his tone a little. "Sorry about my bluntness," he said, "'specially if he's kin to you, but that's the truth. He was a sorry excuse for a man!"

I assured Luke that this wasn't the first time I'd heard that about Milton Parker. No, I was not kin to him—I just promised a friend of mine, she was kin to him—that I'd find out what I could about the old farm while I was up this way from Florida.

He accepted this explanation and went on. "Ah grew up all 'round Hayworth, neighbors to the Whitfield family the whole time. Least until Junior died, and there was no more family around these parts. Guess you know 'bout the relationship between the Whitfields and the Parkers," he put in.

I assured him that I had been told, although I didn't know it when I arrived in Hayworth.

97

Satisfied that I understood what he was talking about, Luke continued, "When ah was a kid ah used to hire on with Edward Whitfield—you know, Junior's father. Worked right here on this farm ever' summer and weekends most of the rest of the year before graduatin' from high school and doin' a hitch in the army. Come back home and been here ever since.

"This here farm was Junior's life. He didn't have no wife, nor kids. Only kin he had left was Milton, and he was down in Florida. They didn't exactly keep in touch, though. Ah do recall when Cecil, Junior's uncle, that's Milton's father," he explained, "died. They brought him back up here to bury him in the family plot over to the church. Ah recollect my daddy sayin' that Cecil knew he was goin' to his reward and had his funeral all set up—already paid for and everything. Reckon that was a good thing, 'cause with what ah know of Milton, it never woulda happened if Milton had to take care of it. Maybe the old man knew it too—that's why he did it all hisself. He wanted to be buried in the family plot beside his wife. She'd passed on years before, ya know."

"Yes, you're probably right about Mr. Parker taking care of his own arrangements," I agreed, "and I've heard that kind of thing about Milton before," I put in, after a long swig of cold drink.

"Anyways, ah was just a kid then—maybe fifteen years old. All us neighbors come to the funeral. Milton was a little older'n me, about twenty, ah think, and he already had a baby boy. Folks said he'd only been married a year when his wife up and left the both of 'em. Couldn'ta happened too long before the old man died. Ah remember Milton standin' there at the grave as the preacher threw dirt on his daddy's coffin. His face was kinda cold lookin', and he was mighty fidgety—like he couldn't get outta there fast enough. The little feller was a good little handful, as I recall, and Milton more or less ignored him, so some of the women looked after him. One of 'em—ah cain't remember who—kept the youngun with her the whole time Milton was here so's the child would get fed right and all. Milton stayed here at their home place with Junior while the woman took care o' the youngun. Junior and Milton was cousins, y'know."

While Luke talked, I watched his face. It was a strong face and a kindly one too. He uncrossed his rangy legs and went over to the refrigerator for another beer. I declined when he held out another "co-cola," so he returned it to the fridge before coming back over to his armchair, scraping his heavy work boots on the concrete floor as he walked.

That's when Sammy showed up. I expected him to be a little cranky when he saw his hired hand hunkered down in an easy chair with a beer in his hand, just chatting away with a stranger. But he smiled as he entered the room, and nodded to me as he walked over to the fridge and grabbed a cold one for himself.

"What's up?" came the cheerful question. "I see you're in here hubbed up with a lovely lady while I'm out keepin' the farm a'goin'!"

"Well, now, Sammy, I was busy workin' on that ol' tractor there when this little lady just showed up. Now, I had to be neighborly," he grinned. Sammy was a big man, and his answering grin took in the whole room. He, too, looked like he easily fit in his skin. Late fifties, I'd say—healthy, but surprisingly not quite as well built as the older man.

I interrupted this good-natured ribbing when I stood up and offered Sammy Martin my hand, introducing myself the same way I had with Luke.

"Your mama sent 'er over here," Luke explained. "I been tellin' her what little I remember about Milton Parker."

"Milton Parker! Why in tarnation would anybody want to know anything about that son of a bitch!" came his surprised reaction. A quick look at me—"Sorry, miss. It's just that he wasn't somebody most folks round these parts really like to think much about. Hope he's no long lost kin a' yours."

I assured him that he wasn't—I was just on a mission for an old friend.

"No offense, ma'am, but you must have some kinda—uh, unusual friends!" he commented.

"Well, I guess I'll have to let the old man tell you about him—I'm too young to remember back that far, ya know," he said with a wink.

Luke ignored the jibe and continued, "I just been tellin' her what I remember. He stayed on a few more weeks here on the farm with

Junior after Cecil's funeral. I remember Junior bein' ticked off because Milton wouldn't help out at all. Just mooched offa him and stayed out late at night, makin' a big ruckus and wakin' him up when he did finally come in. Junior tol' me he had just about had enough when Milton decided to head on back to Florida, thank the good Lord."

Luke took another swig from his beer and scratched behind one ear before going on.

"Then when Junior hisself passed on, Milton come up to take care of his inheritance. This here farm was all of it—ever'thing Junior had in the world was tied up in this place.

"Same routine … drinkin' and carousin' for weeks. Then one mornin' Milton said he was gonna pick up his boy—one of the local ladies was takin' care of him again—and head over to Preacher Fletcher's. Said he had it all worked out. He was gonna marry the preacher's daughter and be on his way back to Florida by noon. We all knew the girl all her life. A sweet, pretty little thang," Luke recalled, "but she was young—just about my age—so why on earth the preacher was gonna allow her to marry up with a poor excuse for a man like Milton Parker was beyond any of us. 'Specially since they hardly even knew him. Later on there was talk that the girl was in the fam'ly way, and the preacher and his wife were well rid of her. Bad seed, they called her. Nobody ever said it in front of the preacher and his wife, though. Far as ah know, nobody ever even mentioned that little girl again around them. 'Fore long, it was like she never even existed. Funny. Ah forgot all about her myself," Luke mused.

I could hardly believe it! But there it was. Almost exactly as Jeannie Sue wrote it in her diary forty years ago. I asked if either man knew of anybody else I might ask about Milton or maybe the Fletchers. Both men thought hard but drew blanks. Most folks who knew them were gone, they said, and they couldn't come up with any names.

Luke had corroborated Jeannie Sue's diary for me, and I needed time to digest this information. In my head I could see Jeannie Sue's own words in her neatly written, tight, even script:

> That was how I came to be. It was how Mama and
> Papa got married. It was how Buddy and me became

brother and sister and it was why Mama "owed" Papa. He had made her "respectable" even though he knew she wasn't and he made sure she knew the $50 her father gave him for his Christian kindness wasn't nearly enough.

Head whirling, I was about to stand up and take my leave, but Luke had one more bombshell to drop.

"Yup," Luke said shaking his head, "I can still see ol' Milton standin' in front of me and Sammy's daddy. It was early mornin' a few days after he and the missus bought the ol' Whitfield place, and we was out in the barn, jus' lookin' things over real good. Junior always kep' the place up, but he'd been sick a while before he died. Anyways, we was 'bout to head out to the field when there was an almighty ruckus outside. Milton pulled up drunk as a skunk and loud enough to wake the dead, singin' some foul song or other. When me an' Mr. Martin come outta the barn, Milton come unglued—demanded to know what we was doin' on his propudy. Threatenin' to beat us both senseless."

My hand shook just a little, and my heartbeat sped up as I listened to his words. I could feel Jeannie Sue's story coming a little bit clearer.

"Well, ma'am, Mr. Martin didn't waste no time lettin' Milton know that this was his propudy now, the deal was done. Milton had his money and had been out carousin' for days, squanderin' whatever profits he hadn't already wired home. They wasn't no hurry movin' onto the place, ya see, so the Martins let Milton stay on there for a few days after the papers was signed."

Luke smiled at Sammy, then, and said, "Yore daddy'd reached his limit, though. Tol' Milton he could sleep it off oncet more, but that was it. By next mornin' he was to be gone, or he'd be asleepin' at the county jail."

Sammy nodded. "Daddy was a tolerant man, but when he was done, that was it."

"Ol' Milton kep' ajawin', though," Luke continued, "Jus' had to feel like he got the las' word, I guess. Puny little cuss. Anyways, he went on 'bout getting on back to—'scuse me, Miss, but this is what he said—I can still see him all but fallin' on his keester, slurrin' his words and smilin' like a Cheshire cat—'Ya'll kin jus' go ta hell anyhow. I got what I come for. Had me a time, but now I gotta git back to my good-for-nothin' wife and those snot-nose kids. Don' worry none. Ain't nothin' more I want 'round these parts. Once I have me a little shut-eye, I'll jump back in my ol' truck and head back to Florida. Ya'll will never see this ol' boy agin!'

Still shaking his head, Luke stared at his hands and said, more to himself than to me, "I jus' hate to think about that little Hannah tied to that sorry excuse for a man."

I remember walking very carefully back to my car, unsure of every step. My brain was reeling. Hannah and Jeannie Sue were more real than ever, and all I could think of was the secrets they had to live with. When Jeannie Sue became a woman, Hannah had to tell her little thirteen-year-old girl about men and what they could do—told her about what her own uncle had done to her so Jeannie Sue could have what she never did—a chance to protect herself.

I couldn't wait to take my leave of Luke and Sammy.

Back on the road, I headed toward my hotel room. My mind was whirling. So far, everything Jeannie Sue had told me was right on the money. But I still didn't know what had happened to the family.

I had to put Jeannie Sue and Hannah and their pain out of my mind. I was finally making some progress, but I wasn't finished in Hayworth yet. I still had to dig for more, and there was only one way I could think of to do that. I had to go honky-tonkin'. Again.

At eight thirty I was ready, though not looking forward to the evening. Loud drunks and louder music just weren't my cup of tea. Still, it was an avenue I had to check out till it ran dry.

So I spent the next couple of hours perched on a bar stool at a rundown place called Bob's Bar. *Catchy name,* I thought, fending off all manner of come-ons. I counted six offers of drinks and two other offers—one invitation for a "helluva ride" and one to spend the night with "the best damn cowboy you'll ever meet." Nobody wanted to talk about Milton Parker or even seemed to recognize the name.

By eleven o'clock I'd had enough—more than enough. I was

ready to admit defeat, for the night, at least. I dodged one last offer, paid the bartender for the two glasses of wine I'd nursed all evening, and headed back to my room.

I was bushed. I never realized what hard work sitting around in a bar all night really was. Too bad ducking clumsy passes by slobbering drunks didn't count as real exercise. Maybe I'd finally figured out a way to lose those extra five pounds!

I undressed, washed off my makeup and as much of the stale beer smell as I could, and crawled under the cold sheets. Damn, I hate cold sheets!

CHAPTER 17

WEDNESDAY.
I'd sure never make a good barhopper. That night pretty much did me in. It was about ten Wednesday morning when I managed to drag myself out of bed. After a shower I went on down to the Hayworth Diner. It was so late that I opted for tea and toast. I wanted to take my lunch over to the pond a little later. Mazie was there again, and we exchanged a few pleasantries. Things were picking up, though, and she was really hopping. I hoped it would be a good tip day for her.

I sat at a single table in the corner, going over what I had found out—again. Then I frittered away a good half hour on a favorite pastime of mine—people watching.

The locals were a fascinating bunch—an array of retired farmers reliving the old days, store employees hurrying through lunch, shoppers enjoying a leisurely meal. When I wore that out, I let my imagination go ... what would I come up with when I finally got out to the Livingston place? Should I call first? No, I decided, better to just show up; then they'll have to slam the door in my face if they want to get rid of me. If I call, they might balk without my ever having a chance at all.

Just before noon I asked Mazie if they had a loaf of stale bread back in the kitchen. She gave me a quizzical look but went through the door to the kitchen, returning with a half a loaf. Reaching for it,

I asked what the charge was. She just laughed and said no charge—they were fixin' to throw it out anyway. So I paid my bill and headed out to the park, the ducks and, I hoped, a nice visit with Glenn.

It was way before noon when I got to the duck pond. The air was chilly—I kept forgetting I wasn't in Florida anymore! March in Georgia can be pretty nippy, but my new sweater mostly kept the chill from my thin Florida blood.

So I sat on the bench alone just watching the ducks' antics: their placid sailing across the pond and their little squabbles—short bursts of quacking and fluttering that sent the others fleeing for opposite shores. I was fighting the temptation to take a few more licks at what was left of my poor nails and doing a darn poor job of the effort. Maybe I just wasn't made for classy-looking, sleek fingernails.

Of course, I had the stale bread, courtesy of Mazie at the diner, but my little web-footed friends were only mildly interested in my offerings. Watching the ducks for those fifteen minutes untangled some of the uptight neurons in my brain, and I was consciously noticing the difference when Glenn wheeled up next to me.

I was glad to see him, but the ducks went wild—converging on him in one great blur of flapping feathers and ear-splitting quacking. I swear they were scolding him for being late. One even flew up into his lap. He stroked the bird's head as the creature snatched a piece of popcorn from his open palm.

"Hey, there, Wilbur! Don't suppose you're hungry!" Glenn laughed and started throwing popcorn out to Wilbur's buddies. Wilbur decided he could get more popcorn on the ground—or maybe he just liked the competition, the jostling for position; maybe it's a game—so he half-jumped, half-flew down into the middle of the fray.

With the initial excitement over, Glenn continued to throw popcorn but looked over at me. "How long ya been here?" he asked.

"Oh, maybe fifteen, twenty minutes," I answered. Then I complained, "I'm insulted! When I got here those ducks barely noticed me. My bread hardly got any attention at all. I think a couple of them just gulped a few pieces out of courtesy," I pouted.

Apparently that amused Glenn, who was still throwing popcorn, working to keep the undulating, squawking mass around him at bay.

"Don't be insulted," he soothed me. "I'm sure it's nothing personal. It's just that I've been coming here just about every day for three years. They look for me."

"I had no idea ducks were such loyal creatures," I said.

We continued in easy silence for a while. The popcorn ran out—my bread was long gone—and the ducks went on about their business, fanning out across the pond, poking their sleek heads under water and popping back up again.

We chatted about our respective mornings and my disappointing evening while we ate our sandwiches. Glenn crunched on the apple I offered him and then had a grand time telling me about a young woman who needed a "little metal thing that goes in a big metal thing to make a bigger metal thing go. You know, it goes on a whatyamacallit. Everybody's got one!"

I marveled at a hidden talent of Glenn's—he did impressions well enough to be on TV. By the time he was finished, I could see this poor woman trying vainly to make herself understood, and the hardware folks politely straining just as hard to make sense out of her descriptions.

After his performance, we were sharing a good laugh when a medium-sized brindle dog—some unnatural-looking mix—lunged out of nowhere. The ducks scattered, some taking to their wings, some moving their little webbed feet as fast as they could, back to the relative safety of the water. But one little baby duck was trapped between what must have looked to him like a barking, lunging monster and a short brick wall that partitioned off the pond and benches from a picnic area.

Glenn and I moved as one. He immediately rolled his chair up to the excited dog, pushing him away while I grabbed the terrified little duck. I turned my back to the dog, who was trying to get around Glenn, and huddled over the tiny creature. I could feel its little heart pounding and cradled it firmly in both hands.

While I tried to calm the little fellow, Glenn managed to chase off the dog, throwing rocks close enough to scare him off without actually hitting him.

The excitement over, Glenn wheeled his way back, and I handed him the little duck. He sat there, just stroking its feathers for a long time.

"People who don't control their dogs shouldn't be allowed to have them," he finally said. After a while we started talking again as the little duck's heartbeat gradually began to return to its normal rate.

Glenn and I clicked right from the beginning, but it must have been the duck episode that pushed him to take the next step. He took a deep breath and said, "I've been in this chair for ten years—a little souvenir from a sniper attack. Vietnam, '73."

It was almost matter-of-fact, the way he said it, as though he'd practiced till he could get it out smoothly. Only his eyes and his shaking hands betrayed the emotions that had to be ripping him apart.

I was stunned. Stupidly, I just nodded, immediately regretting the "hero" comment I made the first day when he wheeled up. But he didn't flinch; he held my eyes with his.

"Sorry. I didn't really mean to just dump that on you. I don't expect you to know what to say. Nobody ever does. I was in counseling for some time. They told me I need to open up and talk about it. Easy for them to say. They damn sure don't know. Anyway, when I saw you sitting here feeding my ducks, I just felt like I might be able to talk to you." Holding up the terrified little duck he added, "He can't say so, but I think this little fella likes you too."

Starting our conversation anew, I began, "I just came up from Florida for the week. I took a few days vacation and promised a friend that while I was passing through I'd try to find out something about a relative of hers who used to live here. Milton Parker was his name."

"Can't say the name means anything to me," he said.

"It probably wouldn't," I said, "It was a long time ago. His family had a farm here, and Milton sold it in 1943. It's a long story."

"1943? Well, I guess that was a while ago!" Glenn agreed.

"It seems ol' Milton was quite a drinker," I continued.

"Been there, done that," Glenn said shaking his head. "It took me a long time to get past losing the use of my legs. I'm still not really 'past' it—but I'm learnin'," he said with a tentative smile.

It was funny how fast Glenn and I connected. I told him everything I could about Milton, but none of it meant anything to him. His folks had moved to Hayworth when he was a kid, so his family wouldn't have any memories of that time. Still, he promised he'd ask his father about the Parker family when he went back to work.

I told him I thought I'd do some more barhopping at some of the older "establishments" in town, to see whether I could dig anything up that way. He warned me to be careful, saying there were a few roughnecks in town.

"Not everyone's as gentlemanly as I am," he joked. "I'd offer to go with you, but I'm afraid I can't trust myself around liquor. When you're on the wagon, you can't afford to get too close to the edge," he told me.

He wheeled over to the side of the pond and carefully placed the little duck in the water. Immediately all the other ducks moved in to check him out. Within a couple seconds he was back in the thick of the flock, and I couldn't even tell which one he was.

Glenn announced, "I have to get back to the store now. Henry— he works the floor—has a doctor's appointment this afternoon so I have to cover for him." He stopped for a second and then added quickly, as though he had to get it out fast, before he lost his nerve, "But I was thinking maybe you'd like to have a bite of supper with me tonight."

Up till then, I hadn't realized how lonely I was. *How sad is that? Gone from home just a couple days and already I'm lonely!* I realized that, although I see and know a lot of people in Oxbow, I don't really have a lot of close friends. Trying not to sound too eager, I said, "Sure! I saw a nice little pizza place—Marino's, I think—just a couple blocks down from my hotel."

Glenn couldn't look away fast enough for me not to see the stricken look in his eyes. I had no idea what I had said wrong, but it was obvious that I had hurt him somehow. My stomach twisted, and my throat constricted. Awkwardly, I waited.

Glenn recovered quickly and said, "How about you just come on over to the house? Mom's a great cook, and she really loves company."

Seeing that I had doubts about a stranger barging in on his family, he said, "Don't worry. Mom and Dad both are always encouraging me to bring my friends home. Please, I'd really like you to come over. Besides, if I actually bring someone to supper, it'll knock their socks off!"

I was a little reluctant but at the same time glad for the offer. I sure didn't relish the idea of staring at the walls in my room, but I made sure that Glenn would tell his mother beforehand. I didn't want to be that big a surprise. He gave me the address and specific directions to the house and we parted, Glenn wheeling the two blocks back to the store, and me walking on to the *Hayworth Bugle* office.

I hardly knew Glenn, but I knew he was genuine. I knew he was exactly the kind of person he seemed to be. And I knew now that he would be my friend.

A community newspaper is a great place to find out about a town and the people who live there. I introduced myself at the front counter to a pleasant–looking, heavyset woman, telling her I'd like to see their bound volumes for the late 1920s (hoping to find something about the Fletchers) and 1943. I had already checked out the current issue of the *Bugle*, which I found had been in business since 1913.

As always, I lost track of time going through old bound volumes of newspapers. The fact that this was a strange place made no difference at all. I had to keep reminding myself what I was looking for; I always get sucked into the black-and-white realities that lie hidden in old newspapers. They are the keepers of the past—the real day-to-day lives of folks as they struggle to be a part of the larger world. Their stories are lost to the history books, but they are the building blocks of that history, forming the continuum of life from year to year, decade to decade, century to century. And their stories are as interesting to me as all the generals and heads of state history has to offer. Enough of my soapbox.

I did find a couple references to Pastor Fletcher and his church in 1929, Randall Martin working with a high school Victory Garden Club in 1943, and Junior Parker's obituary.

But that was it. Evidently, Milton Parker and his doings were of no interest to the local press.

It was midafternoon when I made it out to the Livingston farm, which provided a great contrast to the Martin place. I pulled up to a weathered old farmhouse and waded through chickens pecking at the ground before I could get to the front door. A woman who looked to be in her early forties came to the screen door in answer to my knock. She was a tall, slender woman with a long, pointy nose. She was wiping her hands on a towel as her suspicious blue eyes peered out from under short salt-and-pepper bangs.

"Hello. My name is Molly Martindale. I'm sorry to bother you, but I'm looking for information on a preacher and his wife who used to live in these parts. Name of Sam and Bernice Fletcher. I talked to Miss Clara Baldwin at Belle Wood Nursing Home. She said her cousin, Grace, had been part of the Fletchers' congregation and that she lives here now with you."

The woman raked me with a suspicious glare, and I knew I wouldn't get inside the door unless I thought fast.

"I've come all the way up from Florida. I promised an old friend I'd find out whatever happened to the Fletchers if I could. She's really anxious to find out about them," I said, trying not to sound like I was pleading. Apparently, it wasn't working, and I was about to be turned away when a dusty pickup truck pulled into the yard, stopping next to my well-worn Oldsmobile. A forty-something man in greasy overalls and a sweat-stained cap with the CAT logo emblazoned on the front got out. When he saw me, he pulled off the cap as he walked up onto the porch, revealing thinning, dark-brown hair. He had a weak chin sporting a bit of scraggly stubble and gray-green eyes that seemed to take in everything about me at once. As he walked, he unzipped his thin, olive-colored jacket revealing a blue-plaid shirt under his worn overalls. His old work boots scraped the wooden porch floor as he walked.

Eyeing me up and down he said, "Marty, who's our guest, here?" There was no missing it. Marty was not happy with my presence and even less happy with any attention this man was showing me.

"This here lady just showed up at the door this minute, David, asking about some old minister and his wife. Says your aunt's supposed to know them," Marty explained. "She was just leavin'."

"Well, now, hold on there! Might just be Aunt Grace'd like to talk to this here lady." Looking at me he said, "Come on in and welcome." He flung the next few words Marty's way, "Go on up and fetch Aunt Grace."

Knowing she was beat, she had to get in one more lick. "David, you know your aunt don't like strangers. 'Sides, she's probly sleepin'," she answered while heading for a stairway at the rear of the living room. David crossed the room and turned down the volume on the big, color TV, muting a pitch by a salesman offering "the best deal anywhere on a used car"—but he didn't turn it off. He invited me to sit down on the couch next to him. I opted for a comfortable-looking armchair halfway across the room.

I was explaining to David that Clara Baldwin had told me that Sam Fletcher had been his great aunt's minister years ago; that I was looking for any information I could get on him and his wife and on Milton Parker, who inherited the old Whitfield place in 1943 but then immediately sold it, according to Jean Martin.

David didn't say a word, but I thought I saw a flicker in his eyes when I mentioned the name Parker. He was just asking me exactly where I was from and what my connection was with these folks when—thankfully—it seemed all hell broke loose upstairs.

A very unladylike stream of words came wafting down the stairs from what had to be a very elderly woman, followed closely by a crash.

"Dammit, ah ain't comin' downstairs to talk to nobody! Why you comin' in my room, disturbin' me, anyway? Cain't a body ever be left in peace aroun' here?"

"Now, Aunt Grace, don't take on so. David wants you to come down and talk to this lady. You been cooped up in your room all day anyway. Do you good to come down for a while," came Marty's voice.

Another string of unbecoming language ensued: "This here is mah sumbichin' house. Ya'll are jes' sittin' here, waitin' fer me to go to my glory so's ya'll kin steal it—probly sell it and make a fortune on yore ol' great-uncle's bones. Damn vultures, that's what ya'll are! Don't think ah don' know it! Helluva thang when yore own flesh and blood just circle yore carcass afore yore even dead! You and David both can rot in hell, far as ah'm concerned! Nobody 'round here gives a damn 'bout a pore ol' lady anyway." Followed by "If mah sorry, good-for-nothin' nephew wants me to come down, why ain't he the one come up after me? Git your hands off me, girl, ah can do it! Ah may be ol' but ah can still do for mahsef!"

Then, at the top of the stairs Marty appeared, trying vainly to assist the old lady down the stairs. Grace Livingston, however, would have none of it. It was painstakingly slow, but she took every step on her own. Then she settled her slight weight onto a walker placed at the foot of the stairs. The physical resemblance to her cousin was obvious—and she had the same feisty attitude as Miss Baldwin.

Looking directly at me, she said, indicating the walker, "Ah don't really need this danged thang. David thinks ah do so ah humor him." It was hard to imagine Grace Livingston humoring anybody.

She lurched into the room, stopping at a rocker over by the couch. David sent Marty into the kitchen for some lemonade for their guest and she grudgingly went, but not before she sent me a scathing look.

The old lady eyed me much the same way her great-nephew's wife did—with unapologetic suspicion. "Well, young lady, ya got me down here. Now whadayawant? Make it snappy, girl. Old ladies don't have much time left."

This sure didn't look very promising. The only one in this house with any inclination to talk to me was David—and that prospect was anything but appealing. *Well, Molly, nothing to do here but go for it.* So I took a deep breath and jumped.

"Nice to meet you, Miss Livingston. My name is Molly Martindale. I came up here from Florida looking for information on a family named Parker."

The old lady just glared. Obviously she wasn't going to budge on that one. So I went for the gold. What other choice was there?

"And I also want to know about a Pastor Sam Fletcher and his wife, Bernice," I continued. Hannah's secret had become as important to me as the whole Parker family. It seemed secrets were ingrained in this family.

This time the light bulb went on, and the light was almost blinding. Grace Livingston changed from crotchety to mellow before I could so much as blink. From the corner of my eye, I saw that David was also surprised by her reaction. We both leaned a little closer to her, as Marty placed glasses of iced lemonade on what had to be a family heirloom coffee table, coasters protecting the well-cared-for cherry finish. The beautiful piece of furniture was in stark contrast to just about everything else in the room. Everything was tidy, but the furniture had seen better days. Marty sat down on the couch next to David, obviously protecting her territory from a possible interloper.

"The Fletchers," Miss Livingston breathed reverently, her gray-blue eyes awed. You could actually see the years melt away from her, as fond recollections gathered in her heart.

Then came the thunder. "Hallelujah!" We all jumped as she shouted much louder than any of us thought a ninety-year-old lady could. "Sam Fletcher! Now, there was a preacher! None of this mealy-mouthed stuff you hear nowadays, no sir. That man knew how to get a crowd on its feet a'shoutin' and a'prayin', givin' the ol' devil hisself what fer!

"Ah remember once, it was at a big revival. Ah musta been oh, 'bout seventeen. There was all kinds of preachin' and singin' and poetry readin'. Even a medicine show—'course us church folks wouldn't have nothin' to do with that sort of bidness."

To David, she said, "It was the summer yore great uncle finally ast me to marry him. Took him long enough!" she snorted. "Thought he was agonna swaller his tongue afore he got it out!"

Remembering her real subject, she continued, "Oh, but Pastor Fletcher could put the fire in his preachin'! He made you feel Satan's fire, that's for shore.

"I remember one time when Pastor Fletcher was really agoin' at it. It was a hot summer day, sun beatin' down like hellfire itself, and the revival tent was set up out on the edge of town. Me and my mister was there like always. We always hepped to put up the tent and all—that's how we got to know each other. All day long, startin' from early mornin', folks kept streamin' in. They come in from towns all around here, and farms. Oh, Lordy, but the preachers was fired up that day!" She paused, gathering memories and strength.

"Then it was Pastor Fletcher's turn, and he went at it with a vengeance. I can still hear him—'The ol' devil's acomin'!' he tol' us, apointin' his finger at us all, jus' like this." She mimicked the old preacher's style, jabbing her index finger at me. 'He's acomin' fer yer immortal soul, and he's a tricky one. He's got tricks everywhere, just awaitin' to trip you up and snatch yore soul! Yes, brothers and sisters, repent now. Give up yore wickedness and the ways of the world. Take on the Lord. He'll help ya'll fight off the devil!'" She stabbed at us with one bony finger as the words spilled out of her mouth, and her eyes focused on a scene some sixty years gone.

"Ah was right there, right up front and saw him look right at old Mrs. James. He had deep set brown eyes that just glowed with the Lord's light when he set to preachin' and dark-brown curls that flew around his head when he really got to goin'. And when he talked about sin and the devil, those brown eyes could see right through to yore soul," she warned, poking that bony finger right at me again. "Ol' Miss James got so excited that day she fell right outta her wheelchair! Took three growed men sweatin' in the heat to lift 'er back in, what with her acryin' and ascreamin' how she wasn't deservin' o' the Lord. Mrs. James was a hefty one, ya see. Yes, ma'm, fire and brimstone. Pastor Fletcher knew what that was all about, all right."

The old lady kept spilling memories out like a rusty old pump that somebody finally got primed. It was fascinating, but I was afraid she might wear out before I got what I came for. So when she stopped to catch her breath, wheezing as she fanned herself with a magazine, I asked, "Miss Livingston, do you remember their daughter?"

Her eyes turned cold again, and she stabbed me with them, but then the fire was back, and her voice got even stronger.

"Ah was a young mother then. It was before we bought this here farm. My Harold—your great-uncle, David—ran the hardware store for Mr. Custis and did odd jobs for lots of folks around town. Pastor Fletcher included. We was faithful members of his congregation. When Pastor Fletcher was just a youngun, he had a vision, see. He tol' us all about it. He saw the Lord in all His glory, jus' like he was asettin' in front of him. An' He tol' Pastor Fletcher to start a church. He didn't need no special books to know the way Home, the Lord tol' him. Jus' read the Bible—it's all in there. Preachin' the Bible, Jesus said, is all there is to it. Yessir, that's jus' the way it was too. It took a few years, but Pastor Fletcher and his wife, they done it. The Hayworth Holy Jesus Church, that's what they called it. A few of us started meetin' regular at their place. After a while they was jus' too many of us, and we built us a church with our own hands. Didn't need no fancy stained-glass windows or nuthin'. We had Pastor Fletcher to preach us right up to Heaven, we did.

"Truth be told, it was jus' a tiny buildin', but there was some mighty powerful preachin' there. The Fletchers did a lot of travelin', did a lot of revivals and such."

I had to get her back on track. "Miss Livingston, do you know anything about their daughter?" I asked again. Well, it was now or never.

"You got some nerve, young lady, comin' here and astin' about that little tramp. Yes, ah know about her, all right! She was the shame of her blessed mama and daddy. Little hussy, she was. We all knew about her, a' course, but nobody ever brought her up to that godly preacher and his wife. I'll tell you jus' how good those folks was— even though she got herself in the fam'ly way, and her nothin' but fourteen or fifteen years old, they married her off to that Parker boy you ast about before. He weren't much, but a darn sight better'n she deserved! The Fletchers never talked about her again. She was dead to them. Turned her back on her upbringin' and the Lord, so you couldn't expect God fearin' folks to put up with the likes a' her."

I was stunned. The old lady gave me a lot more than I ever expected to get. My mind was racing. So I said my good-byes. Grace Livingston ignored me and Marty Livingston glared, but that was fine. I just wanted to get out of there and somewhere where I could digest all this.

I picked my way back through the chickens, opened my car door, slid the key in and turned the ignition, anxious to head out.

Dead.

Damn! I don't believe this! I thought, slamming the palm of my hand down on the steering wheel. I tried again. Still nothing. The motor just wouldn't cooperate.

David Livingston came out, the screen door slamming behind him.

"Problem, eh, Miss?" His voice turned slithery.

Great. Just what I needed, I thought. Stuck out in the boonies with a hick Romeo and a dead car.

By then, Marty was beside her husband, giving me that unmistakable "hands off my man" look. *No problem, Marty, he's all yours.*

"Ah'll just check under your hood," David said with what he

must've thought a seductive wink. "When ah say so, hit the ignition again," he instructed. We tried several more times, but it was no use.

"This thing's been working fine," I said. "What could've happened?"

"Well, it happens that way with complicated machinery sometimes. Don't you worry, Miss, ah'll have you back on the road in a jiffy," David told me, and he fiddled under the hood for a while. I got out and spent a very uncomfortable fifteen minutes or so being completely ignored by Marty, except for a few suspicious glances trained in my direction.

When he finally came out from under the hood, David's voice had a decidedly cheery note in it when he said we'd have to run into town in his pickup to get a rotor. Don't ask me. It's a little thingy that makes the motor go, that's all I know.

"Come on now, Miss, we'd better get started," he said with a leer. "Ah can install it when we get back. You know, when you live on a farm, a man's gotta know a lot about machinery."

Fighting panic at the thought of a long drive into town and back with Mr. Seductive—five minutes alone with that joker would be way too long—I racked my brain for any other possible way to get my car started.

"I have AAA," I began. "If I can just use your phone, they'll come out and tow me in to a garage. I don't want to put you folks out."

Obviously that plan had Marty's vote, but David wouldn't hear of it.

"Now, don't you worry, Miss. It'll take hours for AAA to get here, and it won't be but a jiffy for me to do it," David said.

Searching for any other solution, I said, "I won't be any good picking out rotors. How about if I just give you the money and wait here till you get back? It'll be faster that way. Are you sure we couldn't just get a mechanic to come out here? This is so much trouble for you." *Mental note: make sure I never, ever let my AAA membership lapse!* Marty was quick to agree. I have a feeling it would be one of the few things we could ever agree on.

"Why, ah wouldn't think of it. You just come along so's we can make sure you know what you're getting. Won't be no bother, a tall," he said.

Promising myself I'd learn more about engines, I reluctantly agreed, since I could come up with no other solution. I climbed up into the cracked vinyl seat on the passenger's side of his well-used pickup as David jumped in behind the steering wheel. Like a shot, Marty was at his window reminding him that supper would be at five o'clock sharp. "And you know how your aunt gets if meals aren't on time," she warned him, but she was looking at me.

"Don't you worry, woman," he said, "we'll take care o' our bidness and be back in plenty o' time."

"It's 3:30 now!" she hollered as we backed up. Mentally figuring ways to keep this trip from getting out of hand, I calculated that it took about twenty minutes to get to town. Twenty in, twenty back, ten in the store, thirty minutes to install the whichamajigget. That's eighty minutes. We had ninety minutes till five o'clock. And it gets dark early too. With a little luck, there wouldn't be enough time for David Livingston to get too amorous. Especially if I could drag things out at the store a little.

The ride into town started off with a bang. No sooner had we turned the corner onto the highway than David reached over and patted the seat next to him.

"You kin move on over a little closer, ya know. Ah won't bite," he said.

Thinking a bite from David Livingston would probably be preferable to whatever was going on in his head, I answered, "That's all right. You just keep driving. I really need to get back on the road home this afternoon." Okay, so that last part was an out-and-out lie, but I was ready to use any excuse to get my car fixed and this trip over with.

I was pleasantly surprised when he left it at that and drove straight to Lou's Auto Repair Shop. Maybe he was more concerned about what Marty would say when we got back than he let on.

Half garage and half parts store, Lou's looked to be about thirty years old—with some of the original stock still on the shelves— original dust too.

David walked on up to a man in overalls who looked to be just about retirement age. He had his silver hairs stretched to their limit in a long comb-over, covering a large bald spot. His palsied hands shook just a little, making his magazine page flutter. He stood up slowly and painfully and reached out a big hand to me.

"This here's Judge Cain. He ain't no real judge, it's just a nickname-like," he told me. Looking at the "Judge," he said, "This little lady's been over to the farm. Come up all the way from Florida to talk to Aunt Grace 'bout some ol' Pastor Fletcher in these parts. Imagine that! She also wanted to know about a Milton Parker, used to have a fam'ly farm down the road a ways," he informed him.

Glancing at me with newfound curiosity, the Judge blurted out, "Well, ah'll be dogged! Ah ain't heard tell o' neither o' them for a coon's age!"

"Whatever she needs, just go on back in the storeroom and find it," the Judge said to David, "Ah'd like to talk to this here lady a minute."

David went on back into the storeroom himself, and I could hear him rummaging around back there.

The Judge turned to me and said, "Pastor Fletcher! Who'da thought his name would ever come up agin! Shoot, must be forty-fifty years since I even thought about him! He kin o' yourn?"

I told him the usual story—no, just seeking information for a friend.

"Well, I gotta tell you that ah didn't much care for that man nor his wife, neither. They was the kind that give religion a bad name, in my estimation. They pastored a little church over yonder on Mills Street. Buildin's been gone for years. Some other church took the buildin' over in the '50s. They tore it down sometime in the '70s, I reckon, and put up a convenience store there now. If ya ast me, it's a lot more useful," he said.

I nodded my sympathy.

"Guess you kin tell I wasn't a fan a' the Fletchers. They wasn't my idea of good ministers o' the Lord—all that hellfire and threatenin' folks with damnation if they didn't see God their way. No, ma'am, not my cup of tea. My folks was always reg'lar churchgoers. Sunday was a day of rest, yes ma'am. Some folks, like the Fletchers, say you gotta go Wednesday nights too. Well, ah used to like to do a little fishin' on Wednesday evenin's. Ah was 'bout ten, ya see, and me and my buddies would meet down by the ol' bridge Wednesday evenin's.

Weren't doin' nobody no harm, but Pastor Fletcher would always stop me as ah walked past the church, headin' on down to the creek with my fishin' pole. Threatened me with all manner of damnation because ah'd rather go fishin' than to church."

"Sounds like Pastor Fletcher had it in for you," I said.

Shaking his head at the memory, he added, "He'd corner me ever' time! I even tried different routes, but it was like he was lookin' 'specially fer me, and he found me, too, near ever' time, till ah finally told him what he could do. Shocked him, it did, but ah didn't care. He tol' my daddy what I said, and even that didn't bother me. It was worth the whoopin'! Daddy didn't much like the Fletchers' church ideas neither, but he wouldn't allow no back talkin' to an adult, 'specially a preacher.

"Yep, that was a long time ago, all right! You say a friend of yours knew the Fletchers?" he asked.

"Well, yes. When I said I was headed through here she asked me to find out what I could about them," I explained. "Milton Parker too."

"Oh, yeah, Milton Parker," he repeated. "Another winner. Your friends sure can pick 'em. Don't rightly know how it all happened, but Milton married the Fletchers' daughter—can't recollect her name, but she was no doubt one of the purdiest little thangs I ever saw. That was a real strange situation. Most folks around here don't have nothin' good to say 'bout her either, but I remember her as a nice little gal. Kind of quiet."

David came back with the rotor, and I paid Judge Cain.

"Nice to meet you, ma'am," Judge said as we left, "and thanks for the conversation."

Fortunately, the return trip was only slightly more painful than the trip in. David made a few clumsy moves, which I adeptly foiled, and I kept the focus of the conversation on his aunt and Marty. That seemed to work—with all his macho posturing, I think ol' David was more henpecked than he let on. The David Livingstons of this world never appealed to me much, but in this case it worked out just perfectly, and I thanked my lucky stars for overbearing women. As I finally drove out to the highway, I also made a mental note to talk to my mechanic when I got back to Oxbow.

In spite of the little side tour with David Livingston, I was glad I had gotten to talk to Judge Cain. His "testimony" made me a lot more comfortable. Once again, Jeannie Sue was dead-on. Hannah's parents had been ultrafundamentalist preachers. Grace Livingston and Judge Cain underscored that. Jeannie Sue's words about her mother chilled me to the bone:

There was an awful lot of God in her own house, but no joy, Mama told me, and I could see that the pain was still there.

CHAPTER 18

I T WAS TIME TO get ready to head over to the Morrisons. Even at home my wardrobe was hardly exciting. But I pulled what I deemed to be my best choice out of the closet, an aqua-colored slacks suit that everyone said brought out my eyes. I did what I could to smooth out any wrinkles. I showered and washed my thick mop of chestnut hair, blowing it dry. Peering into the full-length mirror on the bathroom door, I turned around slowly, taking a critical look at what God gave me and what I'd added to it. *Damn, one of these days I've just got to lose five pounds* I told myself—again—as my eyes rested on my backside. Glancing over my shoulder into the mirror, I looked into my own eyes. *Why should that be so damn hard, anyway?*

A quick look at my watch on the counter, and I knew I'd better get moving. Bellyaching about those five pounds would just have to wait. So I did my best to comb out my mop of shoulder-length chestnut-colored hair. It was streaked with highlights from the sun—well, at least it's nice and shiny—and I always thought it was my best feature. I applied a little mascara to my stubby eyelashes and was ready to get dressed.

By the time I was finished, it was 6:15. Glenn had said 6:30 sharp. So, I took the little scrap of paper on which he had written the address and directions and went out to my car. I had remembered to gas up when I got back from the Livingston place, so I headed right out to the Morrisons. In just about five minutes, I pulled up in front of a nicely kept, red-brick ranch house with a wheelchair ramp leading up to the front porch. This had to be the place.

At home the world was green with spots of color, but in Georgia, Mother Nature had a different flavor for March. Still, I could see that the yard was well cared for and that the Morrisons were very fond of growing things. Bare-limbed trees were spaced throughout the yard, many of them ringed with flowerbeds that I knew would provide little moats of color around the tree trunks in a few weeks.

I had just stepped up onto the porch when the front door opened, and Glenn appeared.

"Been waiting for you," he said. "I'm really glad you came. My folks are too. Well, actually, they're a little nervous, I think, but I told them about you, and they're anxious to meet you."

I'm not sure if that made me feel better or not. But I thanked Glenn and complimented him on his directions.

"Just one of the things you learn in the army," he said. "Uncle Sam has lots of things to teach you."

I wasn't exactly sure how to take that last comment, but by then I was in the door, and Glenn's father, a tall, spare man pushing fifty, I'd say, with a sprinkling of gray flecks at his temples, was introducing himself.

"Hello there, young lady. Ah'm Brad Morrison, Glenn's dad. He's told us some nice things about you. We're glad to have you in our home." Brad Morrison was a pleasant-looking man. Medium build, dark hair, and lively, smiling, gray-green eyes. His firm handshake matched his voice—in fact, everything about the man seemed to fit together exactly.

I introduced myself. Glenn took my sweater, and Mr. Morrison indicated that I should sit on the couch. It was a large, comfortable room, done in greens and blues and furnished in a homey, traditional style. Very open—I realized this was to accommodate Glenn's wheelchair. Family pictures dotted the walls. I recognized Glenn's baby picture right away. He was sitting in his stroller with what appeared to be a big, chocolate-smeared grin on his face and ice cream dripping down his arm all the way to his elbow. The comparison with the present struck me—Glenn was still on wheels—but I was sure his eating habits had improved. Then again, I had never seen him with an ice cream cone …

Glenn's mother came into the room and sat beside her husband with the easy familiarity cultivated by years of sharing fortunes, good and bad. She smiled Glenn's smile and looked at me with Glenn's eyes. She was about average height, well proportioned, with a lovely, inviting smile—easily her most engaging feature. It began with the broad, upward curve of her lips but was joined almost immediately by a lively sparkle in her sky-blue eyes. She was "the lady next door" who made you feel like an old friend from the first hello.

"It's so nice to meet you. Ah'm Harriet, Glenn's mom."

In their late forties, I guessed, the Morrisons just seemed to fit. They fit their surroundings, they fit their son, and they fit each other. Spending just that one evening with them, I am thoroughly convinced that they are completely at home in their lives. Sad that that should seem exceptional.

Mrs. Morrison said supper would be ready in just a few minutes, and the conversation turned to me. *So soon?*

"Glenn tells us you're up here from Florida, looking for information about a man named Milton Parker," she said.

"Well, yes," I answered, "I'm sort of on a quick vacation, just looking around, seeing what there is to see." This lying thing got easier all the time. "An old friend asked me to see if I could find out anything about him, and about a Pastor and Mrs. Fletcher. She wondered whatever happened to them. Turns out Milton inherited a farm up here but sold it in the '40s, I think. The Fletchers had a small church around here in the '20s and '30s."

It was Mr. Morrison's turn. "It might be a little hard to find out anything about folks from that long ago."

"Tell me about it!" I said. "But I did talk to some folks today who remember them. I think I'm making some progress."

Mrs. Morrison got up to check on supper. She turned down my offer to help, saying it was all under control, and I should stay and chat with the men.

Glenn took pity on me then, turning the conversation to the hardware store. He and his father talked easily about the business.

Glenn wanted to expand the lumber side of it, but his father wasn't quite convinced.

Mrs. Morrison was back—time to eat. The dining room table was laden with food—a crusty, brown roast beef at its center. Glenn wheeled himself into his customary place, and Mr. Morrison indicated a seat directly across from Glenn for me. I joined hands with my hosts, and we all said grace. The cordial and homey clatter signaling the beginning of a shared meal followed. I was used to eating alone and this was a real treat. I found that Glenn was right—his mother was a terrific cook.

"Mrs. Morrison, this really is great! I eat most of my meals alone and—well, I can cook, but I'm afraid I usually take the easy way out by just grabbing something quick," I told her. "I can't remember the last time I had homegrown green beans!"

"Well, thank you, Molly," she beamed. "Yes, those were homegrown green beans. I canned them last fall."

It was Mr. Morrison's turn to beam. "My Harriet has the best backyard garden in the neighborhood and cans her own vegetables."

"Yeah, Mom's always doing something in the garden or in the kitchen," Glenn chimed in. "It's a wonder Dad doesn't have to waddle when he walks!" he laughed.

"Good genes, m'boy, good genes," his father returned.

"Well, that's good news! Means I shouldn't have to worry, either! Pass me some more of those potatoes, please!" Glenn grabbed up that opportunity as though he'd just been waiting for it.

"So, Mol', you don't do much cooking, eh?" Glenn shot me an amused glance with the question.

I wasn't deterred. "Nope, not too much. But I do like to bake bread."

An admiring look came from Mrs. Morrison's direction.

Oh, no here it comes. Center stage.

"Really?" she asked. "I've tried for years but can't get the hang of bread baking!"

"Not much of a trick, really." I explained. "Some of my first memories are of my mother and grandmother baking bread. It was a kind of tradition for them. Nothing smells like fresh baked bread."

"You got that right!" Glenn put in, with a grunt of agreement from his dad.

"So you got it from your mama and grandma?" Mrs. Morrison asked.

"Yes, they used to give me a handful of dough to play with—make shapes and things. It kept me busy while they were talking and baking. Then, when Grandma died, it was Mom and I doing the baking. Those were some of the best memories I have of my mother." I could feel myself slipping close to tears and searched for a new subject, but Mrs. Morrison picked up on that last comment.

"Oh, so your mother is gone?" she asked quietly.

"Oh, yes, my parents were killed in a car crash when I was thirteen," *Too many memories sneaking up on me, I guess. I've told people about this lots of times over the years—why am I letting it get to me? Get a handle on it, girl. Don't embarrass yourself by blubbering now!*

I trudged on. "Yes, I was just thirteen. We lived in Pennsylvania. My brother was in college. I went to live with an aunt in Florida." I got it out as fast as I could. *Damn! Why is it so hard now?* This time it was Mr. Morrison to the rescue.

"So, Molly, what do you do in Florida?" Mr. Morrison asked. It was quick and very obviously intended to change the direction of the conversation. *God bless you, Mr. Morrison!*

I launched into my spiel: "I work at a small community newspaper in Oxbow ..."

The meal passed just that way. Good food, cordial conversation. As I recall, it was one of the most pleasant evenings I've ever had.

When the meal was over, without a thought I just naturally got up and started clearing my dishes. Mrs. Morrison got up at the same time and did the same. She started to say I shouldn't bother, but I just told her not to say a word; I was, after all, raised properly.

She smiled, and we finished clearing the devastation left from our feast, stacking the dishes up on the drain board. Mrs. Morrison took the lead, running the water till steam rose from the sink, then stopping and filling it. As mounds of tiny bubbles erupted in the water, she handed me a dishtowel, and we got down to the business at hand. She kept her eyes on her work as she began talking. "You know, it's been a long time since Glenn brought anybody home. He's had a tough time these past years, since he lost the use of his legs."

"Glenn talked a little about what he's been through," I told her. A quick look up from the sink told me that surprised Mrs. Morrison, but she let it pass and continued.

"When they told us he was wounded, our first reaction was 'Thank God! He's alive, and he's coming home!' You can't imagine how tough it was seeing him for the first time at the VA hospital. At that time, he hardly looked like himself. Ah'm his mother, and ah swear when we walked up to his bed, my first thought was 'Oh, God, look at this poor boy! But why did they send us to this room?'"

She paused, holding her dishrag suspended over the hot, sudsy water and stared out the window, out to her garden area, still covered with straw for the winter. I wondered if I should comment or just stay quiet till she could continue. I opted for silence. In just a few seconds she was back from that VA hospital room.

"Then ah realized it was my boy—my boy—lying there all shriveled and empty-looking. It felt like that sniper's bullet blasted its way into my body too, right then. Ah could see it was affecting Brad the same way. We'd already discussed it and decided that, no matter what he looked like, we wouldn't say or do anything to make him feel worse. We decided to put on a happy face and pretend like everything was normal."

"But it wasn't, was it?" I put in.

"No, it wasn't. That was obvious enough, but we kept acting like the bottom hadn't fallen out of our world. Glenn too. Ah know he was trying to be brave, for us. By the end of the first week there, it was no use. Glenn was sullen. He hardly talked at all. And when he did, it was something ugly—sick words from a sick soul. Ah can't tell you some of the things he said to us—but for a long time he couldn't see any reason to try. He just gave up on himself, on his life. Nobody could say anything that got through to him—not the doctors, not counselors, not us. He didn't even want to see us after that first week. He just curled up and turned his back to the world."

"I can understand wanting to close yourself off from the world," I told her. A gentle pat on the arm with a wet, soapy hand told me she appreciated that.

"It took years for him to decide to live his life again, but he's finally really alive again. Ah know you and Glenn just met a few days ago, and ah know ah shouldn't be talking like this, but ah have to tell you this."

She was shaking slightly now, tiny bubbles sliding down her dishwashing-reddened fingers. She looked directly into my eyes and said, "You seem to be good for him, but please, don't do anything that might set him back. He's worked too hard to get where he is now."

I still held the glass I'd been drying, part of the towel stuffed inside as I twisted it around. What could I say? I could see that this family had been through hell and was finally coming up on the other side. They did not need anymore snags in the process. I knew where Mrs. Morrison was going with this. She didn't have to spell it out. She was afraid of a "quickie" romance between Glenn and me—afraid he could lose all the hard-won self-confidence he'd finally managed to gather if it didn't work out.

"I know you're concerned about Glenn. He's a really good guy, and he's on his way now. I have no intention of doing anything that might stop his progress, Mrs. Morrison. I really like Glenn, and we seem to be good for each other, but I'll be leaving soon. You don't need to worry about anything I might have in mind, and Glenn knows exactly where he's headed. I can't see him letting anything get in his way now," I told her. "We're just friends, that's all."

She smiled, and we finished the dishes. She wiped her hands as the Mr. Coffee machine gurgled, and the unmistakable aroma of fresh coffee filled the room. She took plates and coffee cups out of the cupboard and asked me to grab the cake on the counter. Back into the dining room we went, to a very appreciative couple of fellows. While she cut the cake—a luscious German chocolate layer cake—and passed the plates around, I poured the coffee.

"Well, now, Harriet, looks like you've outdone yourself this time," Brad said with a glance that just oozed affection. Glenn's praise was muffled through a mouthful of cake. Harriet tried to ignore them but beamed all the same. Somehow, we all managed to squeeze cake into our overloaded stomachs—and no one grumbled one bit—except for Mrs. Morrison's complaint that she wouldn't be able to fit into her slacks the next day. I wasn't quite so open about my fears in that regard. Those five pounds would never go away if I kept this up.

What a great family, I thought and tried to imagine how they must have dealt with the past ten years. With a pang of envy I realized that this is what family is all about.

"So tell us about your life," Bradley invited me.

It wasn't such a strain for once, telling people about myself, so I told them about my life as a kid and then about my boring existence now—about bike rides with Dutch.

We talked a little about living in Oxbow and how it was the same or different from living in Hayworth. We chatted for another twenty or thirty minutes and then Harriet and Bradley both got up and said they were going to take a walk. It looked pretty suspicious, but I never saw the high sign.

To my mind it was more than a little chilly for a walk, but then I am a Florida girl with no defense against the cold to speak of. As they turned and walked out the door, Glenn rolled his eyes and I—well, I think I giggled! How embarrassing. When they were safely out the door, Glenn shook his head.

"I guess parents never give up," he mused.

I assured him he was safe with me—"Damn!" was all he said, and we both laughed. Glenn got very serious very quickly, though.

"I guess I owe you an explanation—why I got so funky when you suggested going to a restaurant," he began.

He shushed me when I started to protest that no explanation was needed and looked down at his wheelchair.

"You know, this chair is my freedom. But it's also my prison. When I was a kid, I loved baseball."

I had a quick flashback of Glenn aiming that rock at the dog in the park and placing it exactly where he wanted it.

"Man, the hours I spent out on the ball field!" He was lost in his memories now.

"My high school coach even said I had a good shot at the big leagues. But that was another life. When you're sentenced to one of these," he patted the arm of his wheelchair, "you just automatically divide your life into two parts. The one that's normal for everyone else, that was normal for you—and the one that gradually becomes your normal. That other life almost seems like a dream now. It's over, I've come to accept that, and I have to say that my life is really pretty good now."

"Yes, I do understand what you mean," I told him, praying that I didn't sound condescending.

"For a long time, though, I didn't think anything would ever be okay again, ya know? But it is. It really is." He marveled at his own resurrection. Then he looked over at me. "But it's been a long, hard run, let me tell you!"

I watched my friend as he spoke, taking in every word, every expression, looking for every nuance. I couldn't remember the last time I'd listened so hard to anyone.

"It comes in stages—acceptance does. It's like going through school. You go through elementary school till you finally make it to eighth grade—the top of the hill—only to get knocked back down to the bottom again when you start high school. Same thing happens then, whether you go to college or a trade school or go on to work. Whatever you do, you're at the bottom again, starting all over."

"But you had your folks to back you up, and the veterans had to be a big help," I put in.

"My folks tried hard but, hell, how could they know what to do? At the VA, I learned to cope—oh, I was hardheaded all right, and so I had to do it the hard way, fighting every step. Fighting the therapists, fighting myself, fighting the enemy and the army and the government—even God. I watched all those other guys. Laughed at the ones who were trying so hard, 'cause I knew it was useless. I just knew everything was useless." He shook his head at his own stubbornness. "Our lives were done, and that's all there was to it. Why couldn't they see that? What made them put themselves through that hell day in and day out?" The anguish kept pouring out.

"The doctors and nurses, the therapists, my folks—they all meant well, but what did they know? What the hell did they know?" he asked bitterly.

Glenn was beyond me now, feeling things, remembering things I knew I could not really understand no matter how hard I tried or how sympathetic I was. I could see the pain twisting in his gut. He was doing his best to show it to me, and I did my best to share his private hell. I just let him talk.

"I watched and struggled against it all, till one day it finally dawned on me that those guys were making it. While I was wallowing in self pity, they found a reason to get up in the morning and keep going. They found strength where, up till then, I had only found despair." The memories closed in around him again.

"I think strength is centered deep inside a person," I ventured quietly, "and sometimes it takes a long time and a lot of effort to tap into it. A lot of things get in our way."

His eyes were focused somewhere else, but he slowly shook his head in agreement. "Well, anyway," he pulled himself back out to the world where I was, "I didn't want to go into all that. It's not what I wanted to tell you, but that's where it starts. I finally got it together and stopped fighting it. I worked my heart out and found a way to make this chair work for me—make my life work for me again."

"Well, it looks to me like you've really done a fantastic job—on your way to being a lawyer and all," I tried to sound upbeat.

"Yeah, but after all that effort, just trying to get home again, it was another struggle here. Back down at the bottom again. I wasn't prepared for how hard it would be to just be back. Mom and Dad redid the house to make it easy for me to navigate in this chair, and they were pretty cool about everything. Truth be told, I was the one who kept throwing up roadblocks—for myself and for them. I was a real SOB." His lips formed a pathetic little smile that was gone almost before I recognized it.

"I wouldn't be too hard on myself over that—we all seem to have a talent for that from time to time," I said.

"Maybe so, but Mom and Dad didn't deserve that. Anyway, after a while it was okay as long as I was at home. Going out—that was the biggest hurdle of all. I hated going out where people could see me. I was afraid I wouldn't be able to function out in the real world, and I was afraid of what I might see in people's eyes."

The room was charged with Glenn's intensity. My hands were clenched, my fingernails were digging into my palms, and I could not stop it. I could focus on nothing but Glenn's words.

"A couple of friends from high school had started coming by, calling, that sort of thing. They'd ask, but I wouldn't go out anywhere. Well, I went to work, to the store sometimes with Mom, that sort of thing. But I never went out socially. Finally, one day I just decided it was time. I don't know. Maybe I finally felt strong enough, or maybe it was just the boredom—but the next time they suggested going out, I agreed. We were going out for pizza and a couple beers at Marino's.

"They came to pick me up, and I pulled myself into the seat of my buddy Joey's old Chevy. Funny, he still had that old station wagon! It was a bit of a production getting my chair into the back, but they managed okay. Getting the chair out went a lot easier … I guess they figured out the combination.

"It was like old times, except for the chair. It felt really good. I wheeled myself in through Marino's door thinking 'What was I afraid of, anyway?'" Glenn smiled at the recollection.

"We were laughing and talking as we came in. Then I looked around. It was Friday night, and it was wall-to-wall people. The tables were jammed together, and there wasn't a clear aisle anywhere to be seen. So there I sat … in my prison on wheels. People were jostling behind me trying to get in. Somebody yelled, 'Come on, come on! What's the holdup in there? Move it, will ya? People are trying to get in!' I couldn't move—literally. I couldn't go forward or back. It was too jammed.

"The manager came over grumbling about 'the holdup,' and when he saw me he kind of looked over my shoulder and mumbled something about being very sorry, but there wasn't any room for me there—maybe I should call for takeout. He pushed his way to the door, and I could hear him telling people to stand clear, a guy in a wheelchair was coming out.

"My friends weren't much help—not that I blame them. They didn't have a clue what to do. When the manager cleared the door, I turned around and wheeled myself out as fast as I could. I looked straight ahead. I knew everybody was looking at me. I just wanted to get the hell out of there. I started to wheel myself down the sidewalk, thought about wheeling myself all the way home. But, you know, sidewalks and roads just aren't made for wheelchair traffic. I don't think I'd been that frustrated since the first time they put me in this thing, and it sank in that it would be my legs for the rest of my life. I hated this chair. Hated my friends and the pizza place, the world. Most of all I hated myself. But I had no choice but to pull myself back into Joey's car and let them stow the chair back into the wagon. They dropped me off and I—as sarcastically as I could—thanked them for the night out and got back in the house as fast as I possibly could." He paused for a short time and said, "They still come by every now and then, or call. But nobody has ever suggested we go out again."

I didn't know just how long it had been, but the bitterness of the experience, I could see, was no less potent now than it had been then.

Beginning to relax a bit, he looked at me. "So that's why I overreacted when you brought up Marino's. Sorry, I guess it's still a little raw."

I had no idea what to say to him. There was nothing I could say, really, so we sat quietly for a few minutes.

I'd only known Glenn for a couple days, but I felt closer to him than I had to anybody since Aunt Nell died. He just let me see a small portion of the toll he paid every day for doing nothing more than what he believed to be his duty. This Glenn Morrison was really something, I thought, wondering where on earth he got the strength to go on. After what he had just shared with me, I felt it was only right to offer him some small token of my own vulnerable humanity. Without actually thinking about what I was doing, I told him the whole story of my trip to Hayworth.

Actually, it was probably the best thing I could have done for Glenn. It took the painful spotlight off him and allowed him to close that door quietly again. And it gave him something decidedly different to think about.

It was obvious that Glenn was merely being polite as I started to tell him about my mystery; however, I opted to leave out the part about the faces until the end; I didn't want to lose him before I got started.

"Okay, I guess it's my turn," I began. "This whole trip is a little more complicated that I told you. Actually, somehow I've got myself stuck in the middle of a forty-year-old mystery that I can't let go of. It started out with this family—the Parkers—that lived in Oxbow. The family was there for a good thirty years, and nobody seems to know much about them, including our museum, which has pages and pages about people who only lived there for a handful of years."

"Nobody?" Glenn asked. "Folks in any small town I ever knew anything about all have very long memories about that sort of thing."

"Exactly!" I said. "People will admit to knowing the family, but nobody seems to be able—or willing—to answer any questions about what happened to them. That's my problem. What I do know just doesn't add up," I told him. "I have the daughter's diary—Jeannie Sue Parker. Her last entry was in October 1943. She gives no indication that the family would be moving, just days before they supposedly left for the family farm here in Hayworth. Milton, her father, was no farmer, by all accounts, and even if he had been, I can't believe the family ever came here because Milton came back here and sold the farm when his cousin died. A lady named Jean Martin told me that. She and her husband bought the place from Milton. That was right before the Parker home in Oxbow burned down. I figure that their house, as of October 1943, was maybe a bit rundown from lack of attention, but by all accounts it was very well built. It caught fire—right after they supposedly packed up to head for Georgia."

"Now that's some 'coincidence'," Glenn commented.

"Well, yeah, that's my point. The fire that gutted it shortly after the family left supposedly started from an oil lamp somebody left burning. The newspaper says the fire department finished the job in a training exercise a few months after the family left because it was 'structurally unsound.'" I stopped then. "Putting it all out like that, it doesn't sound like much, I admit."

"Well, it does sound a little fishy," Glenn conceded, but my big mystery certainly didn't ring his chimes. Anyway, I knew I was holding out on him. Glenn had opened his guts and let me see a small bit of his pain. I knew I couldn't make him understand my obsession until I opened mine to him. I had to tell him about my faces.

Taking a deep breath I began. "Well, there is one more thing ... there are these faces ... that I see up in the orchid tree across from my office—well, sometimes I see them." I took a quick glance to see how Glenn was reacting to this one. He was a blank. I trudged on.

"Apparently, I'm the only one who can see these faces"—another look at Glenn, still no reaction, so I rushed on before I lost my nerve.

"I know that sounds crazy. For a long time I felt something drawing me to that lot, but I always ignored it, you know? Put it down to a trick of the light and breeze manipulating the leaves. But a few weeks ago I ... they were just there!"

"Well, light and shadows can play tricks on your eyes," Glenn began, but I cut him off.

"I swear, Glenn, they're real. They must be the Parkers, don't you see? They're the only ones that ever lived there—I checked— and after the house was burned down, there's never been another building there of any kind. The St. Claires, the family that owns the property, are planning to put in a doctor's office there. That must be why these faces are showing themselves now. I don't know what it's all about, Glenn, I just feel that something happened. Something bad." I looked at Glenn, and I know my eyes held a plea for help.

He reached out and touched my arm. "I'm sure there's a perfectly logical explanation ..." Agitated, I cut him off again.

"I'm not prone to seeing things—I can tell you I've never had an experience like this before. I see them, Glenn, and they can see me. They even contacted me. Twice. Well, sort of," I backtracked. "The one that looks like she must be Hannah—Milton's wife—she seems so lost, so tormented. The one that must be Milton, though—Glenn, he came to me in a dream! The cold was numbing—it took me hours to get warm again—and evil just radiated from him!"

I was shaking by then, but I looked Glenn dead in the eyes. "The evil was real. It penetrated my whole being, seeped in with that unnatural coldness. I felt defiled." I had to make him understand. "Sometimes I still do."

Glenn moved his wheelchair a little closer and behind me, leaned over, and gently rubbed my shoulders. "Ease up a little, Molly, you're so tense!"

"So that's the real reason I came up here. I'm looking for the pieces that will make whatever this is make sense."

I was afraid to look at Glenn again. Afraid I'd see disbelief—or worse, humor—in his eyes. I'd been following this mystery for weeks all on my own. This was the first I'd told anybody the whole story, and I needed to be believed—even if I knew I wouldn't be understood.

Glenn was every bit the man I thought he was. He wheeled back around in front of me and touched my hand. I hadn't realized it, but I was crying. When was the last time that had happened?

"Don't worry," he said, "I happen to have a soft spot for crazy women."

We sat for a while then. He was turning this information over and over in his brain, I could see, looking for some logical explanation for what I'd just told him. Finding none, he said, "Tell you what. I have my AA meeting tomorrow night. There are a couple old guys there—in their '70s I guess, must've been in their prime about the time this Milton Parker came back to sell the farm. Maybe one of them remembers him."

"You mean I might have spent every evening this week fending off drunks in seedy bars for nothing?" I asked. The laugh we shared then was the exact medicine we both needed at that point. The world became clear again, mysteries and wheelchairs notwithstanding.

"Do you have that diary with you?" The question surprised me but I told him it was in my room.

"I'd really like to see it, if you don't mind," he said. I hesitated just a moment, but promised to bring it to the duck pond the next day. I knew I had to commit myself completely.

Harriet and Bradley came back in from their "walk," and I decided it was time for me to take my leave of these good people.

So I said my good-byes, thanked them all for the really lovely evening, and headed back to my hotel. Back in my room, I felt better than I had since this whole thing started. Maybe, just maybe, I could get this thing unraveled and return my life to normal after all.

Back in my room, I was exhausted but couldn't sleep. What I needed was a good long soak in a hot tub. I undressed as the steamy water filled the tub. The mirror in the tiny bathroom was opaque from the steam rising in the air, so even those five extra pounds didn't taunt me for once. I slowly lowered myself into the almost scalding water, and the moist heat seeped into my body. There is nothing like a good, long soak in a steaming hot tub to make the world go away. It was heavenly. No Parker family. No mystery contorting my brain. No faces bedeviling my soul. I could feel my mind beginning to drift back to another time in my life when everything went haywire. It was time to face my own secrets ...

The bat cracked, the crowd cheered, a tiny figure in a bright-orange baseball uniform dropped the bat, little legs pumped as fast as they could, closing in on first base. Lots of other little legs, clad in dark-blue uniforms, worked hard, tripping over each other to catch up to a small, white sphere, rolling away in the grass. None were even close.

I had my camera out and was taking a couple shots at the beginning of Little League season. Maria usually took this assignment, being the more athletic member of the staff, but she had been out sick all week. I decided we needed a few photos of cute little baseball players putting their all into the great American pastime, so there I was.

"Get a good shot, now Molly. My little grandson is up next. It's his first year, you know," said a familiar voice from behind me.

I turned to see Claude Bristol beaming at me, juggling a duffel bag full of baseball paraphernalia, his three-year-old granddaughter, and what looked to be a half-eaten burger on a plate, chips scattering to the winds. Whistles and hoots from the crowd rose behind me.

Claude owned the welding shop in Oxbow, took it over when his daddy died some twenty years ago. He did good work that he stood behind, so he gained a good reputation with all the growers around, and he did quite a bit of work for the city and county. He was also the driving force behind Oxbow Little League. For Claude, Little League wasn't a "season"; it was a passion he kept burning all year long. During the off-season he was always planning or fundraising, doing what he could to keep up the ball field. He and his wife, gone these ten years now, practically raised three sons and a daughter on the ball field. All three of their sons coached Little League teams, and their daughter helped coach T-ball. It was her son who was about to take his at-bat.

Claude was introducing the really great-looking guy standing with him now. Greg Richards was his name.

The water had turned cold, and so had my world—again. It always did when Greg surfaced in my mind. I snapped out of my dream world, grabbed a towel, and climbed out of the tub. So much for my nice, soothing soak. I knew there was no way around it. My brain—or was it my heart?—would not let go until I had rehashed the whole mess again.

So I sat in the middle of the bed wrapped in blankets, steeling myself for the memories I knew I could not keep at bay. The sooner I dealt with them, the sooner I could get on with what I had to do.

I let myself remember that first meeting with Greg at the ball field. I remembered the look Claude gave us—that knowing look that says "these two were meant for each other."

Or so it seemed. Didn't I think exactly the same thing?

Greg was new in town, up from Ft. Lauderdale. He was a welder, and a darn good one too. The biggest complaint of Claude's life was that he could never find good welders to work for him. The really good welders usually went to the big cities where the pay was better, so Claude was always looking to hire someone.

I could hear Claude telling me, "Greg, here, is a top-notch welder—just the guy I been lookin' for. He's only been with me now for a couple weeks, but it's easy to see the man's got a good touch. Even better, he's a Little League man too! Talked him into coachin' the Bears. You know about Ernie's heart problem this year," he said, referring to the Bears' traditional coach's recent quadruple bypass.

Passing my camera over to my left hand, I shook Greg's hand, and he held mine just a tiny bit longer than was really necessary. Yes, it was unmistakable. I wasn't all that experienced, but even I knew I was falling hard. Those soft-green eyes with the devil shining through had me, already.

It was time for the Bears to play, and Greg asked me if I would stay and watch. Was there any doubt? I had already taken enough pictures for the paper to do right by my conscience. I put the camera away so I could concentrate on the game. Who am I kidding? I put the camera away so I could concentrate on Greg.

And he did put on a show, fussing over the players, gently correcting their stance in the batter's box, checking their swing. Once, when a rather hefty little player was hustling into home base, bearing down on a scrawny little runner who obviously wasn't going to make it out of the way in time, Greg simply reached down and grabbed the hapless runner by the shirt, pulling him up and out of the way just in the nick of time, to the hoots and applause of an impressed crowd.

Greg, the hero in a Saturday-afternoon matinee.

He followed up that impressive show with the kids a few days later by rescuing me when my car broke down. I didn't have to think about it too hard—I could still feel the warm wind wrapping around me as I straddled his motorcycle on the way back to town. We left my old Oldsmobile dead—or at least in critical condition—by the side of the road, and he took me to Crowley's gas station. It would be about an hour before they could get a tow truck out to pick it up.

Greg stayed right with me, over my protests that it wasn't necessary. After a while, Ben Crowley said they were having a problem with the tow truck, and it would probably be a couple hours yet. He'd have his wife take me if I needed a ride home, then he'd go pick up my car and give me a call when he knew something. Greg stepped up to say he'd be glad to take me home, he wasn't doing anything anyway, just taking a ride when he happened upon me. So, it was decided. I took my place behind Greg again. My body was riding, but I swear my heart was flying. Pulling up in my yard, I got off and opened the gate. It was just getting to be dusk, and Dutch came slowly forward, teeth bared and a low, deadly growl just barely audible. I'd never seen Dutch react that way to anyone. It must have been the motorcycle— he'd never seen one before. I shouted at Dutch and grabbed his collar. Greg shut off the engine and eased over to where I was holding Dutch, trying to reassure the dog that this visitor was okay.

Dutch's reaction meant that Greg didn't stay long, but he asked if he could call some time. You know the answer.

Greg, the knight in shining armor rescuing the damsel in distress.

Sitting cross-legged on the bed, hot tears streaming down my face, I vaguely wondered just how many times I had put myself through this, and just how many more I would have to before Greg was finally out of my system.

But I wasn't nearly finished yet, I knew. *Get on with it, girl. Feel the burn.*

I took myself back to the next time I saw Greg. He had called the office to ask me to dinner. Remembering the schoolgirl flutter turning my insides to quivering jelly, I wondered at just how foolish I could be. I had never thought of myself as a foolish person—never was one to go overboard every time a good-looking guy appeared. Even in middle school, when young girls are notorious for their silly vulnerability, I shook my head at just how ridiculous they were. Now, here I was, just another silly girl making a fool of herself. The really sad thing is that part of me knew it.

I recalled the silly moments and the tender moments and let the sweet ache grow. I recalled the soaring feeling that this was it! Greg was the one—my love and my partner.

Then I forced myself to remember how it all began to fall apart.

Greg made good money at Claude's welding shop, I knew. He always had money and spent it freely. It was a new experience for me. I had never been hungry in my life, thank God, and always had what I needed, but money wasn't something that came very easily—not to my parents and not to Aunt Nell, and certainly not to me, working for the newspaper. It was nice, not having to think about whether I could afford a new pair of shoes or a movie. I didn't take advantage of him, but Greg always wanted to buy me things—and he was so hard to say no to.

Then came the day I ran into Claude Bristol at Birchwood's grocery.

"When do you think Greg will be able to come back to work, Molly? We're gettin' a little behind without him." That's what he asked me, standing there next to the frozen vegetable case.

Bewildered, I asked, "What do you mean? Greg left for work this morning and every day this week."

Now it was Claude's turn to be bewildered—and a little embarrassed, it seemed to me. He wasted no time in moving on. "Okay, sorry, Molly. Guess I got a little confused."

I felt my heart frost over like the glass on the freezer door I was still holding open. My heart was fighting it with everything it had, but there was no denying it. Greg was lying to me.

That evening I called Shirley Nelson. She had been doing the books at the welding shop for years, ever since Claude's wife died. She was a nice lady and a good bookkeeper—and it was virtually impossible for her to keep a secret, so I knew she'd tell me anything

I wanted to know. She confirmed my worst fears. Greg had not been to work in two weeks and had missed a lot of days for weeks before that. Good ol' Shirley—she wondered if maybe he was having trouble meeting his bills, since his paycheck was so skimpy these days.

I confronted Greg that night. He had been spending a lot of nights out late, but he always had a good reason. It probably wasn't the way to go about it, but I just couldn't stand not knowing what was going on. And I had a bad feeling about this. A very bad feeling.

If he wasn't going to work, where was he going? I demanded. And where was all that money coming from? I knew I was on shaky ground. His money really wasn't any of my business—or was it? If this man was to be my partner in life, didn't I have a right to know how he dealt with things?

Apparently, Greg didn't think so. For the next week our relationship was touchy. We hardly spoke. They were some of the hardest days I'd ever had, and it was wearing on me. I felt myself beginning to relent. Just what did I think I was doing, anyway? Greg was good to me, and it's not like I had a new guy every few months. In fact, he was the only one I'd ever been serious about.

Then I found that joint when I was weeding around my hibiscus, and it all started to come into focus. I couldn't look the other way. He, of course, denied it was his, but there just wasn't anybody else it could have belonged to. Greg was smoking marijuana—and he was selling drugs too, I knew. It was the only explanation. Where else could all that money be coming from? I was scared, but it almost felt better. At least now I understood the problem. Now maybe we could fix it.

And we did try. Correction. I tried. I don't think Greg saw it as a problem at all. He was hooked on the money. He only smoked "recreationally," he told me, "no big deal." He was too smart to get hooked. Was it his fault if other people were stupid enough to throw their money away getting high? It was human nature, he reasoned; people had always been looking for ways to feel good. He couldn't be responsible for human nature. Somebody was going to make all that money, so why not him?

There was no reasoning with him. I tried everything I could think of—not the least of which was that he could go to jail. His thinking was warped. There was no "fixing" a problem he would not acknowledge.

Sitting on the bed, I mentally went through every argument again, every time he placated me by swearing he'd quit selling and go back to work regularly, every time he failed, every time I believed his lies again.

Then that last blowup, when I'd finally had enough. We were standing in my kitchen. It was late, and he was headed out the door. I knew where he was going—he didn't even try to make excuses anymore. *You've got to try one more time. You've got to get through to him.* I tried my best, but I was out of my league. I could not save Greg. He didn't want to be saved. So I finally kicked him out of my life for good. I would remember his words as long as I lived, I knew. They still cut deep.

"You're such a little dumb-ass, Molly! You just don't get it, do you? The world changed—where were you? You have to take what you want and run. I'm not responsible for those jackasses who use that stuff. I'm just a businessman, filling a demand. It's the American way," he argued yet again, exasperation written all over his face.

"Okay, so maybe you're not responsible for what other people do, but you are responsible for what you do!" I countered.

"Shit, woman, grow up! Get this through your thick head: this is my ticket to the good life. I can have anything I want. You could too, if you don't let that goddamn bleeding heart of yours get in the way. People deserve what they get, Molly. I'm just a salesman, that's all." He had used that argument before. I still couldn't buy it.

"No, Greg, you're not just a salesman. You're a dealer—you're dealing in other people's misery! Why can't you see that?" I pleaded.

He was pacing by then. Picking up the toaster, he threw it to the floor. Dutch apparently perceived that as a direct threat to me. He came unglued then and went after Greg. I grabbed his collar and strained to hold him back, screaming at the top of my lungs, "No, Dutch! Stay!"

Greg was way beyond exercising any caution at that point and continued his tirade, throwing a kitchen chair in the same direction as the toaster.

I was seeing a side of Greg Richards I hadn't believed could exist. An unthinking, violent side that only craved destruction. Up till then I was only concerned about how Greg was living his life and how it was affecting our relationship. Now I was beginning to be afraid— could he actually hurt me? What about Dutch? Would he hurt him if he got the chance? Desperately holding the snarling Dutch back, my heart sank as I realized what I had to do.

"If you go out that door tonight, don't come back," I told him.

Suddenly he was very calm. "Don't threaten me, Molly, you can't pull it off," he sneered.

Somehow, I was just as calm. "No threat," I assured him. "This is it. Leave, and you don't come back. Stay, and maybe we can work it out."

He smiled then, a one-sided, mocking thing. "Okay, sweet cheeks, we'll play it your way. There are lots of other women who don't have your hang-ups. I've wasted enough time with you anyway. If I'd known you were such a prudish little bitch, I'd never have bothered with you at all."

His words cut deep, but I tried my best to hide it. "I'll collect whatever you have here and leave it at the gate. You can pick it up tomorrow," I told him. Dutch had quieted down but was still watching the scene intently. He opted to stay out of the way and returned to his corner, making sure the man he had always seen as an enemy did not get too close to me. Greg stood there with fists clenched, fury blazing in his eyes. For some of the longest moments in my life, I thought he really might come after me. Instead, he took one parting kick at Dutch, who answered with bared teeth snapping just inches from his leg. "The love of my life" turned away, his face contorted with rage, and fled out the door. If the pain hadn't been so deep, I might have thought it was funny. Poor old Dutch knew from that first day that Greg was no good and, as it happened, he got in the last "word."

I let the memories burn, let the acid eat through my gut and promised myself once again never to trust any man who didn't first pass "the Dutch test."

Greg the schmuck. Greg the druggie. Greg the self-centered bastard.

Curling up into a ball, I tried to think about my next step. For now, I was finished dealing with my past. I knew I had it all planned out for the morning, but my brain rebelled when I tried to call it up. I took it as a sign that I should just try to relax and get some sleep. That's what I needed, all right. A good night's sleep would bring things into focus in the morning. At least that's what I was hoping as I closed my eyes, waiting for sleep to overtake me.

And waiting.

Tossing and turning, I checked my watch at intervals. I got up briefly sometime between 1:25 and 2:29 and switched on the TV, but had no interest in anything it had to offer. *Back to bed*, I thought, *before it cools off and I have to warm it up again.*

It must have been some time around three a.m. when I finally drifted off, but not to the peaceful slumber I needed. Little League ball fields, motorcycles, and joints swirled through my head in a grotesque collage. The morning could not come soon enough.

CHAPTER 19

THE NEXT DAY GLENN wheeled up to the duck pond right on time, and an easy smile passed between us.

"I can't tell you how much I enjoyed supper last night," he started. "It's been a long time since I felt really comfortable with company."

"Well, I really appreciated the evening, too. Your folks are pretty special people, aren't they?" I told him. The grin that spread across his face was my answer.

Glenn's eyes flitted over the small, brown book on my lap, but he didn't say anything about it. He was waiting for me to bring it up. I wasn't ready yet. Last night it had seemed like such a good idea. It sounded so easy. Simply hand Jeannie Sue's life and dreams over to someone I'd known for just over three days. Now I wasn't so sure.

We sat in silence—well, except for the hullabaloo raised by the ducks all trying to get to the same piece of bread at the same instant. Finally, the bread was all gone, and it really did get quiet, so Glenn and I headed over to the picnic tables and settled down to our own lunches. Telling myself how silly I was being about letting Glenn see the diary, I picked it up and handed it over to my new friend. It was like giving up a part of myself, but Glenn's hand accepted it with the same love and care with which mine relinquished it.

There. That wasn't so bad! I told myself. And it wasn't. It really wasn't. In fact, now that Glenn had the little book, it felt right.

Still a little apprehensive in spite of myself, I said, "You'll take good care of it?" How foolish was that!

"You can bet on it," was his reply. "Gotta get back to work now, but I'll read it tonight and call you. Promise."

I watched Glenn roll away with what had pretty much become the center of my life in his hands. This mystery had become that important to me—I thought of it as the central point in my life. In spite of that bad experience with Greg, I always prided myself on not jumping too fast no matter how good something looked or how intriguing it was. I had a good, steady head on my shoulders and wasn't prone to going overboard. Nope. Not me! *Right.*

Funny how something can virtually take over your whole being in just a few weeks. I should just have been glad it was a mystery and a book and not a man this time!

I was lying on the bed in my room trying to force myself to think about what I needed to do when I got back home and to work. It was 9:15, according to my old Timex. I jumped when the phone rang. It was the first—and only—phone call I'd received since I got to Hayworth.

When I picked up the receiver, Glenn said, "Hey, there! Didn't catch you napping, did I?"

"No," I said, "I was attempting to do something much harder than that. I was trying to think!"

"I heard that!" He was laughing but his voice was different. Intense. Jeannie Sue had him, too, I knew.

"I read Jeannie Sue's diary this afternoon when I got home." His voice was low but intense. "It's really something! Jeannie Sue must have been something! I can't stop thinking about her and about Hannah. You really sucked me into this one!" he chided.

"Anyway, I might have something for you. I talked to some of the old guys at AA tonight. They're always there, but I never really got to know any of them. There's this one guy, Harley Dothan. I mentioned Milton Parker and—you won't believe this!—he knew him! Better than that, he was Milton's drinking buddy when he came up here and sold the farm. I told him about you—just about you looking for information on Milton Parker for a friend—and he said he'd be glad to talk to you tomorrow if you'd like."

I let his words hang in the air for a few seconds, incapable of really taking them in.

Good thing I was sitting down. I don't think my knees would have held me up just then. *Imagine! Milton's drinking buddy! He's still here—still alive—and he'll talk to me!* When I left Oxbow I had high hopes—maybe too high, but till that moment I don't think I really believed I could get this far. "Great! Where do I go and when?" I asked.

"Tomorrow morning. Most any time is fine. Harley's the caretaker at the Hayworth Baptist Church. It's a little ways out of town. You go about three miles east on the highway and make the turn toward Valdosta. The church is just about half a mile down the road on the left."

CHAPTER 20

I COULD SEE THE slender steeple pointing up to the heavens long before the church itself became visible. At the end of a long, curved drive, the immaculate white building appeared through the pines—small, but well built and obviously well kept. A slender man dressed in a red-plaid flannel shirt and overalls bent over a set of wooden steps. I could see he had been replacing some rotten boards.

He smiled as I came up the walk—a genuine, how-ya-doin'-set-down-and-talk-a-spell smile. With his left hand he reached up and snatched an old red cap off his head, revealing sparse tendrils of white hair sticking out in disarray all over his head, his high forehead crinkled with deep lines. His hand was outstretched before I got the whole way up the walk, and he said in his slow Georgia drawl, "Don't mind a little dirt. It's honest," glancing at the hammer he had just laid down. I liked Harley Dothan the moment I laid eyes on him.

Harley had had a hard life. It stood out plainly in his face and in his battered frame, but his eyes were a mixture of worldly knowledge and compassion. To the brain, that may seem like a strange combination, but it made perfect sense to the heart.

"'Spect it's me ya been lookin' fer. Been a long time now, but at one time I followed the wild side with Milton Parker," he said.

I introduced myself and told him I was just looking for information for a friend.

"Yes, ma'am, that's what Glenn said, though ah cain't for the life of me figger why a nice lady like you could possibly want to know anythin' about ol' Milton. He was near 'bout the sorriest cuss ah ever did see. Don't give me no pleasure to say that, 'specially since we was such great drinkin' buddies for a while. A real hard-core drinker, that one was. He could never get enough—booze, women. He was a real sorry poker player too, but that didn't keep him from it."

He showed me to a couple lawn chairs with faded green webbing set out by the old church. Thankfully, the church blocked the steady breeze, and the sunshine felt good, even with my new sweater covering my shoulders.

"Met him durin' the war when he was up here ta inherit the fam'ly farm. That was some joke—ol' Milton on a farm! We both had a good laugh over that one!" Harley shook his head at the memory, his faded hazel eyes telling a tale of regret.

"Well, ma'am, he unloaded that there farm just as fast as he could. Got somewheres 'round a couple thousand dollars for it, as ah recollect. As you might imagine, all that money near to burnt a hole in his pocket. Good thing that lawyer fella—don't recall his name now—wouldn't take care of no legal bidness with a client drunk on his tail, so Milton had to sober up for it. The way Milton tol' it, that lawyer read him the riot act about not squanderin' all that money and talked Milton into wirin' most of it to the bank in his hometown. But ol' Milton kep' a couple hundred in his pocket."

"A couple hundred—that was an awful lot of money then, wasn't it?" I prodded.

Shaking his head at the memory, Harley continued. "We did have a high ol' time on that money—drinking and carousin' all 'round these parts. Maybe ya heard 'bout some of it down at the White Crown." *Wouldn't you know! The one dive within thirty miles I must've missed!* A quick glance at me. "No, ah 'spect not," he concluded. "But ah still know a coupla fellas that imbibe a little from time to time, and they tell me that ever' now and then them days come up in conversation down there. Drunks like to outdo each other with tall tales, ya know." After a second or two he said, "Ah guess in my time ah was one o' the best at tall tales." He shook his head ruefully, rubbing the wiry gray stubble on his chin.

"Lordy, when ah think back on all that time ah wasted gettin' low-down drunk for days, hung over for a week at a time—well, it jus' seems like somebody else, now, that's all," he said ruefully.

"I guess we've all done things we wish we hadn't," I said, hoping to make him a little more comfortable. Then he told me an age-old story about getting lost and trying to drink your way back to a real life.

"Don't suppose a lady like you could understand all this," he said scratching his head and looking a bit worn. Harley Dothan was a man who had made peace with his secrets, I realized. That was what I wanted for the Parkers. It was what I needed for myself.

But I nodded that I did understand, as a picture of our own "town drunk," Dennis Blankenship, formed in my mind, and Harley continued his story.

Before leaving I had to make absolutely sure—I wouldn't get another chance like this.

"So," I began, "you're sure Milton wasn't coming back here?"

"Oh, yes'm. Ah can still see it. We was both hung over from a couple days of … well, what I thought was a real good time back then … It was the mornin' Milton said he was goin' back home. Not 'cause he wanted to—this is what he tol' me now—he had to git back home and check on that good-for-nothin' woman and those snot-nosed kids."

"That's what he said?" I asked. I wondered if Luke knew how good his memory is.

"Yes'm. Those were his words exactly."

I don't know how long we talked. It didn't matter. Harley Dothan had a lot to say. And Milton Parker was just the beginning.

"Ah know ah took up too much of your time, miss, but you seem so interested. Most folks aroun' here are nice enough, but not many come over to talk, ya see."

Well, I stayed there with Harley for another hour or so. He showed me the proud little church, and around the old graveyard. He showed me the little garden the pastor let him put in behind an old shed. It was obvious that it was Harley's pride and joy. And maybe even a little of his salvation.

CHAPTER 21

BACK IN MY HOTEL room that night I was all primed for a relaxing soak in the tub when I heard a knock on the door. Puzzled, I pulled my top back on—that soak would have to wait a while. I had my hotel room door half way open before I even thought about asking who it was. *Damn, Molly! This could be an ax murderer for all you know!*

No such luck.

I opened the door to David Livingston's crafty eyes boring into me and his cheap cologne overpowering me.

"Well, hello there, Missy! Bet you didn' think you'd be seeing me again now, did ya?" His voice was like a velvety ribbon of rancid butter. He never took his eyes off me as he started through the doorway.

Fear and disgust rose in my throat. Some instinct for self preservation kicked in, and I grabbed my sweater from the hook by the door as I shoved past him. "I was just on my out," I stammered as my brain struggled with just where I might go. *He'll probably want to go with me. Then what?*

"Oh, that's okay. I was just in town and thought, as a gentleman, I should check and see that your car was still runnin' okay." I was trying to put some more space between us, but his legs were longer than mine. I thought about running, but first of all it seemed downright silly, and second, he could overtake me in a flash.

150

"Ever since you were out at the house the other day Aunt Grace has been goin' on 'bout the ol' days—you know—Pastor Fletcher this, Pastor Fletcher that. 'Bout to drive me and the missus batty with all that drivel. But it jus' keeps comin'."

I was almost out to my car in the hotel parking lot next to the street when my unwanted "friend" said something that made my heart—and my feet—stop cold.

"We can't shut her up. Even started talkin' 'bout that blasted preacher's fam'ly. This mornin' she went on about some sainted brother from years ago. Clem, his name was. Had a farm out a ways or somethin' ...

"Clem? Are you sure that's what she said?" I knew I'd just made a big mistake, but I couldn't keep the surprise and the blatant interest out of my voice.

"Why, yes'm." The silky tone in David's voice made me want to vomit. "That's what she said, I'm sure of it. Does that mean somethin' to you? Cuz I'm sure I can get more out of Aunt Grace for you. Just come on back to the house with me. Marty's out for the evenin' and ..."

"No!" I practically screamed. "I mean, no," I said more calmly. *Get a hold on it, Molly! You've got to find out where Clem is and find a way to stay out of David's little plan.* With Marty at home, David's advances were a pathetic joke. With her out of the picture for the evening, his attitude didn't seem so laughable. *Think, Molly! Get him to tell you where Clem is, then get in your car and drive anywhere—to the nearest police station, if you have to!*

"So, do you know where Clem is? I'm sure my friend would love to hear a little more about him." I prayed the desperation didn't come through.

Sensing he had some leverage now, David moved a little closer. "Well, now, I'm not rightly shore. Seems like she said somethin' 'bout some nursin' home or t'other in Wooster County I think, but I cain't seem to recollect the name ..."

Where were my keys? They had to be here in my bag! I remembered that when I got back from talking to Harley, I slid my bag across the dresser and ... oh, no! ... dropped my keys beside it. *Damn!* I was on foot, and it was starting to get dark. David kept moving in a little more ...

It was only getting dusk but there was very little traffic. Folks were already home with supper on the table. My head was fogging up, so it took a few seconds to realize that a van had pulled up to the curb beside us.

"Hi, Molly!" Glenn's voice sounded like an angel of mercy. "I see you're already out here waiting for me. Sorry I'm a little late." Moving his attention, he added, "Hello, David! What brings you into town?" I didn't know Glenn knew David Livingston. Guess when you run a hardware store you know most everyone around. Anyway, it was all right by me!

Now it was David's turn to be uncomfortable. His transformation back into Marty's mealy-mouthed Greek god was almost visual.

"Evenin', Glenn. How's your daddy? Haven't been in the store in a while," was all David could respond with.

"Come on, Molly, hop in! I'm starvin'!" *Were those wings folded up behind that man in the heavenly chariot?*

I set a speed record for running around a van and jumping into the passenger's seat, saying something like "Thanks for the information, David. Give my regards to Marty!" as I settled into my seat.

David's eyes turned angry, and an edge crept into his voice. "Oh, sorry. Didn't mean to interrupt no plans. Y'all two go on an' have a good time and tell your daddy hello for me."

Glenn was masterful. His tone managed to be polite and to put David in his place at the same time. "I'll surely tell him, David, and you do the same with Marty."

We were a couple blocks down the road when I finally exhaled.

"You okay, Molly? Your hands are shaking." Concern marked Glenn's words.

I looked down, and he was right. I couldn't control my hands. "I'll be okay in a minute," I said. "That man's just more than I can deal with. At the farm he was just kind of pathetic—a joke. But when he came to my door, it was like he was a whole different person."

"You didn't let him in, did you?"

"No! Of course not. But I opened the door without checking who it was—you just don't have to do that kind of thing where I come from—and when I saw him, it was too late to shut the door. I just grabbed my bag and pushed past him, but when we got to my car, I realized my keys were still on the dresser," I told him. It sounded even more stupid out loud.

"Good thing I came along. I always thought David Livingston was harmless, but he sure didn't look that way back there," Glenn mused. "I was headed to class ..."

"Oh, yeah! That test is tonight, isn't it?" I put in. Now I was interfering with higher education.

"Not to worry," he said, "I can make it up. Besides, I know the material." Seeing my discomfort at interrupting his evening, he deftly changed the subject. "It's about time I played a little hooky anyway, and I have a sudden craving for a burger. There's a drive-through just a couple blocks down the road. How about it?" he tempted me.

I told him I didn't care what we did as long as it was as far away from David Livingston as we could get. So we picked up a couple burgers and fries and Glenn drove over to the duck pond. We sat in his van eating and talking as the moon made its way up over the tall pines, spilling faint rays onto the unblemished surface of the water.

Glenn left me to my thoughts. After a short silence, I began. "I know you read the diary, so you know about Uncle Clem and Hannah."

Glenn nodded.

"David just said his aunt told him Uncle Clem is still alive and in a nursing home in the next county." My words were tentative. I was struggling to decide what I should do.

"Alive? He's got to be in his nineties!" Glenn calculated. "He was a real piece of work, that one. My God! Still alive! Are you planning to go talk to him?"

"That's just it. I don't know what I should do. You're right, Clem was worthless—worse than that. But it was so long ago. Who am I to go busting in there and hit him with all that now? I'm not a confessor or anything. Maybe he's changed. Hell, at his age, he might not even remember it! Is it right to dredge something like that up after all these years? What if he has a heart attack or something right there?"

Quietly, Glenn picked up my hand in his. "Molly," he said, "What did you come here to do?"

"I came to find the truth about the Parkers," I said, looking into his eyes.

"Well, that includes Hannah, doesn't it? And what happened to her?" I nodded.

"It all works together. All part of the same story. Maybe Clem is out of it, and you won't be able to get anything from him. But just maybe Clem can shed some light on something. Okay, so Jean Martin, Luke, and Harley all said the Parkers never came back here. I'm sure that's true; they're all honest people and I can't think of any reason why they might not tell you the truth. But Clem was family. Maybe he knows something. Maybe they went somewhere else when they left Oxbow."

"That doesn't seem likely," I said.

"Maybe not, but you'll never know what Clem does if you don't go talk to him."

Why did Glenn have to be so clearheaded, anyway? He left me no way out. But he was right, I knew. No matter how distasteful it would be to talk to the man who cost Hannah so much, I had to do it.

The nursing home wasn't hard to find. Turns out there was only one in Wooster County. Good thing David wasn't smart enough to keep his mouth shut. He gave me just enough information to figure out what I needed to know. The attendant gave me a strange look when I told her who I was there to see. Apparently, I was the first personal visitor Clem Fletcher had had in the two years he'd been there.

It was hard to find the man lying in that clinical-looking, impersonal room. He was just a pile of frail, deteriorating bone, thin, blue pajamas draped over them, the unmistakable brown splotch of a tobacco stain above the pocket. A tiny skull wrapped tightly in opaque blue-lined skin and set with watery gray eyes was poking out from under a thin white sheet. Oxygen tubes protruded from both nostrils. A tray with the remnants of lunch—most of an egg salad sandwich and a puddle of partially melted green gelatin—was still in front of him.

He didn't look up when he said in a soft, weary voice, "Take this thang away, will ya? I cain't look at it no more."

"Here, Mr. Fletcher, I'll move that out of your way," I said.

"You new here?" he asked, fixing me with a glare from those beady eyes.

"No, sir," I answered, "I don't work here. My name is Molly Martindale …"

"Never heard of you! What you want anyways?"

Well, Uncle Clem certainly seemed to be aware of his surroundings. I wondered how his memory was.

"You're right, sir, you don't know me. I'm up here from Florida, and I'm looking for information for a friend of mine who used to live over in Hayworth." I decided to jump in with both feet. If he didn't remember anything, well it wouldn't matter to him what I said, and if he did remember—then maybe I'd learn something important.

"Her name is Hannah. Hannah Parker."

Both hands jerked violently under the sheet and fear—or was it shame?—emanated from those tired gray eyes.

His voice became sharp, and suspicion crept into his eyes. "Who did you say you are?"

"My name is Molly Martindale," I repeated. "I'm here to find out what happened to the Parker family. I understand you are Hannah's uncle." I struggled to keep my voice and my questions matter of fact.

"They're gone. All gone. Now you need to go too," he said, dismissing me.

"What do you mean, they're gone?" I ventured. "They all lived in Oxbow, Florida, but no one there knows what happened to them. They supposedly left town to come back here when Milton inherited a farm over in Hayworth."

"What in hell are you doin' here, lady? That was all a lifetime ago! Go away and leave an old man in peace."

"Are the Parkers in peace?" I asked. "Is Hannah?"

The fear was back in those old eyes. "Just what do you think you know, miss?" he asked.

"I think you know," I baited him. "I know you know."

"I have no idea what you're drivin' at," he said, but tears belied the words. He was very distressed at this conversation. Should I drive the nail through his heart? Should I point-blank ask him the question?

I decided not to take his heart in my hands (*what possible good would that do?*), but I couldn't just let him off the hook, either.

"Everybody Hannah cared about did her wrong, didn't they? You were just one of the many." *How could it be? He seemed to shrink even further right in front of me.*

"Hannah was such a sweet young thing," he recalled from another lifetime. "I was … well, let's just say I wasn't what I should have been. My brother and his wife sent her away. Married her off to that good-for-nothin' Milton Parker, and they went to Florida. Never saw either one of them again."

"Yes, so I understand. Hannah and Milton lived in Oxbow with his son, Buddy. And with her daughter, Jeannie Sue," I could not stop myself. Jeannie Sue needed to be recognized too.

"A girl?" Clem stared at me for a long moment and then closed his eyes, tears dampening his cold, white cheeks.

"So, I'm here to see if I can find out what happened to them. I think they may be dead, but I can't seem to find out for sure," I told him.

"Dead? Could they all be dead?" he mumbled. He was talking to himself, I knew, wondering aloud. "Only me left? For a while yet. Just a while."

I had heard all I could stand and mumbled good-bye. I turned to go but was held fast by an icy hand gripping my own.

"You won't tell nobody, will you?" He was pleading. "I guess it don't really matter no more. Nobody left to care. But I just don't want nobody else knowin'. I'll be facin' my Maker soon enough."

He was more afraid of facing strangers than he was of facing his Maker? After over fifty years, this old man was still twisted.

I had to get out of there.

My questions weren't all answered, but I knew I had learned everything I could in Hayworth. Even Uncle Clem seemed genuinely not to know whether or not the Parkers were dead. It was time to go home. Monday would be a crunch, for sure. Funny, I don't think I had thought once about the paper since I'd been there. I called Glenn

Friday night to let him know, and he promised to meet me at the duck pond and bring Jeannie Sue's diary.

So, I lingered a while over breakfast at the diner. Mazie was her cheerful self. Over the last week, I had learned a little bit about her. She had a baby girl at home—no daddy to go with her. Mazie's mama took care of the little girl while she worked. She'd just gotten her GED and was trying to get some money together to start college. She wasn't exactly sure what she wanted to do, but she knew that college was the starting line for her.

The place was pretty empty, and I hoped business would improve with the lunch crowd. Mazie would never get to college on tips from this bunch.

Sitting there, I wondered at people's resilience. Maybe youth has something to do with it, but I've known many an old-timer who managed to keep his smile and—well, pluck—through a lifetime of trouble and pain. I offered a little prayer that Mazie could shape her life the way she wanted it. I was betting that she was tough enough, but a little divine intervention never hurts.

Heading over to the department store, I found a nice thank-you card for Mr. and Mrs. Morrison and some lovely wooden wind chimes I hoped they would like. The metal ones are nice, but after a while they tend to irritate me. The wooden ones have a nice, mellow tone. Of course, when that soothing tone starts to become noise, you can just take the darned things down! The lady behind the counter wrapped them for me.

Back outside in the crisp morning air, I wandered around the town that had made what I knew would be a lasting mark on my life. It was different from Oxbow but had a lot of the same intimacy about it. And I had met some people I knew I would never forget.

Just before noon I walked over to the bench by the duck pond and found that Glenn was already there.

He must've heard me coming, although I don't know how, and called out, "Mornin', Sunshine," as I came closer. Well, technically it was still morning for a few minutes.

Sitting on the bench, I returned his greeting, but then neither of us spoke for a few minutes. Glenn handed me a bag of popcorn, and we both fed the ducks till the popcorn ran out.

Finally, I said, "You know, these must be the best-fed ducks in the world!"

He chuckled and said, "You might just be right, there, Molly."

It got quiet again as the ducks turned and stepped back into the water, zigzagging their way to the other side of the pond.

Watching them go, Glenn said, "Those birds are so stuffed, it's a wonder they don't sink!"

We both smiled again, and I said, "This trip has been really special, you know. I feel like I made a good friend." He smiled and looked away for a second. "And I actually got answers to some of these questions that've been rolling around in my head. I had no idea what to expect when I decided to come up here. I just knew that I had run out of options in Oxbow and was praying I'd be able to find something here."

"I'm really glad this trip helped," he said simply.

"You've got to know that you've been really important in all of this, Glenn. You and your ducks"—it was only half a joke—"helped me keep my perspective. I've been struggling with this by myself, and staying grounded has been a real problem for me. Ghostly faces and forty-year-old mysteries are kind of new to me, you know?"

"I didn't do anything special," he protested. "You would have gotten your answers even without me."

"Maybe," I said, "maybe not. You sure helped when you put me in touch with Harley Dothan! And from the beginning, you were just what I needed, when I needed it. I want you to know how much I appreciate it."

Glenn was looking a little sheepish, and I didn't want to embarrass him anymore, so I grinned at him, and said, "Just say you're welcome!"

He complied, and the conversation got easier.

I handed him the wind chimes and the card for his folks and asked him to please apologize for my not bringing them myself. It was time for me to head back south and see whether I could finish unraveling this thing. Besides, I had real work to do at home!

"You know, I don't think I've ever met anyone I felt so easy with, at least not since this," he patted the arm of his wheelchair. "And I've got to say that helping out with your mystery has been an experience

I won't forget, either. Maybe you were just what I needed, when I needed it too."

He handed me back the little brown diary that had set me off on this wild-goose chase, and I tucked it into my bag. Then I pulled one of my business cards out. I didn't often get to use them—pretty much everybody in Oxbow knew who I was and that I was with the paper. I carefully wrote my home address and phone number on the back and handed it to him.

"You have my number too, right?" he asked. "After all, I expect a call when you finally get this thing unraveled. I'm hooked too, you know!"

So I promised to let him know how it all ended—if I ever found out myself! Then I stood up and, on an impulse, bent over and gave him a hug. To my surprise, he returned it.

Glenn waved as I turned to go and then sat there in his wheelchair, watching the ducks bobbing in the water.

CHAPTER 22

ON THE WAY BACK to Oxbow, my brain went round and round, coming back to the same thing time after time. A thought had occurred to me while I was talking to Harley Dothan. I wasn't sure how much he and Dennis Blankenship had in common, other than that something in their lives had apparently made them "fall into a bottle." For the past few weeks, when I pictured the lot across from my office, my faces were always there, lurking among the orchid tree branches. He had always been part of the background—there but not there. Now, in my mind, Dennis was always a part of the whole picture, hunched down on the ground, back by the oak tree. I knew I had to talk to Dennis. Somehow I felt he was the only one who might be able to make sense of this whole thing. Dennis was the key, I was sure, although I wasn't sure how I knew it. Very likely it was just the desperation of coming to another impasse with every discovery. Like a Chinese puzzle, layer upon layer, each revealing just a little bit while concealing still more.

As mile after mile of pine trees, palmettos, and malls slipped by, my thoughts kept coming, kept revolving around Dennis. It was time to catalogue everything I knew about the mysterious Mr. Blankenship.

"Dennis Blankenship, just how do you fit into all this?" I thought. Dennis was an enigma that most folks—including myself—had always just ignored. I'd talked to him enough to know that he was a lot smarter than he wanted folks to think. He seemed to be content with his life the way it was. He didn't require much. A warm, dry place when it was cold. A cool one when it was hot. And a bottle. He tolerated other people most of the time, it seemed. He was always polite, but he stayed within boundaries of his own making. He was distant, that's for sure. I'd seen him often enough. Wondered what caused that unusual, rolling kind of gait he had and those scars around his eyes, down his cheek and neck. I'd wondered often enough what had happened to him. Something terrible, for sure.

I'd mentioned it a couple times to different people in town. Nobody seemed to know. Nobody seemed to care.

Well, that's not really fair. Dennis wasn't exactly good at allowing people to care too much about him. Aside from Mattie Lou and Franklin, he didn't seem to have anybody at all that came close to being a friend. He kept everybody at arm's length. Mattie Lou, well, she was just one of those almost perfect human beings who are too rare on this earth. A widow since I'd known her, on a fixed income, she'd gladly share anything she had. I often wondered how it was that no one had ever done her serious harm by taking advantage of her nature. If ever anyone walked around with the word "target" printed on her forehead, Mattie Lou was it. And she had a special fondness for Dennis, it seemed. Or maybe my mind was just seeing connections that weren't really there. Mattie Lou was an absolute friend to all God's creatures, large and small. Maybe that was the end of it, right there. Maybe I was trying too hard to find a reason.

That brought me back to Dennis. He worked on occasion. Did odd jobs for me at the paper, washing windows, general fix-up, that sort of thing. He was really good at working with his hands. Once when he was at the office fixing a hole in the old flooring (it was, after all, an old building, built in the '30s, and something was always going out of kilter), he saw me struggling with the phone. I could hear the person on the other end, but apparently he couldn't hear me. Dennis just reached over and took it apart. Don't ask me what he did; he just fiddled with it for a minute and—it worked!

Okay, so he was good with his hands, and he knew something about telephone systems.

"Well, that really tells me a lot," I muttered to myself, as Willie, Waylon and the Boys serenaded me from my car radio.

"What do you think, Willie?" I asked. "Where's the magic button to make all this come together? Or am I just too tangled up with my secrets to see? Am I headed nowhere here?"

As usual, Willie was no help at all.

And so it went, all the way back to Oxbow. As I always do, I flipped the radio dial around from station to station, seeking wisdom from all my friends.

Mama Cass's strong voice came through, and Bob Edwards on public radio had a lot to say. Even Elvis chimed in. We all put our heads together, but—sorry to say—we ended up not knowing anymore than when we started. Kind of like the lost soul in an old country song who never wins but can't give up the struggle, either.

Back at home. Finally. Still daylight. I stopped at Frank's place—he had kept Dutch for me while I was gone and caught me up on the news. Dutch almost knocked me over when he jumped up to say hello. Yes, Dutch had done just fine, Frank said. He got along great with Fred and Barnie, Frank's two cocker spaniels. Everything at the office went just fine, he assured me. Looking at me, he said, "Molly, you look bushed. You know, things are really on track at the office. Why don't you take another day to rest up before coming in? I don't mean to say anything ugly, but you look like you really need some rest. Too much fun?"

"Well, I don't know about that, but I really am wiped out," I said. Knowing what kind of razzing I'd be in for if I took another day off to recuperate from my "vacation," I decided it was worth it. "Okay, you talked me into it," I said. "I'll be in Tuesday—but call me if you need anything."

Frank said he would, and Dutch and I headed home.

Driving into the yard, I pulled the key out of the ignition and grabbed a stack of drippy Styrofoam coffee cups and several candy bags—empty, of course. Dutch could hardly contain his excitement at being back home. He barely waited long enough for me to open the door before he practically launched himself out of the car and made a circuit around the yard, checking out his territory, before coming inside with me. I threw my ratty old bag on the floor—the dirty clothes would wait till tomorrow—and headed for the kitchen to pour a nice glass of wine. (Did I tell you that long-distance driving always wipes me out?)

The next thing was to give Glenn a call. I was suddenly all nerves and it took three tries to get his number right. I knew he had a big test coming up so I decided to keep it short. *Who am I kidding? I was all but desperate to hear his voice again.* He picked up on the third ring.

"Molly?" He sounded anxious.

"Hi, Glenn! I just got in ..."

"I was hoping it was you. I figured you should be back home about now," he said. "How was the trip back?"

He was timing my return trip. I took that as a positive sign.

"It was okay but I'm about wiped out," I told him. "I just can't take that much driving. It always tangles me all up inside."

"Yeah," he agreed, "and you've got a lot of other stuff tangling your insides too. Any revelations on the way home?"

"Not really, but I did realize something that probably should have occurred to me sooner. There's a man here, Dennis Blankenship —kind of the town drunk. Really, he's a nice guy," I rushed to add. I didn't want anybody to think badly of Dennis. I knew his life had to be tough. "I think I'll have a talk with him. He's always kind of the background, keeps to himself, but he seems to like that lot. It's a long shot, but I guess my short shots are all used up!"

Glenn chuckled. My pulse started to pick up as I pictured his impish little smile, the mischief in his eyes. *Hold on there, girl! Get your head back on! Glenn is a great guy, but he's a couple hundred miles away, remember? And he's in the middle of law school. And he's got his own inside-tangles he's still working through. It's slow-down time!*

"Don't worry. You'll get it figured out. I'm sure of it," he soothed.

We chatted a little about his parents—they were fine and sent their greetings. When he began talking about his classes I figured it was time to cut it off for the night but Glenn beat me to the punch.

"Guess I better back to the books." I was pleased that his voice betrayed a little reluctance. "And I know you're ready to get some rest."

So we said our good-byes and Glenn promised to call.

I poured a little more wine and I fled out onto the back porch to watch the river flow. Why is it that the slow meander of water is so calming? What is it about that steady fluid movement that drains away cares, as though someone has pulled a plug in your brain and they have all seeped out, dissipating like dreams that were never real in the first place?

Except something was real, here. I could feel it, even taste it. My faces made me see it, forced me to—no matter how hard I tried to turn away. I didn't have to be near the lot or even close my eyes anymore to see my faces—moving, living masks of lavender orchid shells and leaves concealing a truth I knew they wanted me to uncover. It—whatever "it" was—stayed right in front of me. Maddeningly just out of reach. I could feel it but couldn't touch it.

Wine—just two small glasses—on an empty stomach did me in. By the time the sun was pouring a glorious tint across the western sky, touching the river and the tall oaks with gold, spattering the sky with puffs of pink and lavender meringue, it was impossible for me to keep my eyes open. So, placing my glass in the sink, I headed for my bedroom. At that time there was no thought of locking the doors. No one in Oxbow ever did. What for? I crawled under my covers—I *have* to have a blanket, no matter how hot it is. I don't know, maybe it's a security thing. Don't really care. Just give me my blanket, that's all. Dutch curled up at the end of the bed, happy to be in his rightful place again.

Sleep came quickly, gently, till something jerked me right up out of it. It was so quick I couldn't comprehend what had happened. I was asleep. Then I was sitting up, my eyes straining unsuccessfully against the dark. Moonlight was streaming in through the window and outside the world was covered with a kind of opaque cloak. The trees, the white moonflowers at my back porch, the ever-flowing water all took on a kind of glow. Inside, all was black, at least until my eyes started to adjust and familiar shapes began to materialize. I could feel the numbing chill before I saw the shimmering, shadowy face or feel the aching sadness, the loss, an eternity of hopelessness cascading through me. No dream was this. I could hear the low growl—half whine, really—at my feet. Poor Dutch. He had to be terrified, confronted with such an unnatural presence, but he was still ready to defend me.

I knew I should try to reassure him somehow, but my mouth was so dry I was incapable of making a sound, much less any comprehensible words.

Smoky wisps curled in the air above my head, entwining, coming together, forming two chilling gray eyes, malevolent and foreboding. Cold. So cold. I wanted to pull my blanket around me but found I couldn't move. A curl of smoke twisted into a hard mouth spewing words I could not hear.

Deep and intense was the pain transmitted to me when I came face-to-face with Milton Parker—I was sure now that it was Milton who had accosted me under the trees—although this visit didn't have the sharp edge that other one did. It produced a kind of soft, smothering sensation. Though I wasn't gasping for breath, I felt like I was drowning ... straining with everything I had, I could see the life-giving air, my world waiting for me, but I couldn't get back to it. I struggled against the oppressive cold, against unseen hands pulling me down.

Then he was gone, and she was there. Unlike the apparitions in my orchid tree, I could see these faces almost clearly. I could see that she had once been very pretty, but any youthful promise there may have been had shriveled up and died long before the body followed. I was afraid, but this presence helped quell the panic Milton produced in me.

Hannah. That was my only thought. *Oh, Hannah, what did they do to you?*

Was that a response? The face shimmered in the moonlight, and the eyes—the same troubled eyes that had been tormenting me since I first saw those faces among the orchid tree leaves—spoke to me. I heard no words, but my body was almost physically battered, then invaded, by an overpowering need to know, to understand what had happened to these people. Hannah was telling me, the only way she could, to continue my search—pleading with me to find the truth. She desperately needed someone to know what had happened to her family.

The ache was unbearable. "Hannah, let me go! I swear I will find the truth. I know how you were abused all your life. I know how you worked to make things better for Jeannie Sue and Buddy. I know how you suffered from Milton, your parents, Uncle Clem. I feel your torment still. But, Hannah, please, let me go now. I can't fight your hell anymore."

Those eyes held me for an eternal second and then their presence slowly, slowly began to fade, the unbearable cold slipping away with it.

And then I was alone again. Dutch jumped up on the bed with me, shivering as I was, and whining softly. The moonlight was as soft and reassuring as before. The whiteness of my moonflowers still glowed, and the shining river kept to its westward journey. All the familiar objects in my bedroom were just as they had been only— what—minutes, seconds, hours before? I couldn't tell.

But I was different.

I realized that it was the reality of hell that broke over me, hard and cruel, with Milton's visit. Hannah brought me another view of eternity. And I wasn't anymore prepared for it than I had been for my first searing look. I was a living, breathing human. I wasn't supposed to know this much. How was I going to live with this kind of understanding, if that's what you could call it?

I wrapped my blanket as tightly as I could around my body and burrowed deep into my bed, my arms around Dutch. I tried covering my eyes but that only made it worse, so I stared out the window, gripped by shivering more violent than I ever thought possible. My mind numb, I lay there for a long time, praying and shivering. "Lord, what has happened to my life? I've seen things I don't believe any human was meant to see. So, why then? I know something happened to the Parker family. I know it was something terrible and that, even after forty years, there are people in town who must know about it. I've been working hard to find out what it was. I don't know why You gave me this task—surely there are people much more qualified to dredge this up. Just one more thing in this world I don't understand, I guess. Please, give me the strength to complete this, and guide me down the right path."

The prayer must have calmed me, because I actually did fall back to sleep, though it took a while. It was late morning when I opened my eyes again. I emerged from my little cocoon and stretched out my cramped limbs. Dutch's sleeping body was still sprawled out next to mine, his breathing deep and rhythmic. The sunlight was the most beautiful sight I'd ever seen. It was glorious! Pulling on the first old housedress I came to and a sweater to protect against the cool March morning—since that first nocturnal visit from Milton I'd been much more susceptible to the cold—I headed out to my back porch swing to revel in the morning glow.

The morning after Milton's first visit, the world seemed dark in spite of the southwest Florida sunshine pouring down all around me. Even the birds were subdued—or so it seemed to me. This morning, though, things were normal—better than normal! Way better than normal! Cardinals and mocking birds sang; Dutch pushed his way out through the screen door behind me and ran out into the yard. He barked frantically as a frog jumped from the high weeds into the river; squirrels darted through the trees chirping their joy or squawking their disapproval, insects hummed. I could hear the short, husky blast of a horn from a boater upriver demanding that the bridge be raised so he could pass under it. The world seemed right again.

Even so, I felt somewhat removed from it. I had a big job ahead of me and no clue as to how to get it done. All the way back from Georgia, I racked my brain about how to proceed. I laid it all out for myself time and time again the whole way back. One more time:

1. Hannah was raped by her uncle; got pregnant and was forced by her parents to marry Milton Parker. He took her and his young son, Buddy, back to Oxbow with him. Milton's first wife had left him and their son for another man.

2. Milton was an excellent carpenter, like his father, but liked the bottle a whole lot more than he liked to work.

3. Hannah had a daughter, Jeannie Sue, in 1929, the result of the rape by her uncle. The family lived in the house Milton and his father had built on the southeast corner of St. Claire Avenue and Baines Street.

4. The house was across from the *Oxbow Independent* and just down the street from Ruby Mae's Café. The family lived there until October of 1943. Sometime before Milton sold the house to Anderson St. Claire and rented it back from him—presumably because he needed money very badly. Well, that was certainly in character.

5. Milton worked, off and on, at a sawmill just south of town. In spite of his drinking, he had an excellent reputation as a carpenter and did quite a few jobs on his own throughout the county. During one of his sober spells working at the sawmill, he met a man named Charlie Weaver and brought him home as a paying boarder. Charlie Weaver had been in the army but got hurt working on vehicles in England and was discharged. He was working his way back home to Indiana or Illinois.

6. A lot of this information came from Jeannie Sue's diary, which my friend Barbara had given me. Barbara was Jeannie Sue's best—maybe only—friend when they were kids, and Barbara let Jeannie Sue keep her secret diary at her house so Milton would never find out about it.

7. In fall, 1943, Milton inherited the family farm in Georgia. He went up there to take care of his inheritance and sold the place. He sure wasn't going to work a farm! He wired most of the money he got from the sale to the Oxbow Bank and kept a couple hundred as "pocket money," according to his drinking buddy, Harley Dothan. Milton hung around town with Harley, drinking and carousing for a few weeks before heading back home.

8. Okay, here's the kicker. There was no reference to the Parker family at the museum, where virtually *every* early family at least rates a mention. I'd found nothing official to support their existence except a couple very cursory items in the county records. According to the *Oxbow Independent*, Miss Jolene, and Billy Brownly, the family moved up to Georgia to the old farm Milton inherited, and a few months later the fire department burned down the "ramshackle" house on the corner in a training exercise. I've known these people for years—can it be that there's a conspiracy around this family? Could this be an ugly secret nobody wants dredged up?

9. And then there were my faces. Okay, I didn't have a clue how to quantify them and I wasn't sure I wanted to go around letting people know about them. I only knew that they *were* real—I'm not creative enough to conjure up anything that terrifying in my head.

10. Oh, yeah. And one more thing. Just what could Greg Richards have to do with all this? That note and that ambush in the park—I didn't see how Greg could have any real connection to the Parkers, so someone else had brought him into this. Someone who knew I was

looking for answers about the Parkers and also knew that no one in this world could terrify me as much as Greg. Somebody was really serious about stopping me—and knew exactly how to get to me.

So that was the sum total of the facts I had. And they didn't add up. The question was, *where do I go from here?*

I kept going over and over my facts, looking for a connection I might have missed. Something that would make it all come together. But there just wasn't any real link. Finally, an idea crept into my overworked brain. I wondered how it had never occurred to me before. Maybe the lot itself was the key. That's where the faces clung to the trees. That's where I saw them—well, except for the times when Milton and Hannah paid me more personal visits. Dennis Blankenship was the only other person who ever seemed at all interested in that lot—except for Oliver St. Claire, and he owned it. Every now and then Oliver would be over there raking and cleaning up the lot. He did like a tidy place.

And that "tidy place" was about to become something entirely different. After allowing it to remain empty for some forty years, Oliver St. Claire had finally decided to make a change on that corner lot. It didn't take him long to get moving on building the doctor's office once this Dr. Michaelson committed himself to opening his practice in Oxbow. Within a few short weeks, the good doctor was already making himself known to the townspeople.

I'd met Dr. Arthur Michaelson one afternoon as I was leaving the office. Oliver was showing the lot across the street to a spry-looking older gentleman. Naturally, I had to go check it out.

Dr. Michaelson had lively sparkling gray eyes encircled by old-fashioned wire-rimmed glasses. Strands of white hair were displaced by the slight breeze, giving him a look somewhat reminiscent of Albert Einstein. In spite of his disheveled hair, one got the impression that there weren't many things out of place in the good doctor's life.

He reached out his hand to me as Oliver introduced us.

"Dr. Michaelson is the one who's going to set up his practice here," Oliver informed me. "He's a pediatrician from West Palm Beach."

The doctor and I exchanged greetings and a few basic facts about each other.

I asked, "So, what do you think of our little town?"

"Oh, it's just what the wife and I were looking for. We've been on the coast for a long time now and, you know, we really love it there, but it's just getting so crowded. And we're ready to start slowing down, enjoy life a little more. My wife has people over on the west coast and our son is down in Lauderdale, so we think this is a good compromise," he told me.

Oliver took over. "The doctor and I are just checking out the lot. The doc here already has plans for his office. Rex Dunham is on his way over and we're going to talk some about construction."

"Yes, I want to make sure we leave all these beautiful trees on this lot. Over in West Palm we had a nice office, but the whole place was concrete. We want to keep all the nice green things around us over here," Dr. M. said.

That made me feel much better, and I let him know that right away. "Great, Doctor! You don't know how relieved I am to hear that! Ever since I heard Oliver was going to build a doctor's office on this lot, I've been worried that these trees might go. I've looked at this lot for a long time, you see, and I'd sure hate to lose my view," I told him.

"Oh, we think these trees are the lot's best selling point," he said.

"We're glad to have you here," I said, "but I'm not sure how 'slow' it will be for you. I'm sure you know the only pediatrician we have is at the health department," I commented.

"So I hear. It just sounds like job security to me!" he quipped.

"So, is your wife with you this trip?" I asked.

"No, Verna stayed in West Palm. She's getting things ready over there. You know, it takes a long time to pack up thirty-five years of life. She'll be coming along next time, though," he responded. "And I want our goddaughter, Dana, to come and get a feel for this place and the folks who live here too. She's taking over my practice on the coast, but I'm really hoping—well, I'd just like her to get the feel of this place," he finished.

It was a couple months later when I finally met Verna Michaelson. She had accompanied her husband over to check on the construction. Mrs. Michaelson was in her early sixties, a cultured lady, but down to earth. She was quick-witted and spoke kindly to everyone, with a cheerful attitude that shone through her sky blue eyes. Her high-pitched voice had a kind of lilting quality that betrayed an Irish heritage. She had an avid interest in plants and was already asking about the local gardening club. Verna Michaelson was one of those women who seemed to be born with good taste and an easy grace.

I'd been watching the construction from my office window. It was moving along very quickly, and I was having a hard time getting used to the new view. Every time I looked up from my computer, I got a surprise. Oliver St. Claire, the Michaelsons, they were all ruining that lot, but I was trying my best to look at the whole thing in a positive light. The town certainly needed a pediatrician and Dr. M. seemed to be just the kind of man who would fit in nicely. Having met both the doctor and his wife, I was beginning to feel better. But, damn, I didn't like the idea of losing that little patch of serenity outside my window.

CHAPTER 23

Sitting on my back porch, staring at the dark water silently gliding westward, I felt—I knew—I was at an impasse. I could not go forward; I would not go back. Standing still was not an option.

Okay, Molly. So, what do you do? I asked myself.

There was only one answer. Forward it would have to be. The question I could not answer was: how? How does one find a path to the truth when surrounded by walls? Big, tall, blank walls.

My attention wandered to an osprey gliding peacefully over the river. I watched as it swooped down to the surface and plucked its slithery, dripping lunch from the gently rolling waters.

That's what I needed to do—pluck a squirming, unwilling truth out of the murky depths of forty years. And I had to do it without the osprey's keen eye and ability to pick out its prey from a clear, overhead view. The thought was appealing, though.

I imagined myself effortlessly gliding—gliding high over the waters, then veering south, off toward the lot that was the focus of the mystery. My imagination took me over the treetops to a totally new vantage point where a clear view down to the leaves came into focus. Below that, though, all was obscure. I was seeing forty years into the past.

Flames were roiling upward toward the lush, green canopy. I could see that some of the leaves were beginning to blacken from the heat and smoke. The rest of the scene, below the heavy tangle of leaves and branches, remained obscure—the thick smoke a curtain between me and the truth below.

What was happening down there? What could be hiding amid the billowing black mass? I wondered.

Try as I might, I could not see through it, so I cast my gaze across the street. There was the *Oxbow Independent* office—several renovations before "my" *Oxbow Independent*, but recognizable just the same. Even the cabbage palms were there, the most photographed trees in Oxbow—somewhat smaller, somewhat shorter—but there they were.

And on the other end of the block, back across St. Claire Avenue, there was the landmark St. Claire building. As ever, it sat grandly, marking the intersection—claiming it and the town for its own. The air was clearer on that end of the block, just a few stray clouds of black smoke drifted over the empty sidewalk.

No, wait! The sidewalk wasn't empty. There was Oliver, broom in hand. Imagine that! Forty years ago—and the man still had a broom in his hand. For a fleeting moment I wondered just how many brooms that man must have gone through in forty years.

Oliver! He must be back in town by now. He'd been out to some art show with his daughter, Callie. I could ask him about this whole thing. He had been there—right there—the whole time the Parker family lived there, probably with that same broom in his hands. He was the "hands-on" manager for the St. Claire family businesses. Anderson was the brains; Oliver his hands and legs; Elwood was the legal mind, though his son, Kyle, carried the mantle these days. With the trip to Georgia and all, I'd almost forgotten about Oliver. Of course he would know something, and he was always been amenable to talking about most anything.

Face it, Molly, you'll never be a master detective. Hercule Poirot has nothing to fear from you!

I hoped my little gray cells were recharging, because I had to keep digging. Tomorrow I'd approach Oliver—see what he could tell me.

Coming in that morning felt really odd, but I soon fell into step. During the day I got the lowdown on what had happened while I was out. Maria got cornered by Jack Taylor, a retired civil engineer—always complaining about something the county was doing, or shouldn't be doing or might do or might not do. I was usually his sounding board but, in my absence, poor Maria took the hit.

"Don't worry," I counseled her, "it only hurts while he's complaining."

Lunchtime usually meant a cup of soup and a container of yogurt at my desk. But that day was different. Today, I thought, I would unlock those voluntary chains and head across the street to Ruby Mae's Café. Hoppin' John—a Southern concoction of hamburger, chopped tomatoes, and onions over rice—was on my menu today. Hoppin' John with forty-year-old information for dessert.

Walking into Ruby Mae's Café, I looked around the familiar room—the original soda fountain and counter along one wall, the old telephone booth still in use, albeit with a modern telephone installed—the original shelves along another wall stuffed with old medicine bottles and curiosities, remnants of the time when a drug store shared the premises.

The place surely looked much the same as it had in the '40s.

But Oliver was nowhere in sight. The hair stood up on the back of my neck when I saw Oliver's painting of "my" lot. It appeared quite normal now—no ghastly images lurking there, waiting to pounce. Uneasy, I sat with my back to it, fighting the urge to turn and glance at it constantly; ready to flee at the first appearance of anything unusual. My seat was across from the round table where groups of regulars—some "movers and shakers" and some "shovers and makers"—gathered every morning to discuss the latest news of the town.

I finished my Hoppin' John between greetings from several townsfolk. As always, I picked up bits of news and gulps of gossip: the high school would be getting a new principal next year; two longtime school administrators were on the short list for the position; it was rumored that the mayor would have some competition this time around, after almost twenty years at the top city spot.

I was just about to pick up my check and leave, disappointed, when Oliver walked out from the kitchen. Broomless for once.

I waved him over.

"Molly!" he began as he sat in the chair across from me. "We don't see you here often enough!"

"I know. I don't usually take this much time for lunch," I explained.

"So, what's different today?" he asked.

I took a deep breath. "I've been going in circles with a sort of little mystery," I told him, "and thought maybe you could help me with it."

"Yes, I heard you were asking questions about some of our former residents," he said. "Sounds interesting."

"You've been in Oxbow a long time, right?" I began.

"Nearly all my life," he said proudly.

"And you've seen a lot of people come and go."

"Oh, yeah, of course."

"Your family has been at the heart of this town for a lot of years," I continued, sidling up to my real subject.

He smiled. "Yes, my dad put his mark on this town early on, guess you'd say."

"And your brother, Anderson, too?"

"Oh yes! He had the brains and the know-how to build things—not just bricks and mortar—but a real town, a good place to be, a town with a future. Anderson built a lot of the buildings around here and did a lot for the people. You never knew Anderson, Molly, but he had a kind of energy that most folks only dream about. Just being around him could energize you. Yes, ma'am, my brother Anderson knew how to get things done and always worked for what was good for the town. He was always like that; he'd do anything for "his" town."

"I guess Oxbow was a lot different then."

"Not really," he mused. Gazing through the large plate-glass window that looks out onto River Street, he continued, "You know my family is responsible for a lot of what the town looks like. My dad and my brother Anderson, mostly. They were two-of-a-kind—both had the natural ability to lead. Other men just naturally followed them, had confidence in them, you know? They could take in a situation at a glance—brains and intuition and leadership. Everybody just naturally looked up to them; did anything they asked."

"And what about you?" I asked.

He chuckled. "I was just the muscle. You see, I could always get the job done. Anderson would tell me what he wanted, give me direction. I just carried out his orders. Elwood, well, you know he always had the legal mind." He let his thoughts, his memories carry him to a place I couldn't quite follow but tried my best to see with his eyes.

"Right over there is the first piece of property my family gave the town." He indicated the park at the north end of the street down by the river. "My family's always been at the heart of this town. Of course, you know my dad donated the land for that park—wouldn't let them name it after him, though. Dad said it was the town's park and not about one man."

Everybody knew the St. Claires donated the park to the town. The family was virtually legendary in Oxbow.

Oliver didn't stop there.

"I think you would have appreciated Anderson's abilities, Molly."

"You were really crazy about your older brother, weren't you?" I said.

He smiled. "I guess this sounds like hero worship but ..." He stopped for a second and continued, a little sheepishly. "Well, I guess maybe it is. But Anderson had something special, even as a kid. He was a good ten years older than me. Elwood came a couple years after me. Anderson always looked out for us. He always knew what was best. And we just always understood that."

Something about all this hero worship brought out the twinge of perversity in my makeup. Mom always did say I was contrary—"just like your father!" And I don't think she meant it in the nicest possible way! I just couldn't help myself.

"Anderson sounds like he had a halo." It was mild but still a challenge.

That rated a semi-disgusted look from Oliver, replaced quickly by another sheepish grin.

"Yeah, I guess I do sound pretty corny, but to answer you, Anderson did make a few mistakes."

A shadow crossed his face then, and the years crept up on him as old memories crowded in. It was time.

"You must remember a family named Parker." There, I finally threw it on the table.

Oliver gave me a startled little look, even though he had to know it was coming, and then let his feelings loose. "Milton Parker! What a waste he was!" he began.

"Sure, I remember them. The Parker family rented the house on the corner, right across from the newspaper office. Milton took his family back to Georgia one night. Never heard anything more about them, not that that's any loss," he almost spat.

"Well, yeah, that's what Miss Jolene told me," I said. "She didn't think much of Milton Parker, either. But I was kind of hoping you might be able to tell me a little more about the family."

"More?" he asked. "Believe me, there's nothing about Milton Parker you'd really want to know."

"What about his wife?" I pushed, as lightly as my anxiety would allow. "And their kids? What were they like?"

That rated an inquiring look, but he answered just the same, "The wife, Hannah, was a special lady," he began, staring out the window. "She'd do anything for you. And she sure didn't deserve to be saddled with Milton. The kids—Buddy and Jeannie Sue—they were just kids, like the rest. Buddy was always out huntin' or fishin', Jeannie Sue was kind of sickly and quiet. What's so important about these people, anyway?" Oliver squinted at me as he asked the question.

"Well, I don't know that there's anything important," I lied. "It's just that they seem to be a mystery. Nobody seems to want to talk about them."

"Maybe 'cause there's nothing to say," was his answer. "Take my word for it, Molly, Milton Parker was never worth even this much conversation."

Getting up, he said to me, "You need to get over here more often, Molly. It's good to see you." Then he started back to the kitchen, whistling "Amazing Grace."

Okay, so Oliver didn't really give me anything substantial. Not exactly a surprise. It was the way this whole thing seemed to be going. The shadows seem to be more substantial than the facts—at least the few facts I'd been able to ferret out.

Face it, Molly, talking to Oliver was pretty much a bust, except he did get a little creepy on me there for a minute. He had a bad case of hero worship where Anderson was concerned. Okay. And he didn't care for Milton Parker. That part of the story didn't ever change— everybody had praise for Anderson; nobody had anything good to say about Milton.

"My" lot was being changed forever. After virtually forty years it was about to become "inhabited" again. It wouldn't be the quiet island of peace it had been. Progress is inevitable, I guess, and maybe nobody really cared. I'd miss it temporarily. But it wasn't just me. Dennis would miss it too. It was time to get serious about talking to Oxbow's gentle misfit.

Dennis had been in Oxbow for—oh, twenty years or so. The "town drunk," he was part of the background. Quiet, harmless. He was just there, and nobody paid much attention to him. A lot of folks seemed to like him well enough. The others tolerated him, although some of the more affluent ladies weren't inclined to display too much Christian charity toward him. Basically, Dennis didn't bother anybody, and nobody bothered him. He seemed to like it that way.

I realized that the lot was one of Dennis's favorite spots. Occasionally, I'd see him picking up a pack of hot dogs, crackers, or an apple at Birchwood's or a bottle at the Saddle Up Bar, and then walking back to his camp in the woods. Every now and then he'd be coming back from doing some handyman work somewhere—there were several folks in town who swore Dennis was the best handyman they'd ever had. That's how he made enough money to survive. That lot and his camp were the only places I could think of where Dennis spent any time, though. And of course, I saw him from time to time at the post office and the bank. But it was the lot I kept coming back to in my mind. It was, after all, a nice spot. Covered with oaks and that orchid tree, a couple palms and a locust tree—even a stand of bamboo. I wondered if Hannah had planted them.

So, was this place somehow special to Dennis? Or was it just a nice spot where he could get a different view of the world from his camp and let the world turn around him? Yes, I had to have a talk with Dennis. So, why was that such an unappealing prospect? I'd talked to Dennis lots of times, exchanged meaningless pleasantries.

"Morning, Dennis, how's it going?" "Not bad a'tall, Molly, not bad," he'd always reply.

"Better find a nice, dry spot, Dennis, it's surely fixin' to pour!"

"Yes, ma'am, think you're right about that."

I think I was afraid of another dead end. Still, what else did I have?

CHAPTER 24

I WAS THE FIRST one in the office the following Monday morning. I switched on my computer and made the morning coffee. Just as the first good whiffs drifted up from the pot, Frank came whistling in the door.

"Mornin', Molly," he called, "you look nice today!" (One of Frank's little ongoing jibes.) Then he came through the doorway into the production room, where we pasted up the paper every Tuesday night, and actually saw me for the first time. "Have a good weekend?"

I answered with my usual rhyme: "Same ol' stuff, but it didn't last long enough."

About that time, Minnie came in, and it seemed like all of Oxbow was right behind her. Yep, Monday mornings. Ya gotta love 'em.

There had been a fatal crash out on the state highway south of town over the weekend. A woman and her young son were killed. That meant a call in to the Florida Highway Patrol. Otherwise, things were pretty normal. Maria had a story about a new music program at the middle school, complete with pictures, and Frank went out to get a quick photo of Mr. Gonzalez with his latest catch out of the river. Snook.

At eighty-three, the only thing Mr. G. loved as much as fishing was getting his picture in the *Independent*—right by that old cabbage palm next to the office. It's sabal palm to most folks, but around here we still call it by the moniker the old-timers attached to it.

Anyway, that old swamp cabbage tree has been the backdrop for untold numbers of "grip and grins"—quick, set-up photos—by who knows how many *Oxbow Independent* reporters over the years. In Oxbow, anybody who is anybody has had his picture taken by that tree.

It wasn't long before there was no room in my brain for anything but getting the paper together. The day passed quickly, and I found myself alone in the office about dark, keeping an eye on the vacant lot across the street. Sure enough, I detected movement just behind and to the left of the foundation for the new doctor's office. It was ever so slight—Dennis never called attention to himself. He just hunkered down in the far corner and sat there.

Okay, Molly, it's now or never, I thought. Early April—the evening was a little cool. I grabbed my sweater and two cups of coffee—I knew Dennis took it black because that's how he always drank it when he did handyman jobs for us—and headed across the street.

Wishing I'd thought to bring an old newspaper to sit on, I plunked myself down next to Dennis and handed him his cup. Li'l Bit sat up and begged for the scrap of hot dog I had grabbed out of the refrigerator for him. Dennis had done some job, teaching this little pup to do tricks. But then, Dennis had a lot of time on his hands. For his part, Dennis accepted the steaming cup with a slight nod of the head but only said, "Heard you were at the beach."

"Well, I was out of town last week," I shied away from an out-and-out lie. Well, another one.

Silence. Dennis sat, apparently pondering the infinite mysteries of Florida's sandy soil, while I tried to come up with a way to introduce my subject without scaring him off. After all, he wasn't much for conversation, and if he didn't want to talk, his usual reaction was just to say good-bye politely and go on his way. So we sat and listened as an occasional truck headed down River Street, or an owl hooted from an unseen resting place.

"I like this place," I finally said. "I've always liked this place."

No response.

"You know, for as long as I've worked at the *Independent* I've always wondered about this lot. It looks so pleasant, you know? With the trees. I've found myself wondering about who lived here, what they were like."

That rated a glance in my direction and sparked a flash of inspiration in me.

No! It couldn't be!

"You see them too, don't you, Dennis?"

No mistake. That was definitely a glance in my direction, so I continued. "The faces." There. I had finally committed myself.

Now Dennis's hands were shaking so much he had to put down his cup or spill his coffee on the ground. He looked away for a long moment and made a low moaning sound I've never been able to adequately describe. Guttural. Primal.

"I thought I was the only one," he whispered as much to himself as to me. "Are you sayin' that you really see them? How can that be?"

"I'm sure I don't know," I said. "But I know that something really bad must have happened here. It's only been a couple months that I've really seen these faces but, thinking back, I know there was something about this place that drew my attention from the first time I came here to live with Aunt Nell. I didn't really see anything but, you know, little flicks of light, sort of. Distortions—I don't really know how to describe it." It was time to lay it all on the line. "I tried my damnedest to ignore them, but a few weeks ago I knew it was no use. So I started looking into the people who lived here. The Parker family."

I was trying hard, and, for my reward, I got a little grunt out of Dennis.

"You know, nobody in Oxbow will talk about that family," I continued. "None of the old-timers. There's nothing in the museum about them—and that little museum has information on every last family that lived here in the early days. Miss Jolene told me the family went back to Georgia to work the family farm. That's what old editions of the *Independent* said too. And that their house burned down that same night they packed up and left, and the fire department finished the job in a training session a few months later."

I could see I had Dennis's attention so I pressed on.

"I just came back from up there—Georgia," I fessed up. "I didn't really go to the beach. Went up there last week to see if I could find any answers 'cause I sure wasn't getting anywhere here. And I did find some people who shed some light on this for me.

"I know Milton Parker went up to Hayworth when he inherited the family farm. I know he sold it right away because he didn't want to work it. He wired most of the money back here to the Oxbow Bank. After hanging around Hayworth for a couple more weeks with a drinking buddy, he left to come back here. That's where everything dead-ends. The diary ends with October 1, 1943. Nothing anywhere in it says anything about moving to Georgia or anywhere else."

I looked at Dennis to see how he was taking all this information. He had lost all color and was almost as pale as "my" faces. Where his hands had been shaking before, now his whole body trembled. I almost screamed when his hand shot out and grabbed my arm. My coffee was a rapidly diminishing brown spot in the sandy soil. Dennis's haunted eyes practically glowed, and he whispered—demanded—"What diary?"

My arm was beginning to get numb where Dennis had it in a vice grip, but I barely noticed it.

Li'l Bit squirmed, sensing the sudden tension.

"Jeannie Sue's diary," I told him. "She was Milton and Hannah's daughter, and she had a diary she kept at her friend Barbara's house. Barbara—you know, Miss Jolene's daughter—gave me the diary a couple weeks ago. Said she never had the heart to read it. The family must have left in an awful hurry, because she was sure Jeannie Sue would never have left it if she had the chance to pick it up."

Dennis was anguished. Dazed. Energized. He was on his feet, pacing. "Yes, Jeannie Sue did have a diary. I'd forgotten all about it. Miss Johnson gave it to her," I heard him say.

Realization washed over me, and I came up sputtering from the truth. I heard myself say, "Tell me what happened that night, Buddy."

Li'l Bit and I just watched as Buddy—the man I'd known for years as Dennis Blankenship—walked over to the orchid tree that I was so pleased would remain where it had stood for so long. I could hear him saying something—talking to someone. I couldn't make out the words. Agitated, he drew his hand through his unruly hair, seemed to search around for—I don't know what—then walked back to me and squatted down in the same spot he'd just left. Li'l Bit settled back down in the exact position he had before.

"Forty years. And in all this time I don't think I ever gave Jeannie Sue's diary a thought," he said.

When he finally began speaking, he was amazingly calm. And it all poured out.

CHAPTER 25

B UDDY'S STORY.
"Papa was a son of a bitch. I know how that sounds, but God help me it's the truth. I never knew him to give anybody one honest emotion except hatred, jealousy, greed. It was always all about him. All the time. Sometimes I'm not even sure we were real to him except as things to be used.

"When Charlie Weaver came into our lives ..." He stopped. "You know about him?" he asked.

"Yes," I said, "he was in Jeannie Sue's diary."

He nodded. "We all thought he was the best thing that ever happened to us. I don't know, maybe he was. It sure as hell was the first time me and Mama and Jeannie Sue felt like real people in our own home. That's why I spent so much time out in the woods, I reckon. It was the only place I didn't feel like I didn't belong, ya know?"

It was my turn to contribute a little grunt to the conversation.

Buddy continued, "I guess school was like that for Jeannie Sue. You know, that's where she felt real, like she mattered.

"Jeannie Sue was so pretty, just like I know Mama must've been till Papa sucked all the life out of her. Funny. After Charlie Weaver moved in, though, Mama changed. There was a spark left in her that Papa hadn't killed after all. I didn't understand it at the time. Hell, I

185

was just a kid. What did I know about men and women—the good things, anyway. Not like I ever learned any of 'em around Papa."

"Tell me about Charlie Weaver," I said, praying I wasn't pushing too hard.

Buddy's gaze remained fixed on a spot up in the orchid tree, but he continued. "Charlie Weaver made me a radio for my sixteenth birthday. Man, what a surprise that was! It was a rebuilt one, really."

I nodded, and I think I murmured something about reading that in Jeannie Sue's diary. A jagged lightning flash streaked across the sky in the west. It was early in the year, but there just might be some rain headed our way. A dank smell in the chilly air drifted up to my nose.

Words kept pouring out of Buddy, sometimes gushing like a pent-up spring that's been uncorked, sometimes slowly. Painfully. Oozing from a long-tortured, festering soul.

"Never had a real birthday before that," he said, "Since, either, come to think of it." His battered face wavered between the softness and the harshness of the memories gripping him.

"That man started a spark in me too—an interest in something. Lord knows I had damn little interest in anything, 'cept hunting and fishing, walking out in the woods, and taking my old flatboat out on the river. If I could do it alone, in my own space, it was okay. I just couldn't take anybody crowding in on me. Guess that's why I always hated school. Teachers are always there, looking over your shoulder. It was even hard to be around Mama and Jeannie Sue too much. Felt real guilty about that 'cause Mama was always so damn good, ya know?" A rueful smile crossed his lips. "But she knew when I needed space and just let me be. I wonder if she ever knew how much that meant to me. Jeannie Sue, she was a good kid. Real pretty and smart. Papa was 'specially hard on her. Guess 'cause she looked so much like Mama."

I suddenly had a thought. Did Buddy know about Uncle Clem? Did he know the secret of Jeannie Sue's birth? I decided he deserved the truth about everything, but now was not the time. I would give him Jeannie Sue's diary when the time was right. It belonged to him, anyhow.

"Anyway, like I said, Charlie Weaver was just about God, I thought. Or at least sent by Him." Chuckling he added, "I wondered at the time what took Him so long. Charlie knew a lot of things, and he was real good about sharing his knowledge."

Getting up, Buddy's eyes swept across his old yard, stopping at a spot just beyond and to the east of that orchid tree. A couple more lavender shells floated down to join the jumble of others on the damp ground.

"That's where the house stood. It was really a good, strong house. Nice place. I guess Grandpa Cecil must've been able to keep Papa in tow. They built the place together when Papa was a kid. Did you know that?"

I nodded, afraid to speak. I don't think he was really talking to me anyway.

"Mama always took good care of it. Cleaned and shined it up like it was a palace. I can still see her with her hair all tied up in that old blue bandanna, sweatin' in the heat, getting rid of every speck of dust on our old furniture, erasing every streak on every window in the house; up to her elbows in hot water scrubbing our dirty clothes—and sometimes the neighbors' too. Jeannie Sue helped out when she was able. Jeannie Sue was always a little sickly. Fragile, you know? Like the blooms on this old orchid tree." The expression in his voice changed again as a new thought hit him.

"Man, she really loved this old tree. It was right outside her bedroom window."

"I got the impression from her diary that Jeannie Sue was a thoughtful kind of kid," I said. He nodded his head pensively.

"Sometimes, this time of year, I'd come into the room, and she'd just be starin' out the window watching these flowers fall to the ground. Used to wonder what she was thinkin' about. I used to drive that poor girl to distraction sometimes." He smiled at that thought. "Like all big brothers do, I reckon. But whenever I saw her in that mood, I'd always give her a little extra space—like I needed sometimes."

Another change in expression.

"Well, anyway, I found out Charlie knew a lot about radios. I was sixteen. It was a whole new world for me. Charlie taught me what radios were all about. He taught me how to build one. Like I said, I thought Charlie was sent straight from God.

"He explained things to me so I, a dumb woods rat who hated the very idea of school, could understand. And for the first time I found out that learning something without a fishing pole or rifle in your hand could be fun.

"One mornin' Mama sent me in to Charlie's room to get his dirty clothes. Charlie was gone on one of his trips, and she was fixin' to do some wash. Mama hated dirty things layin' around, ya know? So she sent me up to my old room—Charlie's room—to fetch them for her. I balked, 'cause I was on my way down to the river to catch some fish, but I went on up to do what she asked. There was a little pile of clothes in the far corner so I went to pick them up. When I grabbed them there was something hard and bulky underneath. Scared the bejeebers outta me. I knew there'd be hell to pay if I broke something. Then I took a better look at this thing on the floor, and I realized what it was. Charlie himself told me all those evenings he spent teachin' me about radios. It was a shortwave radio."

"I thought you weren't allowed to have those things during the war," I said, astonished.

"That's true, and I wondered, 'Now what in the world would my friend Charlie Weaver want with a shortwave radio?' Maybe he was making it for somebody, or maybe he was fixing it for somebody. I was rollin' it over in my head when Mama called me again, waitin' for the dirty clothes. So I just left the radio in the corner and took the clothes down to Mama. But I left a few of the clothes on top of it—if anybody else found it, things could get real serious. It was in the middle of the war and, you're right, civilians weren't allowed to have shortwave radios. I gave Mama the clothes and then I grabbed my fishin' pole and headed off to the river.

"All the rest of the day I sat with my pole in the water, but my brain wasn't on my fishin'. Something was screwy, ya know? About Charlie.

"About a week earlier I went with him and Papa to Sandy Point over on the lake. The sugar company needed some work done, and they always called Papa for any kind of woodworking. Anderson St. Claire—he was the mayor and the biggest businessman in town—

always called Papa when he had carpentry work. He was connected somehow with the sugar company, too, and had recommended Papa to them years before. Guess they liked his work, too, 'cause they kept calling him back, 'specially for a big job. When he worked, Papa was the best there was. It was a pretty big job that time, so he brought me and Charlie along to help out. 'Sugar' didn't care. They were glad to pay, 'cause they knew the job would be done right, and this way it would get done quicker. Papa and Charlie Weaver went over every day for a week. They took me along on the weekend.

"I spent the mornin' being a "gofer," then at lunchtime the three of us went over to the drugstore just a block or so down the road. They had a little lunch counter in there then. The stools were empty, so we all sat down at the counter. There were three British flyboys sitting over in a booth just on the other side of us. You know, from the training camp over there outside of Sandy Point. Man, they looked sharp in their uniforms! I can't tell you how that impressed me, sitting there with guys from all the way across the ocean! I thought I was really in the big time then! They were just mindin' their own business, but I could hear some of what they were sayin'. Sounded real important to a sixteen-year-old boy who'd never been anywhere, but it was just chitchat.

"'Course it would have impressed you," I said, "all kids love new things, things they've never been exposed to before," I said, knowing he wasn't really listening.

"Before we could order, one of sugar company employees came runnin' in. One of the bigwigs needed Papa for somethin' right away. Papa wasn't too pleased, but he got up and went with him. Charlie Weaver and I went ahead and ordered.

"Before our sandwiches got there, though, another man walked through the door. Some guy at the other end of the counter leaned over and said he was one of those German POWs from over in Craven's Corner. Said the guy worked down the street at the dry cleaners. Everybody knew they had a POW camp over there, but I sure never expected to actually see any of 'em."

"I never knew there was a POW camp around here till I read about it in Jeannie Sue's diary," I said, mostly to myself.

"I knew they let the prisoners out of the camp during the day to work all over Sandy Point and Craven's Corner. When the day was over, they all went back to the camp."

"And they trusted them like that?" I couldn't quite believe it.

"They weren't worried about any of the prisoners escaping," Buddy said, "This whole area was pretty far out at that time, and there was just no place for them to go," he said.

"Anyway, I guess those British cadets in the drugstore must've heard it, too, or they already knew who he was, 'cause that German guy didn't look no different than anybody else. No uniform or anything. But you could see that one of those British boys was really getting sore. You could see it in his eyes. He started kind of mumbling; then he started getting louder, sayin' about how it wasn't decent for some blokes to be in regular company. That's what he called them—"blokes." The guys he was with tried to shush him—calm him down."

"I can see how British pilots and German POWs wouldn't mix very well," I put in.

"The German guy had to see what was goin' on but just went about his business, went over and picked up a bottle of aspirin and went to take it to the girl at the cash register. Well, he had to walk back past that booth with the Brits in it again—there wasn't any other way to go—and the one that was carryin' on so stuck his foot out and tripped him. Well, that man come up swingin', and it started to get pretty hot. The other cadets grabbed their buddy and held him back." Buddy's agitation grew as he continued. His eyes glared into his soul, at the memories only he could see. "Charlie Weaver grabbed that German guy and swung him around to the stool on the other side of him and held him there. Those English guys had a time of it, but they finally hustled their buddy out of the store. The third one threw some money on the table and stopped long enough to apologize to everybody in the room before he caught up with the others.

"'Sorry about the row,' he said, 'but my mate here, he lost his fiancée in the Blitz a while back and well, he's still taking it rather hard, you see.'

"Hmph! Sounds strange, what with all that just happened, but that little bit of politeness really stuck in my head."

"Funny the things you remember," I agreed.

"Things were quiet then, after they left. Charlie kept his hand on the German guy's arm for a while before he let him leave.

"My brain was so full of what I just saw that I couldn't eat when our sandwiches arrived. It wasn't the ruckus—that really wasn't much. That British guy's buddies and Charlie Weaver kept it from getting out of hand. It was something else I heard that I couldn't get out of my head.

"When Charlie swung that guy over to the stool I heard him say something in his ear. Couldn't tell what it was, but I knew what it wasn't. It wasn't English. I thought about it all that afternoon back on the job and could only come up with one explanation. It had to be German, right? The guy was German—so why would he talk anything else to him? I knew that POW could speak English because when he came in he asked the girl at the counter where the aspirin was. But Charlie spoke to him in his own language. It all happened so fast, but I knew what I heard.

"When we were alone, I finally got up enough nerve and asked Charlie about it. He just laughed and said, yeah, it was German, all right. Said his grandma and grandpa came over from Munich, and they used to talk German to him when he was a kid. Said he just told the guy to settle down and let it ride.

"So, when I was hunkered down under that tree watchin' my line bounce around every time a boat went by, my mind was goin' in circles. Charlie talkin' German to a prisoner of war. Charlie goin' off for days at a time. Charlie knowin' all about radios. And findin' that shortwave under his dirty britches, like that. Strange place to leave a radio, I thought. A shortwave radio! Now, what would Charlie be doing with such a thing? I wondered. I knew they were used for long-range communication, and you weren't supposed to have that kind of thing during the war. Folks might get the wrong idea.

"So finally there it was in front of me. My friend, the only man who ever really gave a damn about me. The man who made my Mama look like a girl again. The man who made Jeannie Sue smile. That man was a German spy. My enemy. Friend to the man that killed Chick St. Claire, for all I knew—to the men that were killing American boys every day."

Wet, dirty streaks were crawling down Buddy's disfigured cheeks by that time. He wiped his nose on his sleeve and then ran his hands under his eyes, smearing the tears across his cheeks and started again. It was hard going, I could see that. I could feel the strain he was under, and I wondered if I would have the strength to live Buddy's life. Or Jeannie Sue's. Or Hannah's.

He continued, "What was a sixteen-year-old kid supposed to do with that kind of suspicion? Charlie was my one friend, 'cept for a few of the guys that went fishin' or huntin' with me once in a while. What the hell was I supposed to do now?" His agitation escalated. "I studied on it all day till 'bout sundown when I decided Franklin was the only one I could go to. He'd know what to do.

"Franklin would be at Ruby Mae's Café about seven o'clock to pick up Betsy, you know—his daughter—and take her home after cookin' all day. Mama knew I was fishin', so she wouldn't worry about me. I thought then that those next few hours were the longest I'd ever live through," Buddy said. With a wistful kind of sneer, he added, "Yeah, I wish!"

"When I just couldn't stay still any longer, I headed on over to Ruby Mae's kitchen to wait for Franklin. Betsy passed me a biscuit, and I tried hard to eat it, but it just wouldn't go down. Betsy kept givin' me looks like she knew somethin' was wrong, but she didn't say anything. When Franklin finally walked through the door, I ran over to him so fast I almost knocked him over. He started to give me a scoldin', but then he must've seen my face. He took me by the arm, and we went out to the back.

"You know that quiet way Franklin has of lettin' you know you can talk whenever you're ready?"

I nodded. "Yeah, been there a time or two," I told him.

"That's the way it was. We just stood there, out in the dark. Funny. I can still remember how the moon was so dim, and the stars were just beginning to poke out over us. And there was this breeze and the smell of fried chicken from Ruby Mae's kitchen. Any other time it would have been a perfect dusk. We sat there for a while on a couple old milk crates they used to keep stacked up out back. I remember hearing somebody's radio, some comedy show as I recall. Jack Benny, I think. The last thing I could think about was laughing, though. Neither of us said anything for a long time till I just couldn't take it anymore. I was about to bust. I needed to get it said, and it was pushing its way out of me, but I just didn't know how to start.

"I don't even know how I finally did get started or just what I said. I just remember that for the first time—the only time I know of—Franklin looked like he didn't know what to do. At the time it didn't seem strange, but now I look back and wonder how it was that he didn't tell me to go on home and stop makin' up tales. But he didn't. For some reason, he believed me.

"'Go on home now, boy,' he told me. 'You jus' laid some powerful stuff on my shoulders, and I needs to think on it awhile. Don' tell nobody else, hear me? Nobody! We's can talk some mo' tomorra.' I waited till I saw him leave with Betsy. I just hated the thought of going home—worse than ever.

"When I finally got up my courage and started for home, I saw Papa's truck pull up to the house. Damnedest time for him to come home. Gone three weeks, and he had to come back just then!

"So I went back to my spot behind Ruby Mae's to figure out what to do. Mama and Jeannie Sue were over to the Bruners—Miss Bruner'd been feelin' down, and so they went over to clean up the place for her. That always took a while 'cause Miss Bruner wasn't such a good housekeeper, ya know? I can still hear Mama sayin', 'Bless her heart, she does the best she can.' Most folks just said Miss Bruner was lazy. Anyway, Mama and Jeannie Sue wouldn't be back from there till about nine o'clock, shore thing.

"I watched as after a while Papa got into the truck and headed on over to the Red Spot—big surprise. I don't know why he took the truck to go three blocks. Anyway, I just couldn't help myself. When Papa was inside the Red Spot, I headed on over there. I wasn't allowed anywhere near that place, a' course, but I just needed to—I don't know why. But something made me head over there. There weren't many folks around. Just about the whole town was down in Miami to a big war bond rally. They wouldn't be home till 'round midnight, everybody figured. With the war on, gas was rationed, ya know. They all piled up into buses, though, to go to the rally 'cause it was for the war effort. Anderson had set it all up. Those few that didn't go mostly stayed home. So there was a coupla fellas at Ruby Mae's and a couple at the Red Spot, that was about it. Guess Papa just couldn't stay away from that watering hole. Or maybe he just didn't want to come home and be with us," he said bitterly.

Li'l Bit stirred as a lone mosquito flew past his nose. He snapped at the pest but missed. Buddy waved it away and laid his scarred hand down on the little dog's head before continuing.

"So I slipped on over there, across River Street. The Red Spot used to be right over yonder, where the dry cleaner is now," he pointed just down the road. "I knew I'd get my hide tanned good if Papa saw me there, so I hid out back behind the parking lot not far from the back door. For some reason, Papa always used the back door. Wasn't very long till the door opened, and all the muffled noise suddenly got louder, but I couldn't make out anything but little bits of music in the background. Mike Sheffield and Curley Hackett come out and stood by Mike's truck, a couple feet from where I was hiding behind old Mrs. Pringle's fence." He smiled. "I can tell you she put it up right quick when they opened the Red Spot right behind her house!

"They were laughing and walking pretty unsteady, like most of the times I'd seen that pair leaving the bar. I could smell the cigarette smoke and the stale beer. Curley spoke first, through that wad o' tobacco he always had in his mouth. Juice dripped down on his shirt when he opened his mouth, but I'm sure he didn't even notice.

"I can still hear Curley. 'Hoowee! Can't remember when we had this much fun, Mike! Ah thought ol' Milton was gonna bust when he heard us talkin' 'bout Hannah and that Charlie Weaver fella. If ah'd a seen him come in I'd a shore kep' my mouth shut. Still, it ain't ever' day ya get to see a man's face when he finds out his wife's got a likin' fer another guy. Yessir, ol' Milton sure is hot!'

"'Gonna get a lot hotter 'fore he goes home, too, the way he's packin' 'em away,' Mike said."

By this time, Buddy's face had no color in it at all, but he continued, "I guess Curley had some second thoughts, 'cause then he backed up a little: 'Poor ol' Hannah's in for it now! Ya know, maybe we should go on over there an' warn the pore woman. I don't mind gettin' Milton's goat, but I feel kinda bad about Hannah. She took care of my maw before she died.'

"'Naw,' Mike said. 'She's not home anyway.'

"'Oh, yeah, that's right.' Curley wasn't ready to let it go yet, though.

'Guess we could go on over to the Bruner's place and warn her there, though. You know she'll be there a while, yet!'

"'Yeah,' Mike cut in, 'ol' Miss Bruner ain't much for mops and brooms. Pore ol' Hannah and Jeannie Sue'll be a while yet.'"

"Nice guys, Mike and Curley," I ventured.

Buddy took no notice but continued, "It was only a few feet to his truck, but Mike fell twice on the way and near 'bout had to crawl over to it. I don't know how many times he tried before he finally managed to open the truck door—Curley just alaughin' the whole time. God, they were ugly! Any other time watchin' him try to pull himself into the driver's seat woulda been a real hoot! Charlie Chaplin couldn'ta done it better. But nothin' was funny by that time. Once he was finally in, he couldn't find his keys and fell back outta the truck. So Curley took over and got Mike into the passenger's side. He managed to drive off, but I don't know how. Curley wasn't in much better condition than Mike was."

Buddy's ravaged face suddenly contorted.

"Laughin'," he spat out, "all the while they were laughin', knowin' what Papa was likely to do when he finally got ahold of Mama.

"And they both took advantage of her good heart. Lots of times she did for them and their families, and they always seemed grateful. Ha! I remember thinking then I'd never so much as take a drink if that's what it turned people into." He shook his head mournfully, unbelievingly. "Look at me now!"

Silence took him over again. I can only imagine how hard it was for him to say all this. He just stayed there, with his back up against that tree, lichens and airplants sprouting out all over it, watching a couple brown squirrels chasing each other through the branches over our heads. His face was unreadable. Finally, he let out a long, low sigh and then started again.

"So after Mike and Curley left, I decided maybe I should get the law. If Papa come home in that state and lit into Mama, well, that would be it, shore. I was just leavin' my hiding spot when the music and talk got louder again. The back door to the Red Spot was open, and this time it was Papa who come stumblin' out.

"I could hear him grumblin', but I couldn't make out the words. Just as well. I didn't need to hear him to know what he was sayin'.

Anyway, I guess he forgot he had the truck, 'cause he just started walkin' home—clean forgot about some hot poker game Mike and Curley talked about, I reckon, or maybe the thought of somebody actually makin' Mama happy was more than he could take, even fallin' down drunk. I'd seen Papa drunk lots of times, and he wasn't in too bad of shape, not for him, anyway. I knew from experience that, even drunk he could still be real nasty. Especially if he was drunk and mad—he just got meaner, and it seemed to kind of energize him. Still, the way he was walkin', I knew it'd be some time before he got to the house. I prayed he'd fall down and fall asleep right there on the sidewalk before he got to the house.

"When I was sure he couldn't see me, I left my hiding place and ran around the back way, over to Henry Graber, the town marshal's house, just half a block down, but nobody was there. Maybe they went over to the war bond rally, I don't know. I just knew I had to protect Mama somehow. So I ran on home and damn! Charlie's old Studebaker was parked out in the street! Should I warn him? I argued with myself for just a second or two before I jumped up onto the porch on the far side of the house and ran inside. Took the stairs three at a time up to Charlie's room screamin', 'Papa's comin'. He's dead drunk and he's after you and Mama!'"

Buddy paused for a moment. Dully, I realized that my scrubby fingernails were taking a beating through all this. *Damn! Down to the quick this time!* Then he began again, and any thought of my fingernails vanished.

"Charlie was sitting in his room at the shortwave radio spewing out scratchy squawks and screeches. 'Don't you know how to knock?' he snarled, and cut the thing off. I was stunned. Can't imagine it now—what with all that happened up to then, but I sure was. Guess I didn't quite believe it about Charlie—the spy stuff—till that moment. But I pushed it away. 'I know about you,' I told him. 'I know about you! But I don't care 'bout that right now. Papa's back. He's been drinkin', and he knows about you and Mama.'

"Charlie's face changed then. I can still see him runnin' his hand through his hair—he did that when he was thinkin'. Told me to get out, get far away, and see if I could find Mama. 'Don't let her come back home,' he told me. 'I'll handle your father.'

"I think those four words scared me worse than anything else that night, up to then. 'Go now! It'll all be all right!' he told me."

"Damn! What a load for a sixteen-year-old to carry," I said, more to myself than to Buddy.

"I ran outta the house, slamming the screen door, and grabbed my old bike outta the yard. It took me six months to build that thing—tradin' for a wheel or a handlebar. A piece at a time. I was glad I had it that night! Hopped on and pedaled as fast as I could. Franklin was my only hope. If I couldn't find him, I'd just have to come back and confront Papa and Charlie myself, though I really didn't think I could."

Buddy walked over to the orchid tree, caressed its bark with one disfigured hand. Then he went on …

"I made real good time gettin' over there. Knocked on the door as hard as I could. I'd been to Franklin's house lots of times. Used to help him out on his ice run sometimes. Anyway, I reckon they thought I was gonna bust it down the way I was bangin' on the door. They were prob'ly right. Betsy answered the door, and I just got out that ah had to see Franklin before she slammed it again. Wasn't a good thing for a white boy to be seen in that neighborhood after dark, but I just kept bangin' on the door till Franklin came out. I heard him tell everybody else to stay put in the house, and we sat over on the porch swing. Guess everybody was pretty surprised what with me showin' up in such a state, but I really didn't notice. The only thing I remember is Franklin's voice and my fear.

"We sat down, and I started to blurt everything out, but Franklin made me take a couple deep breaths and start slow. Guess it was comin' out all in a jumble, and he couldn't follow me.

"I told him that Papa was back in town. He had been at the Red Spot where he found out about Mama and Charlie Weaver and that he was stumblin' his way home. Told him Papa would kill Mama, for shore. Prob'ly Charlie too. Told him Mama wasn't home yet, but Charlie was. I told him I'd warned Charlie, and he sent me to warn Mama. I went to him first, 'cause it was a lot closer.

"Franklin was thinkin' real hard. I knew what I was askin' him to do. He could pay dearly.

"After what I guess was a few minutes—I know it seemed like

forever—Franklin got up and told me Charlie Weaver was right. I should go warn Mama. He'd go over to the house and see what he could do. I balked at that idea. Thought I should go with him. We talked a little, and he finally said I could go with him but that somebody needed to warn Mama. I had to promise to go when he told me to. He went inside and told his family to stay put, no matter what, picked up his old hat, and we walked out into the yard. Then we threw my old bike in the back of his pickup truck and climbed in. He drove back over to our place, still thinkin'. I don't think either of us said a word.

"Just before we got there he warned me, 'When we get dere, boy, you stay outta the way.' Franklin parked across the street from the house. In those days there was a little cobbler shop there, next to the newspaper office. He parked behind the shop. Franklin got out, and I followed him like a shot, but he grabbed me and pulled my arm hard, keeping me from just shootin' across the street. We hid behind the swamp cabbage tree between the shop and the newspaper office. It was a perfect spot. It was pretty dark by this time—we were behind in the light bill again, and the electric company shut off the power, but the oil lamps were lit in the parlor, and we could see right into the windows. If Mama had been home, the curtains would have been drawn—there was a blackout, you know. But Charlie Weaver didn't take it seriously, I guess, or maybe he was hopin' some of his Nazi buddies would see it. I don't know, but the curtains were still open.

"'Don't you be runnin' up dere, now!' Franklin whispered. 'Ya gotta stay hidden back here, leastways till I's checks the situation out.'

"Franklin looked real hard all around before he started across the street, but he only got a couple steps before a truck pulled around the corner with its lights out. Franklin hit the ground and crawled back over to the cabbage tree where I was, just as the truck pulled up by Ruby Mae's. A group of men—four of 'em—came sneakin' up to the house."

Buddy stopped then, wiping his sleeve across his face, his coffee now stone cold in his cup.

"We were only about forty feet from the house," he remembered. "We could see Papa and Charlie inside. I don't know how Papa did it. When I saw him just a little while before, he could hardly stay upright. I guess the drink and the anger fed off each other. But there he was in the living room, screamin' at Charlie and throwin' furniture. Charlie was doin' his share of screamin' too. We could see their faces, red and all screwed up, plain as day. We could hear them too. If all the neighbors hadn't been at that war bond rally, the whole town would've heard them.

"Then we could see that Mama and Jeannie Sue were in there too! I was supposed to warn them, and instead I wasted time lookin' for the town marshal and gettin' Franklin! Oh, God! What was happenin' right in front of our eyes? Like lightnin' all hell broke loose.

"Papa threw a chair at Charlie Weaver, but he dodged it, and it bounced off Jeannie Sue's head. She fell and Mama grabbed her ... there was so much blood!

"There was a lot of crashin' and cussin', punches were flyin', along with pieces of furniture. Sounded like Mama beggin' Papa—or maybe Charlie—to stop. Then she screamed at Papa, and he had his hands around her neck. I saw Jeannie Sue jump on Papa and him tryin' to shake her off. She wasn't very big, but she held on like a little wildcat. Guess she was a lot tougher than we all gave her credit for. I still remember how she had her nails dug into Papa's shoulders, the look on her face—like she knew there would be no tomorrow but just didn't care anymore.

"Papa managed to shake Jeannie Sue off and kicked her hard in the stomach. I heard Charlie yell at Mama to take Jeannie Sue upstairs—lock themselves in the closet and not to come out till he came for them. Looked to me like Mama was bleedin' too. Charlie held Papa back while she dragged Jeannie Sue up the stairs."

His voice cracked as he spoke, rose and fell—sometimes to just a whisper. His words revealed a world of pain and disappointment. His eyes ... his eyes were desperate. Pleading for relief from the burden of his life.

"That's when Papa broke free, and I saw the knife in his hand. I still don't know where it come from. Then I saw him lunge, and there was blood on Charlie's shirt. He looked to be hurt bad. I don't know how, but he jumped up and grabbed that knife right out of Papa's hands. Then he stabbed and stabbed—I don't know how many times. And then Papa fell onto the floor, and I couldn't see him no more.

"Then Charlie just kinda fell too, but he was on the couch, and I could see he was movin'."

I don't have any idea, truly, how Buddy was feeling, but I was just about exhausted. I know he had to be just running on sheer will and nerves. He kept going.

"All this time Franklin had one arm around my middle, holdin' me back and the other hand over my mouth. Thinkin' back on it, ah don't think that was really necessary, 'cause ah don't think ah was capable of movin'. It was almost like my body didn't belong to me no more. It wouldn't do anything ah told it to.

"All the while Franklin and me was watchin' from behind the tree, the four men that got out of the truck—I recognized it as Bob Handcroft's old work truck—they was watchin' the fight too from the darkest corner of the yard. In the light from the house I could see their silhouettes. And I could tell who they were. Anderson St. Claire, Oliver St. Claire, Bob Handcroft, and Wylie Jenkins—they both worked for the St. Claires off and on. Odd jobs, mostly. All four of them were keepin' to the shadows. We couldn't hear any of what they was sayin'.

"I remembered that Wylie was hangin' around outside Ruby Mae's when I went lookin' for Franklin. I remember, 'cause I almost tripped over his big feet. Wylie spent a lotta time hangin' around there. He was sweet on a little gal that worked there. I think I heard somewhere that she married some guy and left town later.

"I guess Wylie followed me and Franklin 'round to the back of the restaurant earlier and heard what I was tellin' him about Charlie Weaver. He musta went and got Bob, and they told Oliver, and Oliver went and told his brother, Anderson. Anderson prob'ly woulda been at the war bond rally, 'cept since Chick got killed, he wasn't nearly so gung ho about the war, ya know? I guess it was eatin' him up, losin' his only son like that."

Silence again. I think Buddy and I both were thinking about what kind of agony that must be, losing your own child. When Buddy started speaking again, it seemed to be harder for him. Up till then the words were rushing out—crashing into each other. It seemed like he couldn't get them out fast enough. Now it was like he had to pull them out from a place so deep and lonely, even he could barely reach it. His voice was just an anguished whisper now, and his eyes never left his hands. Poor Li'l Bit—I wonder what he was thinking—he whined and pushed at Dennis's hands with his nose, but Dennis didn't seem to notice, so the little guy just settled his head back on his paws and waited.

"So, that's how they knew about Charlie—'bout him bein' a spy. Ah told 'em mahself. Like always, Anderson was in charge. I could tell he was giving orders, but his back was to us, and I couldn't quite catch what he was saying.

"It happened all at once and kind of in slow motion, all at the same time. They went into the house, and I lost sight of Oliver, Bob, and Wylie for a couple seconds, but I could hear glass breaking. Anderson went over to Papa and leaned over him. Then he said something to the others. The only word I caught was 'dead.' Then he went over to Charlie and shook him. He didn't wake up, but he was alive, shore. I think he said something to him, but I couldn't hear.

"The next thing I knew I smelled kerosene and smoke and flames just seemed to burst out everywhere all at once. Anderson, Oliver, and the others come runnin' out and just stood in the yard for a minute, back in the same dark corner they were in just a few minutes earlier. Watchin' those flames get higher. That old cypress wood is hard as nails, but fire near 'bout swallows it in one gulp.

"Franklin was practically sittin' on me by then. He was always kind of a smallish man, but I bet he's one of the strongest men I ever knew. I couldn't move. I couldn't breathe. I couldn't even think. Papa was dead! Lord knows I thought about what that would mean, more'n once. But this was real—only it didn't feel like it somehow. Charlie was all but dead, looked like. That seemed more real. And the thought cut right through me. It couldn't have been more'n just a minute or two and the flames was already goin' up the stairs. Almost flyin'.

"That's when I heard Mama scream. We all heard it—watchin' what was happenin' in front of me, I clean forgot Mama and Jeannie Sue was upstairs! And the St. Claires and their bunch didn't know it at all. They weren't there when Charlie sent Mama and Jeannie Sue upstairs to get them away from Papa.

"Then I could hear Jeannie Sue. Chokin' and cryin'. Screaming for somebody to help—please, God, help! And then through the window I saw Charlie drag himself up offa the couch. He tried, God he tried to get up the stairs, but the fire was eating up the staircase. It was everywhere! He grabbed the ol' rug offa the floor and tried to beat down the flames. He was barely on his feet but he kept tryin'. Then he fell down, and I didn't see him no more."

Buddy was quiet for a while, bitter hell reflected in his eyes. The lightning cracked the sky again, a little closer this time, and a fresh breeze stirred Buddy's dirty-blond hair.

"Oliver was the first one of the four of 'em outside to react," Buddy said. "He ran over to their truck and pulled a ladder outta the back, but he was havin' a hard time gettin' it up alongside the house. None of the others moved. Anderson just watched the fire burn my house and my family into nothin'. Then I heard Anderson tell Bob and Curley to go over to the Red Spot and fetch Papa's truck. He told them to drive it till the gas run out and then push it into the river.

I caught my breath as I realized why Greg was there to threaten me that night. It was obvious now. The St. Claires were involved in the deaths of the Parker family, and they were the only family in Oxbow with enough money and clout to keep it quiet. They brought Greg in to make sure I didn't rock their very expensive boat.

"Franklin jerked his head around so he could talk directly into my ear. 'Stay put, boy. Ain't nothin' you can do now, anyways. Soon's ya get a chance, head on back over to yore camp and stay there. Don't talk to nobody! Don't let nobody sees ya! I'll be comin' when I can.' That's what he said to me. Then he ran over and helped Oliver get the ladder up to the bedroom window. Franklin was the one that climbed up. I could see the flames, though, right in front of the window. It was the only window in that bedroom, and the door was right by the top of the stairway that was choked with fire. There was no way out of that room."

Tears again, streaking down his face. Silent tokens of a lifetime of pain.

"Oh, sweet Jesus!" a tortured whisper. "Can you hear them screaming? Can you hear them? Oh, Mama, Jeannie Sue, I'm so sorry! It was my fault. How was I to know? How could I see where it would lead?" His words were bitter. Condemning. Full of self-reproach.

"If I'd just kept quiet about Charlie, kept my suspicions to myself, none of it would've happened. Papa would've come home and lit into Mama like always. And she would've taken his crap, like always. If it got really bad I could've gone for somebody, anybody—stepped in myself—done somethin', and she'd have been alive. And so would Jeannie Sue. And we wouldn't be sittin' here starin' at Jeannie Sue's orchid tree, tryin' to figure out how to finally let my people rest."

"You couldn't have known," I tried to soothe him. "You did what you had to do." I don't think he even heard.

"Was it even true?" he suddenly demanded of himself. "Was Charlie workin' for the enemy? There hasn't been a day go by in these forty years that I haven't wondered about that. Was I right? Did I jump to a conclusion and end up getting everyone I loved killed?"

He was silent again. Sitting hunched over by that big old oak, he looked so small. Crumpled like an old tissue, used and carelessly thrown to the ground.

And I finally knew the answer to the question that had been driving me so hard. The Parker family of Oxbow, Florida, was dead. All of them. The last one just wasn't buried yet.

CHAPTER 26

I HAD THOUGHT THAT finally having the answer to my mystery would set me free. After all these weeks of jousting with ghostly windmills, I expected to be elated—or at least satisfied. But there was no satisfaction, only a deep sense of sadness. It had been forty years since the Parker family disappeared off the earth with no one to mourn them but one lost soul and a wise and compassionate friend.

Funny. Now that I understood the story of the Parkers, I wasn't all that anxious to share it. Besides, the St. Claires were still afraid of that truth getting out. And Buddy—Dennis—and Franklin were still vulnerable after all these years. I couldn't be sure, but I couldn't take that chance, either.

Bitter though it was, I felt compelled to keep the secret. Still, now that my mystery was solved, I had to share it with somebody. Glenn. Of course! We had kept in touch since I returned, and he very delicately asked how it was going every time we talked. My answer was always the same—slow-motion frustration. Now, at last, I could put his mind at ease too.

He picked up on the last ring before I gave up.

"Hey, Glenn, I had about decided you were out on the town somewhere," I began.

"Molly! Now, how did you know I needed a nice surprise right about now? I've been studying my brains out for a test in the morning, and I'm about to go mad!" he shot back.

"Oh! I didn't mean to get in the way of higher education! Maybe I should call back!" I said.

"Hang up, and I'll call you back every minute till you pick up!" he laughed. "So, how's your world going?"

Suddenly nervous, I didn't know how to begin. "Glenn," I stammered. "I know what happened. I know what happened to the Parkers." It was the first time I'd said it out loud.

Silence on the other end. Then, "Are you okay?"

I smiled. How many people would be concerned about me first, before their own questions were answered?

"I'm fine. Really. But it's strange. I was sure I'd be flying high right now. Sure uncovering the answer would be a release." I thought for a moment. "And it is," I admitted. "It is. But it doesn't feel anything like I thought it would."

Glenn remained silent, allowing me time to work the feelings out.

"They're dead," I finally blurted out. "Hannah, Jeannie Sue, Milton—and their boarder, Charlie Weaver. And you won't believe this, Glenn! Buddy? He's really Dennis Blankenship—or Dennis is really Buddy. I'm not sure if I ever mentioned him. He's kind of an old drunk that came to town a few years before I got here. Lives out in the woods by himself with just his little dog. His whole left side is mangled and scarred. Nobody really knows what happened to him, and he never says much. Never bothers anybody. Just does odd jobs and keeps to himself.

"Anyway, it finally dawned on me to talk to him about the Parkers. He always hangs around that lot. I just thought he liked it because it was quiet and pretty—and close enough to the store to run for another beer."

"So, this Dennis just opened up and told you everything?" Glenn asked.

"Well, pretty much," I replied. "I guess I took him by surprise. As I was leaving the office the other evening, I saw him hunkered down over there like always, under one of those big oaks. I sat down with him and just told him I knew about the Parker family. Told him I went up to Georgia to find out if they were there. Then I told him I could see the faces there among those orchid branches. That's what really got him, Glenn. When he realized I could see them too. And that's when I realized who he was. It all just came pouring out of him then."

"Damn, Molly, that must be a helluva story," he put in.

"It surely is!" I agreed. "Glenn, the St. Claires—the mayor, his brother, and two of their flunkies—burned the house down! They went there because—you won't believe this!—Charlie Weaver was a German spy!"

"What? Molly, are you sure this guy Dennis is for real?" Glenn was supportive, but there were limits to just accepting a story like this one at face value

"Yes, Glenn. There hasn't been room in my head for anything else. It all fits. And sitting there with Dennis—it was just so real. If you could have felt the pain just seeping out of him. Then it was like years and years of venom finally exploding out of him. He is very real, Glenn."

"But a spy? In that little town? What would he have been doing there?" Glenn wanted to understand as much as I did.

"Well, according to Jeannie Sue's diary, he'd come and go—leave for days at a time without saying where he was going. There were lots of military bases all around Florida during the war. I don't really know, but I guess he was gathering information. He had a shortwave radio in his bedroom at the Parker house. Dennis—Buddy—saw it that night.

"Anyway, Milton and Charlie Weaver were fighting in the living room. Buddy and Franklin Brown—he's a great old black man who still lives in town, kind of always took care of all the kids—watched them from across the street, right out by the newspaper office. Milton died in the fight and Charlie was hurt pretty bad. Charlie had told Hannah and Jeannie Sue to go upstairs and stay there till he called them, but then the St. Claires showed up. They had overheard Buddy telling Franklin about Charlie being a spy. Anderson St. Claire's only son had been killed a few months earlier fighting the Germans. They spilled kerosene all around the first floor and up the stairs and set the place on fire."

"Oh my God—and the women were still upstairs," Glenn jumped ahead.

"Yes. Milton was already dead. Charlie Weaver was on his last legs but tried to beat down the flames going up the stairs till he collapsed. The house was all cypress wood—hard as nails, but it goes up in flames like a matchstick. Franklin went to help Oliver—Anderson's brother—try to put a ladder up to the window and get the women out, but it was too late. Franklin made Buddy stay hidden. He knew Buddy would never be safe if Anderson knew he was still alive—not if he knew what they had done. And Buddy surely would never have been able to stay in town, knowing that Anderson was responsible for killing his mother and sister."

"Damn, Molly!" was all Glenn could say.

"I can explain it better later. I'll write you a letter. It comes out better that way. I know you've got to get back to studying ..."

"Now? You want me to get back to studying now? Just how do you think I'll be able to do that?" he wanted to know.

"I know. I'm sorry, but you've got a big test, remember? You'll just have to set this aside for a while. I'll get that letter out to you tomorrow," I promised.

A little more chitchat, and we hung up. I felt better, now that someone else knew too. And I knew that it was all as sacred to Glenn as it was to me. The secret of the Parker family was no longer a secret, but it would never be grist for common gossip. I wanted to make sure Hannah, Jeannie Sue, and Buddy got the respect they deserved.

Life, and work, went on. A week later I was on my way over to the elementary school to get a quick picture of the kids at the honor-roll party. Every grading period the principal threw a little party for the kids who worked hard and made good grades. The kids loved it.

It was unusual, but I was actually ahead of schedule. The school was just down the road, and I had time to kill, so when I saw Franklin in his usual spot, sitting on a box by the old ice house, I just had to stop.

"Well, Miss Molly, I done 'bout give up on you! Thought ya clean f'got 'bout dis ole man," he said with that same mischief in his old eyes that always gave everybody such a big lift.

"Now, Franklin, you know better than that," I scolded, giving him a big hug. "Franklin," I began, not knowing just what to say, "Buddy ..."

"Ah knows, girl, jus' let it be. Time fo' folks to jus' let it go. He goin' be awright now, don't you worry," he told me.

So we had a nice catch-up talk: yes, all the kids and grandkids were doing all right although the family was afraid that young Jamal was heading down the wrong path. He'd been keeping some bad company and staying out late. The fourteen-year-old wouldn't listen to anybody. Franklin was pretty sure the boy was getting involved in drugs and lamented that they couldn't drag him to church anymore.

The old man shook his head ruefully, staring at his shoes, scuffed and worn by walking from his beloved neighborhood to the Hollow Tree Restaurant for breakfast, then to the old icehouse every day of his life. Well, at least the past twenty years.

Franklin shook off his mood and brightened.

"You didn' f'get you're comin' to the special service dis Sunday, did you?" he asked.

"'Course not! You've all worked hard for months renovating the church. I'll be there, and bring my camera," I told him.

"You right 'bout us workin' hard. Near 'bout ev'body in Oak Park did somethin' to git da church done. The paintin' is done inside, and the seats done been stripped and revahnished. Miz Maple and her sister, Miz Carroll, sewed up a storm, makin' new seat covers for the benches, and Miz Briggs crocheted new tops fo da altar table. Young Twanda Little—you know, Bella Williams' oldest granchile—did a powerful good job paintin' the Garden of Gethsemane on da back wall. Looks so real you feel like you could jes' go set under dem trees and cool off a spell," he said proudly.

Franklin was always proud of the hardworking successes his family and friends achieved. Maybe that's why he was so well loved. He made no secret of how much he cared about the people in his life and was always the first to praise a job well done—or even a good attempt that fell short. It was all the same to him. I knew young Jamal's rebellion was a sore trial to him.

It was getting late, and my honor-roll students should be ready for their traditional picture, so we said our good-byes, and I headed on over to the school. Franklin stayed put, waving as I left.

Sunday morning I got up and dressed carefully, mindful of showing proper respect to the House of the Lord and to His people and then drove over to the Sweet Chariot AME Church. The familiar church shone brightly in the sun, sparkling under a new coat of white paint. The grounds were immaculate, and people were arriving, stopping to pass the time before the service would begin. It seemed they all took special pains to greet me, thanking me for coming to the event that was so special to their congregation.

Inside, worshippers packed the little church. Overhead, ceiling fans circled lazily to keep the air moving. The ladies were resplendent in their brightly colored dresses and matching hats, and the well-scrubbed children hardly squirmed at all. The men were also dressed in their very best suits, looking every bit as classy as their ladies. Young Twanda's painting lived up to Franklin's buildup. The girl really did have a gift.

The singing commenced, heartfelt and moving.

Members of the congregation moved in time with the choir's song, clapping and waving their arms. Random "Amens" and "Praise the Lords" erupted from all corners of the little church.

When it was time for Deacon Franklin Brown to preach, he walked slowly up to the podium, and I noticed for the first time that my old friend seemed to be in pain. *How could I have missed that? Is age catching up with Franklin? Or could it be the worry about young Jamal that I know is eating him up?*

Once at the podium, though, it was the old Franklin who lifted his eyes to the congregation, and those eyes shone with the light of the Lord. I had never heard Franklin preach before, and it was a revelation.

"Friends!" he began. "Let's all raise up our hands in praise to da Lahd who has brought us all here to dis place in love and friendship.

"We worked hahd to make dis a fittin' House for da Lahd, worked together, da way the Lahd expec's us to. He's lookin' down now from His place high up yonder, where He's saving a place fo each of us, great and small."

Amens. Praise the Lords.

"Dis here church has a new face, a new life. It has been home to long years o' strife and hard times. Many a tear was shed right under dis here roof, brothers and sisters, many of us hit rock bottom right here and found da true meanin' of faith. We found da true meanin' of fam'ly. We reached out our hands to God and He reached right back, and in takin' His hand we been delivered o' all our sins. We each stahted a new life den," he assured us.

Franklin was preaching to the whole congregation, but I could swear he was looking right at me, touching my heart, my soul.

"It's all brand-new now. We're all brand-new. Da ol' pain is gone. We done been cleansed by da Lahd. He looked down and saw our worryin' and our grievin', and He led us to Him, to a new life. He led us back to each other. See, no matter what we been through; no matter what we done to git on the wrong side o' the Lahd, once we see His light and accept it into our hearts, there's a barrier between our hearts and all the bad things in the world. Oh, they can still hurt us, shore, but we're new—always new. Like dis church. All scrubbed and shinin' with the Lord's glory and with da peace only He can give us."

And I knew Franklin was talking about Buddy. About Dennis. I knew he was telling me that our friend was brand-new, like this beautiful little church, full of new life and possibilities. The old, the worn-down, had been made new again—better, because of what had gone before.

CHAPTER 27

I DIDN'T SEE DENNIS for a while after that night at the lot. I looked for him, but he just melted away again. I was afraid it was for good this time. Then late one Tuesday night I was alone in the office. We had put the paper to bed, and Minnie, Frank, and Maria were gone. I was just putzing around, getting ready to leave when a knock on my window sent my heart to the pit of my stomach. The misshapen face at my window was a very familiar one—and a very welcome one. I unlocked the door and let Dennis in, Li'l Bit in his wake. I couldn't help but notice—something about him was different, besides the fact that he looked cleaner.

"Evenin', Molly. Sorry for the scare," he said.

"Dennis! Do you know how glad I am to see you?" Without a thought, I reached out and gave him a quick hug. "I was afraid you were gone," I said, realizing that the smell of alcohol was completely gone.

As I stepped back, the look on Dennis's care-worn face said he was both pleased and embarrassed about the little hug. He looked away quickly but turned back and trained his slate-gray eyes on mine.

"I know it's late, but I need to talk to you, if you don't mind," he said. *Now, just how in the world could I mind?*

"Of course I don't mind. Come on in. Coffee?" I offered. A little coffee always seemed to put Dennis at ease.

"Sure, if it's no trouble." I could have predicted that answer.

So, I went back to the Mr. Coffee and measured out the water and grounds while Dennis sat in my office. As the coffee brewed, I grabbed a plate, covered it with some of the homemade chocolate chip cookies Maria had brought in that morning, and took them out to my friend. He smiled one of his peculiar, crooked smiles—jagged scars kept the skin on the left side of his face rigid. His scars may have confined the smile to only one side of his lips, but they couldn't keep it from lighting up his eyes. It was a beautiful sight.

We sat quietly for a few minutes while the coffee brewed. Then I went back and poured two cups—mine with everything I could get in it, his black. Another of those incredible smiles when I handed him his cup. Li'l Bit begged for the cookie I offered him and favored me with a little dance.

There it was again! Two smiles in a matter of just a few minutes! I was beginning to feel a lot better about Dennis.

After a little chitchat about how good Maria's cookies were and how the coffee hit the spot, Dennis looked away for a minute, inspecting the wall, and then finally turned to me. The eye contact was both comfortable and a little painful. I know that doesn't make sense, but it's the truth.

"Ah can't begin to tell you what you've done for me," he began. "Ah don't know why you cared, but you have been a lifesaver for me. Ah've been doing a lot of thinking the past couple days. At first ah thought about running. Just getting away from here again. But the past pulled me back years ago. Anyway, this is home. Where would ah go? At one time, all ah could do was run. This time, ah have a choice. And ah choose to stay. Ah choose my life."

He looked at me and shook his head. "Ah owe you a lot that ah can never repay ..." He fended off my protest and continued, "But at least ah can explain ... you deserve to know the whole story."

I nodded my appreciation, and he continued:

"Like Franklin told me to, ah stayed at my little camp in the woods till he came for me. Nobody came around. It was just me, alone. Goin' crazy, ya know? Ah was scared to death. And sick, so sick in my heart. Ah wanted to die. Ah knew ah had no family left.

Every time ah closed my eyes ah could see our house going up in flames and hear Mama and Jeannie Sue screaming."

He had to stop there for a minute. The enormity of it all still overwhelmed him.

"Those pitiful screams are still in my head. Ah think that's been the hardest part of this whole thing. Ah've spent my whole life trying to escape those agonized screams. It never worked."

The pain on Dennis's face was so intense that I had to look away for a minute. He cleared his throat and wiped his nose. He started to use his sleeve and then thought better of it, reaching across for a tissue from the box on my desk. It was a small thing, but a signal. I prayed Dennis really was paroled from his life sentence. He continued.

"Finally, Franklin showed up one day after dark. He brought me some cornbread, a sausage, and an old blanket. Ah hadn't realized it, but the weather had turned a little chilly at night—it was October, after all—and once ah took a bite of cornbread, ah found ah was actually hungry!

"Poor Franklin. Ah don't know where he got the courage to do what he did for me. He was in a helluva position. Ah'm not sure how much the world has really changed. Back then black men did not stick their noses into white folks' business. But he just wouldn't let me down, ya know?"

He blinked his wet eyes hard and waited a minute until he could speak again. I looked away for a minute, trying to allow him a shred of privacy. In due time he continued.

"Franklin talked while ah ate—told me what happened after he made me leave the fire. By that time the few men left in town arrived, and they all started trying to put the fire out. There were a handful of people who didn't go to the rally, you know. They'd seen the fire light up the night sky and come to find out what was going on. Anderson told them we left town—Papa showed up and packed us all up in the truck, he said. Then we headed back up to Georgia soon as Mama and Jeannie Sue got back from Miss Bruner's place. Said we just took a few clothes and headed north. Not long after, the house just went up in flames. Said somebody must've left an oil lamp lit or something. You know how those ol' cracker houses go up like tinder. The house was fully involved when he got there. That's what Anderson told them.

"By the time it was all out, the buses came back into town from the war bond rally. Folks gawked at the house for a while and were told just what Anderson told the first men to get there. Anderson also told them he knew where to contact Papa in Georgia and would let us know about all our stuff. And they all left. The show was over, and they were tired. They all patted Anderson on the back and told him how sorry they were. It was his property, after all, that went up in smoke.

"Only Anderson was left, staring at the glowing embers that had been the only home ah ever knew. Franklin hung back too. He told Anderson he saw what happened—he understood the 'accident' and would take care of everything—get rid of the 'details' for him. Franklin told me Anderson just nodded—didn't say anything except that Franklin knew what would happen to him if the story ever got out. Not much chance of that. Even if Franklin decided to tell anybody what really happened, who'd believe him? Anderson—the big man in town—would make sure no one ever would. And those other two boys—Bob Handcroft and Wylie Jenkins—they were so far down in Anderson's pocket, they'd never be able to crawl out.

"When Franklin told me ah had to leave town, ah knew he was right. No way could ah stay here and challenge Anderson St. Claire's story. So after dark ah took my little flatboat and floated away down the river. Ah made my way doin' odd jobs. Ah decided to call myself Dennis Blankenship—don't ask me why. Ah was signin' up with a shrimp boat headed out on the Gulf—ah wanted to get as far away from everything as ah could. When they asked me my name, I just made it up. Nobody asked how old ah was or anything. The boat was a rickety old tub, and most of the able bodied men were off to war. Ah guess they were glad to get anybody they could to sign on. Did some carpentry at construction sites, stuff like that, till the Korean War. By that time ah pretty much established myself as Dennis Blankenship and enlisted. Told them ah had no next of kin. Korea, that's where ah got my face and leg—my whole left side—messed up. They put me in"—a mirthless chuckle escaped him—"communications, workin' a radio."

Everything was falling into place now, but I still had a big question in my mind. "Dennis, why didn't Anderson come looking for you?" I asked. "Surely you were a loose end he wanted tied up."

"You're right. Anderson couldn't afford for me to survive. He couldn't afford for the town to find out what really happened. So Franklin told Anderson he took five bodies out of the house—told him ah was upstairs with the women. Apparently that was good enough for Anderson. Franklin was always a man you could believe."

I got up to get a refill for Buddy, and when I got back he continued.

"Before ah left, Franklin brought me some more food and a change of clothes. He gave me two hundred dollars and warned me to be very careful not to let anybody know I had it.

"Ah remember staring at that money and then at Franklin. It was more money than I ever saw before, that's for sure. Ah tried to give it back to him, but he told me it was really mine. The afternoon Papa came back from Georgia, Franklin saw him come out of the bank, then burying something in the backyard, out by Mama's old potting shed. While he was cleaning things up after the fire, he remembered it and got curious, so he dug it up. There were a couple cans of money—huge chunks of money! Thousands of dollars! It was what he made from selling the farm. Papa didn't trust banks, you see. It wasn't too long after the Depression and Grandpa Cecil had lost a lot in the bank failure. Franklin told me he'd keep the rest of the money for me. All ah had to do was let him know when ah needed it, and he'd get it to me.

"Over the years ah was gone, ah never contacted Franklin. Not once. Lord knows there were plenty of times ah was desperate to hear his voice or have some contact with him. Ah don't know. Maybe that's part of what made me come back here. But ah started having these dreams—seeing their faces. That's what really led me back. Ah ran as hard as ah could for as long as ah could—and couldn't run fast enough to get away. So ah finally came back.

"A few years ago Franklin asked me about the money Papa had buried. Ah couldn't believe he still had it! It was just like him, though. He'd never have used any of it for himself. So ah told him to use it for upkeep at the cemetery. Ah sure as hell didn't want it."

I didn't really want to bring up the next question I had, but the story would not be complete without knowing. So I asked, "What did Franklin do with the bodies?"

A shadow crossed his face, but Dennis took a deep breath and began: "Late the next night after the fire—in the early hours of the mornin', really, when even the town marshal was asleep, after what was left of our house cooled down, Franklin went over and started takin' the bodies out, one by one. He carefully wrapped them in worn-out blankets and put them in the back of his old pickup. He drove them over to the Sweet Chariot AME cemetery. The church was in the process of makin' that little memorial by plantin' a couple oaks and puttin' in a little bench by a small plaque—you know the place. It had been Franklin's idea. He was always a deacon there, you know. He told them it would always be a place where they could find peace, and the rest of the congregation thought it was a great idea. They'd been plannin' it for a while, you see, and they had already dug the holes for the trees. They were good-sized trees, so they had to be pretty large holes. But then Franklin went out and dug them extra deep. Overnight he put Mama and Jeannie Sue in one grave, Papa and Charlie Weaver in the other and covered them up. Then later the church planted the trees overtop the graves and dedicated that little park."

There was silence again for a minute, and he again covered his discomfort by sipping his coffee.

"Ah've been there lots of times. Ah used to go on Sundays after ah came back to town. But Franklin was wrong—at least the place never gave me any peace—so ah stopped going. After talkin' to you, tellin' you what happened that night, ah finally got up the courage to go over there again. And you know what? It felt right. Those trees grew up strong and beautiful. It's a wonderful place. Ah sat there a long time, talkin' to Mama and Jeannie Sue. Ah even talked to Papa a little, but ah didn't have too much to say, ya know? And Charlie Weaver—God, ah've thought so much about him over the years. Wondered—was ah right? Was he a spy? Or was there some other reason—somethin' else he was doin' and ah just jumped to the wrong conclusion? Could ah have been the cause of all this?"

While he talked, Dennis's face was constantly changing. Pain.

Sorrow. Fear. Even peace. Now it was anguished as he pulled the deepest, shattering fear from his soul. "Could ah have been the cause of all this?" he repeated.

I had no idea what to say. No words would come. No words could suffice. So I just touched Buddy's hand. And he smiled again. A grateful and pitiful thing.

CHAPTER 28

IN THE YEAR THAT followed, the good people of Oxbow marveled at the turnaround Dennis Blankenship had made. He stopped drinking, even picked up a steady job at Chico Flores's electronics shop. Chico was getting on in years and needed some help. He wasn't ready to close up and retire—he was just too full of life for that—but his hands didn't work as well as they did in his younger years, and tinkering with people's radios and TVs wasn't as easy for him as it used to be. He let Dennis live in the room up above the shop, and even little Li'l Bit was welcome. He had to be. Dennis would never have gone anywhere without his woebegone little buddy.

Lots of folks said it was the answer to their years of prayers for Dennis, and maybe it was. Maybe my filmy, opaque faces were an answer to those same prayers.

The world continued to turn, and our little town was beginning to change.

It amazed me how fast the doctor's office across the street went up once it was started. Years of open space were replaced by wood, concrete, and tile in just a few short weeks. I had to admit, however grudgingly, that the overall effect was really very nice. All the large trees, including the oaks and Jeannie Sue's orchid tree, remained intact, and Verna Michaelson's plantings added splashes of hot pink, red, yellow, and blue—in, it seemed, just the right places.

Came moving day. The Michaelsons arrived at the site early.

Dennis was already there. I had recommended him to the doctor when he asked about moving help. I knew what that lot meant to Dennis. We had talked about it over coffee and cookies during one of our late, Tuesday night discussions after the paper was done.

Dennis had cleaned up his act and was thoroughly presentable these days. Gone was the acute smell of alcohol. His gray eyes were clear and even showed signs of good-natured mischief from time to time.

I knew he was a little uncomfortable about someone "moving in on" his old home site, but he was glad that it was going to be a doctor's office. That seemed to please him—I think because it reminded him of the "doctorin'" his mother used to do. Still, the memories were so strong and so painful, I knew it could be hard on him. So, I thought it might be a good idea for him to see the process firsthand and to meet the new occupants. I decided to stay for a while, to keep an eye on Dennis. Okay, maybe I was a little overprotective, but I knew how hard this had to be for him and just wanted to be there if it overwhelmed him.

The Michaelsons greeted Dennis warmly. If they had any misgivings about his appearance—sobriety could not disguise the disfigurement of his whole left side—neither showed it. For once, it was just Dennis. Li'l Bit had to stay home. There was a new face with the Michaelsons, though. A very pretty one, that I soon discovered belonged to another pediatrician. Dr. Dana D'Lorenzo was a protégée of Dr. Michaelson's.

"Nice to meet you, Doctor," I said.

"Call me Dana," she replied, as she stood at the curb sorting boxes coming off the moving truck. Her thick, auburn hair was pulled back in a ponytail. A blue-green baseball cap perched on her head. The way she was handling boxes proved she was a lot stronger than her small frame would indicate.

Before long I found out that Dr. M. and Dana's mother had been lifelong friends, and he had always been the girl's mentor. She was a partner in his practice in West Palm and had come over to help him move into his new office.

Dennis hung back, always uncomfortable meeting new people. He just nodded when Dr. M. introduced him to Dana and mumbled something that sounded like "Nice to meet you, ma'am." He quickly started grabbing up boxes and took them inside.

When Dana finished coordinating things outside, she went in to help Dr. M. set up his exam room and small lab area. Verna was magically creating order from the chaos in the office space. It was easy to see how such a woman would be an asset in any busy office. Things were running smoothly, but when Dana came into what would be the waiting area, she took one look around and was clearly upset. Dennis was unloading boxes, surrounded by books and all manner of papers and medical-looking thingamajigs.

"What are you doing?" she demanded. "Those things should be in the exam room, and the books go in Dr. M.'s office! See, the boxes are all clearly marked! What are they doing out here?"

Looking sheepish and a little confused, Dennis backed off quickly and then started to help her stow the items back in boxes to be taken into the other rooms.

"Don't bother!" Dana told him, her irritability showing. "I'll take care of this!" She indicated a box in the far corner. "You go take that box over there and put it in the exam room," she ordered.

Dennis did as she told him. He was soon out of sight, followed almost immediately by a horrendous crash and a sort of yelp. Dana jumped up and ran toward the exam room. At the end of the hallway, the box was up-ended on the floor and Dennis was helping Verna up. The two had just come face-to-face with the physical impossibility of occupying the same space at the same time. Verna had been coming out of the storage room, heading to her husband's new office just as Dennis was coming down the hallway with the box full of steel instruments. The result was unavoidable.

Dana gasped and ran over to help Verna, almost pushing Dennis out of the way.

"Are you all right, Verna?" she asked, concern written all over her face.

"Now, child, I'm just fine. These bones aren't that old, you know!" she responded with a little laugh, although it was plain that she was a little shaken.

Poor Dennis kept trying to apologize, but Dana kept cutting him off. She didn't say anything really ugly to him but glared at him as she ushered the doctor's wife to the deeply cushioned couch already set up in her husband's office.

"I'll go over to Ruby Mae's and get her a glass of water," Dennis offered and was gone as soon as the words were out of his mouth. The city wouldn't be turning on the water at the office till Monday.

"Now, don't fuss, Dana," Verna scolded, "and don't blame that poor man, either. We just collided in the hallway, that's all. Could've happened to anybody." Looking up at her husband, who just walked in to see what was happening, she said, "I'm fine, Arthur, just a little mishap. Go ahead and finish what you were doing."

"You're sure?" the doctor asked, peering over his eyeglasses. She nodded, and he returned to his new exam room.

Verna looked a little ashen to me, but she was already being tended to by a doctor, after all. There really wasn't anything else I could so, so I returned to my work.

Dennis returned with the water, and Dana almost grabbed it out of his hand. It was Verna who thanked him, and very kindly.

"Thank you, Dennis. That was very thoughtful. And don't worry about this little accident. It was as much my fault as yours. Please, if you don't mind, go back and finish up in the storeroom," she said.

Throughout the day, Dana was trying to keep her temper, but it seemed Dennis was always getting in her way. It happened so often that it was getting downright exasperating. He didn't seem to be doing it on purpose, of course, but he was really getting on her nerves. The man just seemed to be all thumbs and no one heard an entire sentence from him beyond "Where would you like this one, ma'am?" Twice Dana just barely managed to save some of Dr. Michaelson's favorite glass knickknacks.

It was just after lunch when it seemed things between the two would finally blow up. Dana got more than a little testy when Dennis knocked over her handbag and her wallet fell out on the floor, open to a picture of her and her mother. Dennis picked it up and took a good look at the old photo before handing it back to her. Dana was obviously incensed. I saw her open her mouth and just knew something acid was going to come out of it, but before I could react, Verna came to the rescue.

"Dana, child, would you please come help me with these records?"

adding an insistent "now" when Dana didn't react immediately. Quickly, Dana swallowed whatever words were about to overflow, turned, and briskly walked past Verna into the storeroom. Verna took in the stricken look on Dennis's face. Walking over to him, she gently placed a small, well-manicured hand on his shoulder and said, "Please don't take Dana's attitude personally. I think she may be a little upset that Arthur is leaving the practice over in West Palm. It will be the first time she's had the office alone, you see."

Seeing gratitude in Dennis's eyes was very humbling. I guess that having some idea how hard life had kicked him and how much he had always been deprived of, made me supersensitive to his feelings. I silently blessed Verna Michaelson. She surely could not know how much that bit of kindness meant to him, but I thanked God she was the kind of person who treated people with respect and compassion whatever the circumstances.

I went into the storeroom where Dana was, thinking I'd give her a piece of my mind, but she took the initiative.

"What nerve this guy has!" she mumbled under her breath. "Did you see him staring at my picture?"

Mad as I was about how she had just spoken to my friend, I was beginning to see why she was so upset. Dana clarified it for me while Dennis went out to the moving van for something, and in all honesty I guess I'd be a little leery if some stranger stared at my picture that way, too, so I held my tongue and let her vent a little.

"I know he's your friend and all, but the guy's just creepy!" she half-whispered to me, her expressive hazel eyes seeming to plead her case. She really did look disconcerted.

"I know," I heard myself say. "Dennis is a little strange, but he's totally harmless. He's had it really tough—you can't imagine—please, don't judge him harshly. He means well," I told her.

Dana accepted my explanation and seemed calmer.

"Okay. But I'm having a hard time dealing with him, so I'll just stay in here and work," she volunteered, and turned to unload more office supplies.

I stayed in the storeroom helping Dana, thinking I'd be handy to cut short any possible further misunderstandings between Dana and Dennis, when about midafternoon she turned to me and asked, "Do you run?"

I know the look on my face was as blank as my mind as I repeated dumbly, "Run?"

"Yes, you know, like in 5-K races. Well, you don't really have to race, just run. I started running about a year ago and I'm absolutely addicted to it now. I run about three times a week. I usually try to run a couple miles in the morning—it's just too hot during the day most of the time. But I didn't get a chance to this morning, so I'm thinking maybe I could have a run a little later," she explained.

"Later?" I repeated. "You mean you'll have enough energy left after this to actually run a couple miles?" I couldn't quite believe my ears.

"I know it sounds strange, but once you're out there you'd be surprised how invigorating it is! You just have to get used to doing it every day and not let yourself wimp out because you're a little tired," she explained, adding, "Do you know of a nice trail to run?"

"Trail? Well, no, not really," I said. Thinking for a minute or two, I added, "There are some runners around here. I see a couple sometimes kind of jogging through some of the nice, tree-covered streets and then down the trail by the river," I told her. "I can show you where … it's just a couple blocks away."

"That sounds perfect! Hey, how about you come with me?"

Responding no doubt to what had to be a seriously incredulous look on my face, she continued, "Oh, you'll love it! It takes a little effort to get into running, but once you do, you're hooked! It's great exercise for your body and even helps clear your mind. It's great for relieving stress. Come on. I'll run alone if I have to, but it's more fun if you have company." She really looked like she wanted my company, and her argument was so sincere, I said okay. What was I thinking? I knew very well I couldn't keep up with a seasoned runner. Hmph. Another fine mess I'd gotten myself into …

The rest of the afternoon passed without any further unpleasantness. For the most part, Dennis kept his distance from Dana. He was always polite, but he backed off a little further. It really hurt me to see him shunned that way, but I guess it was better than being verbally abused, so I just left well enough alone. I did try to give Dennis a little extra attention, though, to make up for it.

As we were winding down for the day, the Michaelsons asked us all—Dennis included—if we would like to join them for dinner. Dennis declined, as I knew he would, and Dana told them she and I were going running. We'd grab something to eat afterward. Now that was a surprise to me! But it sounded good, so I went along with it.

Dennis disappeared, and the Michaelsons took their leave. Dana, who had volunteered to lock up, turned to me as we placed the last reference book on a shelf.

"Do you have some running shoes?" she wanted to know.

"Running shoes?" I asked, feeling like a complete moron. Obviously, there were such things, and they were very important, judging by the exasperated look on Dana's face.

"Yes! You really need good running shoes to protect your feet and ankles," she informed me.

"I'm afraid all I have are some beat-up old sneakers," I told her, feeling like I was completely out of touch. Where was I when running shoes became a necessity of life?

"Those'll do, especially for a first time out," she concluded.

First time? I thought. *Doesn't that imply there would be a second time? Am I getting myself into more than I bargained for?*

Dana locked the office door behind us and headed over to her mint-condition '65 Mustang. The car was a thing of beauty—even I could see that. My knowledge of cars, vintage or otherwise, was limited. If it got me where I was going and back again, I was happy, but this cherry-red 'Stang was a real classic.

"C'mon," she said. "I'll take you back to your place so we can change." I slid into the passenger's seat, relishing the classic feel of this really cool car.

"This is a great car!" I breathed. "I haven't been in a classic Mustang since I don't know when."

She smiled appreciatively. "Yes, isn't it? I always wanted one. I'm not really what you'd call a 'car person,' but I still remember the first time I saw a '65 Mustang. It took my breath away. I was just a kid, but I promised myself that some day I'd have one of those. After I got my MD license and got settled, this was the first thing I bought." The wistful smile that deepened the slight curve of her lips accentuated her lovely features. I didn't know whether to be jealous of her or like her even more. Dana D'Lorenzo seemed to be a hard worker, intelligent, and down-to-earth. The more I learned about her, the more I liked her. So far, the only negative in her character was her apparent inability to see any redeeming social value in Dennis. Well, maybe that would come later. On the other hand, what difference did it make? She'd be gone by Sunday evening, back to the pediatric practice in West Palm that was all hers now.

We pulled up into my yard, and Dutch greeted us at the front gate. My chocolate-colored Labrador always acted like he hadn't seen a human being in years whenever anyone pulled up. He looked a little confused when I got out of the passenger's side of a strange vehicle but recovered quickly, gently placing his paws on my shoulders to offer his sloppy greeting. Then he loped around the car to do the same to the newcomer. Dutch was a very affectionate dog and always showed proper enthusiasm for anyone he knew was "okay" with me. Had Dana not been with me, he would have been standoffish—barking a warning while he held back, waiting to see if the stranger could be trusted. I'd had Dutch for four years, and I had never known him actually to bite anyone. Well, he did come close with Greg a time or two ... I could see, though, from Dana's reaction, that she was a little disconcerted by Dutch's forward behavior.

"Don't worry," I assured her, "Dutch wouldn't harm a flea."

"That may be," she observed, "but I'm not a flea."

Laughing, I called Dutch back over to me. He gently laid down at my feet a stick he'd picked up on the way, and I obligingly threw it to the back of my old cracker house. Dutch barreled past the front porch with the vine-covered railing, past the salmon-colored double hibiscus at the corner, and plowed headfirst into my gardenia bush. Dana and I laughed—full-throated guffaws—as we watched poor Dutch lose and regain his footing at least three times in his single-minded attempts to bring back his woody prize. True to his kind, he did just that, proudly placing it directly into my outstretched hand. Then he sat, trembling, barely able to contain himself, till I finally threw it again. We went through this ritual innumerable times, with Dana taking over the honors several times. I knew I had to put an end to this, or Dutch would go on till he quite literally fell over in a big, brown, air-gulping heap, unable to move.

So I put the stick on the porch and commanded Dutch to stay with me. You could see the struggle on his beautiful face but, obediently, he resisted his natural instinct to run for the stick.

Opening the trunk, Dana reached in and pulled out a bag she said contained her running clothes. Dutch walked sedately with Dana and me into the house.

Inside, I fed Dutch and made sure he had clean water and then offered Dana a cold glass of tea. We quenched our thirst out on the back porch, and Dana voiced her appreciation of the view.

"This is great! The river is so peaceful, with all the trees along the banks. It almost gives you the feeling that there's no one else in the world. Like it must have been years ago, before cars and roads and airplanes—before people choked the world up with temporary … stuff. It's not at all like the East Coast, although I suppose it must have been a lot like this there before people took over," she mused.

"I suppose that's true. This really is a special place. But we better get moving, or we're going to run out of daylight," I cautioned.

So we got up, and I showed Dana to the bathroom where she changed, and I went into my bedroom to do the same.

In a couple minutes we were ready, said good-bye to a doleful Dutch, and headed back out the driveway.

I directed Dana to the parking lot at the bank where she could leave her car. As I slammed my door behind me, I caught sight of her doing the most curious thing. She was locking her doors!

"What are you doing?" I asked, amused. "I noticed when we got in at the doctor's office that they were locked. Really, Dana, there's no need. Nobody here locks their doors."

I should've been used to it. Oxbow folks always had to explain to big city folks what an unnecessary mechanism locks were around these parts. Well, businesses were an exception, but not having to lock our houses and cars was a point of pride for locals that outsiders just didn't seem to get. They always insisted on locking up, no matter how silly the procedure seemed to us.

Her incredulous look was expected. City folks are so predictable.

"You can't be serious!" was her less-than-original comeback.

She proceeded to lock up—again, no surprise—and I followed her around back. Realizing debate was useless—city folks are very fond of their locks—I reminded her that I had not a clue what I was doing, except putting one foot in front of the other. She explained that that was all there was to it, and we hit the road.

We ran through a lovely residential area covered by a thick, oak canopy.

Almost from the starting point, we passed my neighbors as they went about their business. Miss Palmer waved as she searched for nonexistent weeds around her prize rose bushes. Little Shelly Brooks raced us on her tricycle, trailing giggles and ponytails, as her mom laughed and kept a watchful eye on the tyke.

"Mind, now, you stop at the corner, Shelly," she warned. And the little girl did.

Old Mr. Cox greeted us as he picked up his mail from the box at the road.

"Sorry I can't stop to talk, Mr. Cox," I explained, "but I'm getting a lesson in running."

"Really?" he asked. "I thought you were more advanced than that! In my day, we learned how to run a lot sooner!" he quipped. "But don't let me hold you up. If your development's that far behind, you need all the practice you can get!"

Most of the folks we passed ended their comments with a cheery, "Evenin' Dr. Dana."

Finally, she could stand it no longer.

"Just how do all these people know who I am?" she demanded.

I just smiled at her. "Small town," was all there was to say.

We continued that way for a while, bobbing our way along under the green oak canopy, past petunia-splashed yards, neighborhood basketball games, and folks just sitting on lawn chairs or swings, making the most of the cool late afternoon. The summer heat would be brutal, they knew, and would bring Florida's legendary mosquitoes out in force—so they would take advantage of every minute of this pleasant time.

In spite of her original advice—just put one foot in front of the other—Dana offered tips along the way as we continued through the park and down to the trail by the river.

I had been struggling to keep up for some time, but about halfway down the trail at the river's edge, a cramp in my left leg stopped me cold. Dana wasn't even breaking a sweat. To her credit, she didn't comment on my lack of stamina. I was beginning to really like this girl.

"Let me take a look," she said, as she bent over and reached for my leg. "I *am* a doctor, you know," she reminded me.

"Just a little cramp," she pronounced. "Keep walking, and it will work itself out." Smiling, she continued, "If we were in my office, I'd charge you forty bucks for that bit of advice!"

I jumped right in, "Nice to know you got something out of eight years of medical school."

Without missing a beat, she gave me an incredulous look and said, "Medical school?"

Yes, I was beginning to like this girl, all right. I just wished I could get her to ease up on Dennis a little.

Turning our heads westward, we both caught sight of the luminous pink-orange glow at the same time. The whole sky was streaked with gentle colors no human palette could duplicate. Oranges melting into pinks, shading into purples, and a glorious pearly softness overall that enhanced the scene before us. The glowing disc itself was dipping silently into the slow-moving current, becoming one with the water as it journeyed to the Gulf and beyond.

Neither of us heard him. Suddenly he was just there behind us. I could see Dana's indignation rising, but Dennis cut it off before it had a chance to break the surface.

Gazing with awe at the westward sky, he almost whispered, "This must be the most beautiful thing in the world. I think if people could see the love around them, this is what it would look like."

The hush returned, and we all drank again from the pink-orange wine surrounding us. Then he turned and walked away alone, with a dignity that even his peculiar rolling gait could not diminish.

The sun was part of the river now, and the array of hues would soon begin to fade. My cramp had eased—or maybe I just forgot about it—and we jogged back to Dana's incredible cherry-red '65 Mustang without another word. We continued in silence for the few blocks to my office where my own vehicle was parked.

Hating to break the awe-inspired silence, I started to open my door when Dana began.

"I don't mean to be harsh with Dennis. I'm not really that way. I do feel bad about my reaction to him," she said and then pleaded, "but come on! Just how clumsy can one man be, for heaven's sake?"

"All I can say, Dana, is that you should just give the man a chance. He's really a good person. He's just not good at being around strangers," I tried to explain, feeling just how feeble and inadequate my effort was.

"Well, anyway," she continued, "I'll be leaving tomorrow afternoon. I'll probably go to church with the Michaelsons in the morning—they're my godparents, you know—then go back and do whatever I can at the office. Will you be there?" she asked.

I had a lot of things I had to get done at home, but if Dennis showed up I figured I'd better be there—just in case—so I told Dana I'd probably be there after noon sometime for a while. Then we went our separate ways—Dana to the Oxbow Motel to stay with the Michaelsons and me to make up to Dutch for leaving him alone. Driving away, I realized that we never did get our dinner. PB & J again.

Two weeks later the good doctor was booking appointments. Verna handled the appointments till he could hire an office clerk. She didn't mind—said it reminded her of "the old days" when her husband was first starting out as a young pediatrician. They were on a shoestring budget and she had served various functions in his office when he was working hard to get his practice going. She wasn't even above cleaning the toilet—and it was a point of pride with her.

She enjoyed the chance to be of tangible support to her husband once again, although she made it known that she was glad she didn't have to clean the toilet this time around!

"That nice Dennis Blankenship down the block," as Mrs. M. always referred to him, was temporarily taking care of a lot of those kinds of tasks.

CHAPTER 29

A S A NEWSPAPER PERSON, I argued long and hard with myself about putting the whole Parker family story to rights. The truth shall set you free, they say.

And it did. It had set Dennis—Buddy—free. Did it really matter if anybody else knew the whole story? Almost everyone involved was long gone. Anderson St. Claire, Bob Handcroft, Wylie Jenkins had all died years ago, long before I came to Oxbow. Oliver had suffered a heart attack a while back. He still kept things tidy over at the lot, around the doctor's office, and I saw him at Ruby Mae's Café, but he'd cut way back on what he did. Besides, he was the only one of Anderson's bunch who even tried to help that unholy night. Only Dennis and Franklin just seemed to keep on going. I think Dennis was making up for lost time, and Franklin, well he just doesn't let anything stop him.

Even my faces were gone. Since that night at the lot when Dennis opened his soul to me and together we watched his demons escape, I'd never seen those hazy apparitions again. I've thought long and hard about that, and I think I've found the reason my faces were there—the reason they reached out to me. They wanted peace for Buddy, at last.

Buddy—Dennis—lived and worked in this community but always kept his own counsel about the past. He finally chose to let the ghosts of his life rest. How could I do any differently?

Those fragile lavender shells on the orchid tree have bloomed once again since that night I finally learned the truth about the Parker family, brightening the corner across from my office, then shivering down to litter the ground around the doctor's office that Oliver St. Claire built there last year. It was strange, getting used to seeing a building there after all these years. Life in Oxbow had been pretty much the same for a long time, but then the changes all seemed to come at once. I guess that's the way of it.

Dr. Michaelson's practice took off like a flash, and the couple was accepted into the Oxbow "family" quickly. Mothers instinctively trusted him with their precious children, and the kids responded to Dr. M.'s gentle ways. Yes, the new doctor and his office were exactly what this town needed.

I had just locked up my office one afternoon. I was actually leaving at five—well, shortly after—and was about to settle into my car. My mind was on having a romp with Dutch when I got home. Poor Dutch had been neglected for a few days—again—so I jumped when Verna gently touched my shoulder as I pulled the key out of the lock.

"Oh, I'm sorry if I startled you, Molly," she apologized, "but I'd like to talk to you privately for a minute," she said, glancing back over her shoulder at the doctor's office. Her lovely face was drawn, and her eyes bored into mine as she firmly gripped my arm.

Somewhat confused, I mumbled something like "of course" as I opened the door. Verna was almost pushing me as we headed back to my office.

In my office, she dropped her delicate body into the old office chair I know had to be one of the building's original pieces of furniture. I took a chair next to her and waited for her to begin. It took a few minutes.

She kept staring out the window at her husband's new office before finally beginning. I waited, wondering what this could be about.

"It's such a pretty lot. This is where we needed to be," she said cryptically, "but that's what sold us on it, you know. It was a real plus for us. In West Palm we had landscaping, of course, and it was very nice, but man-made—sort of artificial looking ... not really natural like here." In the few months they were here, Verna herself had planted some hardy bromeliads whose splashy colors lit up that lot even more. "Arthur ... this is just what he's wanted for some time. I've never seen him happier," she mused, more to herself than to me.

From the moment I saw Verna's strained look, I knew this wasn't just going to be a friendly little chat. Something was up, and I didn't know what. But I was pretty sure that I wasn't going to like it. I waited for the lady to continue.

"Well, I suppose there's no point in shilly-shallying about this," she finally began with a slight tremor in her voice. "I've been diagnosed with a malignant tumor. It's a slow-growing kind, and I'm told I might have as much as a year or more."

I just sat there, dumbly. I guess concern must have registered on my face because Verna—steadier now—leaned over and patted my hand like a mother offering emotional support to her child.

"Now, now, don't fret about this, Molly. We found out a couple weeks ago. I've had a good cry and did my ranting at the Lord—tried making a deal with Him—but I'm beginning to accept it. I've had a good life—so much better than many others. At least that's what I'm telling myself, and I know it's true.

"But enough of that. That's not what I came here for. No, I'm worried about Arthur. I think he's taking this harder than I am."

I seemed to be having a little trouble breathing myself all of a sudden, but managed, "Yes, I did notice he seemed distracted—really down—the other day. He hardly said a word, and that's not like him. He always has some cute little story he wants to share about one of his patients. When I asked, he just said he was tired," I told her. "I didn't think anymore of it."

"Arthur and I have always said that when he retired, we'd travel. I've always wanted to see the village in Ireland where my mother was born, and, well, there are a lot of things to see in this world. We've never taken much time for a real trip. Arthur has always been so caught up in his practice. Not that I minded. It's always been his passion. It's what he is. Anyway, now Arthur wants to give up the practice. He wants us to do the traveling we've always said we would," she told me, keeping her eyes on mine.

I didn't hesitate. "I think that would be just perfect!" I said. "If you're worried about the practice, well, don't be. Oxbow has done without a pediatrician for years. People out here learn to adjust— make do with what they have. It's more important that you take care of yourself and enjoy ..." I broke off before actually blurting out "the time you have left," but, with a rueful smile, Verna finished the sentence for me.

"Don't feel bad, child." There she was, taking care of *me* again, when she had to be in such turmoil. "We all have to face the inevitable."

There was silence for a while, as we left each other to our own thoughts. Then she began again. "Arthur and I want to offer the practice to Dana. She won't have any trouble finding someone to take over in West Palm—several doctors were interested before. I'm just not sure she'd want to come over here." She gave me an apologetic look. "She's used to a much bigger city, you see."

I assured her that I understood perfectly, and that she was right. Small towns are great places to live but aren't necessarily for everybody—especially if you're young and lively. My impression of Dana D'Lorenzo was that she was definitely the lively sort.

"I noticed that the two of you get along quite well," she said.

It was true. Since the day we helped the Michaelsons move in, Dana had been back several weekends to visit them. She always invited me to run with her, and I did, although I was seriously thinking about suggesting I ride my bike while she ran. It was too hard on the knees and ankles for me.

"We were thinking of asking her over this weekend to tell her about my illness and to make the offer. What I'd like to know is, do you think she'll be interested?"

Now that was a tough one. Would Dana be at all interested in picking up stakes—leaving the place she had lived her whole life, except for her college years, an exciting place that has movies and theaters and beaches and, and, and—and move to a one-horse town with not much more to offer than an endless stream of tots with runny noses? Especially after having just taken over a lucrative medical practice. I also knew she had an aunt there whom she would not want to leave—the only family she had, I believe. It didn't sound promising, and I had to be honest with Verna.

She agreed but was determined that, if at all possible, Dana would have her husband's practice. Arthur, she said, would feel much better if she took it over. He'd already fallen in love with Oxbow's children, she explained, and was feeling guilty about leaving them so soon. Besides, Arthur is adamant that this is where Dana needs to be, and I agree. She asked me to help her convince Dana to come to Oxbow. I didn't think I had any real influence with our mutual friend but promised I'd do my best.

A month later the Michaelsons were on their way to Ireland, and a reluctant Dana D'Lorenzo was spending two days a week at the Oxbow office. She had taken on a partner in the West Palm Beach office and was splitting her time between the two offices. She confided to me that it was only to please the Michaelsons but the children of Oxbow adored "Dr. D.," like her mentor before her, and it was pretty obvious that the feeling was mutual. "After all," Dana explained curtly, "kids are kids."

CHAPTER 30

YESTERDAY, BUDDY FINALLY CROSSED over into the peace that was denied to him for so long in this world. Chico found him in his spartan room above the electronics shop, lying on his bed. As always, Li'l Bit was by his side, lying quietly with Dennis's hand still gently caressing his scruffy head.

Franklin quietly asked to bury him in the Sweet Chariot AME cemetery, in a small lot close to the little park with the bench. Folks were a little surprised at first, but then everyone knew Franklin was the closest thing to a friend Dennis had since he came to Oxbow. And there was no family to protest.

I went to see my friend tonight, to say a private good-bye. Brian Masters, our funeral director, let me go in alone before the few townspeople who would be coming to the short viewing showed up.

As I looked down into the modest casket, Buddy's heart spoke to mine. "I am safe. I am happy. I am at rest."

And his face confirmed it.

It was a short ceremony that laid Dennis to rest in a shady grave close to the little park area at the cemetery. Franklin did the honors himself while Mattie Lou, Chico, and I kept our thoughts to ourselves. Only Franklin and I understood that this was as much of an earthly homecoming as Dennis would ever have. As Franklin ended the little service, each of us said a few words about our friend and then walked away without speaking, each going back to our own little corner of the world.

My emotions ran deep. Dennis had been a very special friend and his loss was a hard one to accept. It just wasn't fair and I needed to talk to someone. I needed to talk to Glenn. He was fast becoming my rock, my touchstone, who could bring me back to solid ground. So I called and he, as always, was there for me. He listened quietly and I cried soft bitter tears for a life that had been so lonely, so bereft of light. And I thanked God for life, for hope, and for good friends.

Sitting on my back porch that evening, I stared at the ink-black sky, liberally sprinkled with tiny, white pinpoints. Away from the bright lights, we are blessed with awe inspiring night skies that folks in big cities and towns probably never know exist. I often sit out there by the river at night, covered in the blanket of chirping insects, hooting owls, and the occasional splashes of unseen critters living out their lives at the river's edge. That night, all the natural sounds seemed muted. Even the volume of my thoughts was turned down, and my heart was left to sink and swell by turns, reacting to my memories and my unanswered questions about life.

Dennis—Buddy—was gone and I couldn't help feeling bitter that his temporal peace had been so short. Yes, I believed that he was in a better place and that he was finally reunited with Hannah and Jeannie Sue. In fact, they were probably having a group hug and big gab-fest right about now, I assured myself. Still, the man who ultimately became my friend had lost so much time, suffered so much. To this day I cannot understand why life is so hard on some people.

It was the end of a long journey for me, from my first niggling suspicions about the Parker family, through the emotional explosion that was Jeannie Sue's diary, to the trip to Georgia that moved me further down the path to the truth that ultimately released Dennis from his soul-searing pain.

When my doleful thoughts finally subsided, I left the chirping insects and the gator croaking from the other side of the river and fell into bed, sinking into blessed oblivion.

But it was not a night for sleep, after all, and once again a familiar presence crept into my consciousness. I tried to wipe the cobwebs away, out of the thin air overhead, but they just kept reforming into a familiar pattern.

It took a while to realize that I was, in fact, awake. The image before me was the same as before—deep, sad eyes—so sad they were actually painful to look at. The deep-seated ache of loss, of soul-wrenching tragedy, was still there.

Hannah was back.

But she was different this time. In spite of the underlying pain, there was a more tranquil overall feeling, a sense of wholeness that she did not exude in her previous visits.

"Hannah!" I whispered, feeling a profound reverence. "You have your son again. Buddy isn't suffering anymore, and I can feel the peace that gives you, so what is it? What keeps you from your rest?" I knew there would be no answer, but it couldn't keep me from asking the questions of those grief-laden eyes. For a moment—or an hour—Hannah silently made her plea for my help once again. And then she vanished in a wispy swirl.

Wide awake, I sat up in bed, pulling the covers around me. The lingering chill these visits always left soaked through my bones, but it somehow didn't have the power it had before. Still, the visit took me by surprise.

I had done all I had been asked, hadn't I? I had uncovered the tortured story of Hannah's family, freeing Buddy to live what remained of his life. What could possibly be left? Could I have been wrong? Could it be that Buddy himself had been wrong? I had accepted everything he said—it all fit into a complete, if grotesque, puzzle. Now what was being asked of me? I had no clue, and it kept me from any semblance of rest for the remainder of the night. Dutch moved closer to my bed, laying one big paw on my pillow. I petted him and let him know everything was all right. He was obviously aware of Hannah's presence but was not alarmed as he had been before.

I slogged through the next day, writing, editing, and preparing photos for the week's edition. When I found myself back in my kitchen that evening, the day was a blur. After so many years at the paper, I could do it all by rote, although I knew it didn't really do justice to my craft or the paper's readers. This "crossing over" business numbed body and soul, and I was running out of the strength necessary to cope with both worlds.

As it happened, that week turned into a "feeding frenzy" for news, and I didn't have time even to think in depth about my ghostly visitor again.

It was early Thursday evening. I experienced no more visits from Hannah over the week, but there was a faint aura of unfinished business cloying at my heart and mind. I went over it all again. And again. Nothing. The feeling could not be dispelled. Then, the faintest tickling sensation started in the corner of my poor overworked brain. Undefined, but there nevertheless. It was maddeningly elusive, but I knew I couldn't will it to the forefront. Then, the tingling slowly spread downward. By the time it worked its way down to my toes, I was on my feet. I could feel something coming closer—nothing frightening—something exciting, something reassuring.

Then it came to me. The box! Whatever Hannah wanted, it had to be in the box!

A few weeks after Dennis died, I got a call from the Oxbow Bank to tell me that the rent on my safety deposit box was due. The recollection of that afternoon jumped into my mind. It had been a shock, to be sure. I remember the weight of the receiver in my hand, suspended between its cradle and my ear. I had forgotten about that safety deposit box. When had it been? A year ago? It was late one night—it always seemed to be late when Dennis came to the newspaper office. I could still hear the conversation and feel the calm, warm glow our friendship had developed into.

"Evenin', Molly. Ah see you're working late again," he had said as Li'l Bit settled into his usual spot in the corner.

"Just tying up a few loose ends ... still," I said with a weary smile. "Coffee?"

"Now you know me, Mol'. Ah never turn down a hot cup of coffee," he said.

I went back to the little kitchen area and dumped the dregs out of the pot, refilling it halfway with water and coffee. Dennis always had at least two cups, I knew, but I was coffeed out. Returning with a steaming mug, I apologized, "Sorry, no cookies tonight." Li'l Bit lifted his head as I went by and then just laid it down again when no goody was offered. I bent down and patted him apologetically. "Sorry, boy, fresh out of goodies tonight," I told him.

"Coffee's fine," Dennis answered, accepting the cup with obvious relish. He grew quiet then, sipping the hot brew before launching into the chitchat he always did when he first got there. He was on his second cup when he finally got to the point.

"Got a favor to ask, Molly," he began tentatively.

"Name it," I said, and I meant it. If Dennis had a favor to ask, it had to be serious. He'd never asked anything of me before, but I would have done anything he asked without hesitation. Dennis was, indeed, a very special friend, even if our relationship was—well—different.

"Ah've had a safety deposit box over at the Oxbow Bank for years. Ah'd like to put you on the account too. You'd have full privileges, a key and all," he said. "Ah pay the rental every year. Not much in it, you know, just a few personal things. Ah just think it would be good to have a second name on the account."

I was astonished. Well, Dennis was nothing if not full of surprises. A safety deposit box? Well, I'll be! Whoever would've thought? It seemed an odd request, adding my name to it, but it must have been important to Dennis, or he certainly would never have asked.

"Of course! I can go over tomorrow to sign the paperwork," I agreed without hesitation. There was a little more small talk—how were things going at the electronics shop, what would be the big story in the paper this week—then he and Li'l Bit took their leave.

I met Dennis at the bank the next day, added my name to the account, and picked up my key. I had a few brief thoughts about this odd request as we parted company, then thought about it no more.

I had picked up the contents of the safety deposit box—a plain gray shoe box with white letters—from the bank the day after I got a call saying the rent was due and brought it home with me that evening. I stared at the box for a long time before deciding I just didn't have the heart to open it yet. Dennis had been gone for a couple weeks, and I knew I should be better prepared for this "job"—after all, Dennis certainly must have wanted me to have whatever was inside. But I had to admit that I just couldn't do it yet. So I took it to my closet where I made a special place for it on the shelf.

There it remained, until I connected the little shoebox to Hannah's last visit. I wanted to have a clear head and an open heart when I finally sat down to reopen Dennis's life, so I retrieved it from the shelf, set it down on my coffee table, and just looked at it. It sat there, just waiting, as it had ever since Dennis died—until Hannah prompted me again a few nights ago.

I went out on the back porch to stare at the river and gather up the courage to open the plain box that held Dennis's earthly treasures. When I finally felt ready, I got up and went back into the house to reveal them.

I thought about him now. We had only really gotten to know each other a little over a year ago. But when we did, our friendship held fast. The secret we shared—the story of Dennis's family tragedy— was a strong bond.

The same gut-wrenching sadness I always felt when I thought about the Parker family enveloped me. I couldn't think of a more solitary human being than Dennis Blankenship—Buddy Parker—the sole survivor of the forty-year-old tragedy that left him alone in the world. But in his last year, Dennis finally managed to shed some of his lifelong pain. The struggle had been eased once the pain was shared.

I knew that when the box was finally opened, Dennis's most intimate treasures would be unveiled. What he held so dear had been locked away in a secret safety deposit box, only to be taken out and viewed occasionally—lovingly, I could only believe.

Now that I finally felt ready to open the box, another old pain crept up from the depths of my soul. I felt closely connected to the tragedy of the Parker family and thinking about it always brought unbidden the recollection of my own loss.

It had been many years since my own life was shattered, yet sometimes the pain still chews into my heart with razor teeth. I was just thirteen then.

I remember begging and pouting and cajoling till Mom finally relented. I recalled well savoring the flying feeling when Mom told me I didn't have to go bowling with her and Dad for once. It had been a family treat just about every Sunday afternoon for as long as I could remember. This time, however, I could go to the movies that afternoon with my friends.

"Don't be late," Mom cautioned me. I distinctly recall rolling my eyes. "Your father and I will be home early."

But they weren't.

With the stark melancholy of hindsight, I remembered the stolen enjoyment of those few extra hours of freedom when they took longer to come home than expected. Then the annoyance. Then the growing fear. Daylight was waning when the two officers came to the door of our home, and the fermenting fear roared to life. My brother Paul was out with his mangy old girlfriend—I never did like that girl; she was such a stuck-up little bitch—why couldn't he see that? I was alone when the word came.

Now the sense of enormous loss came back, full force. With it came the tears. Silent, cleansing. I still wrestled with the guilt as well as the loss. I should have been with them when that semi crossed the centerline, bearing down, head on, right into the center of my life. But I wasn't there. I was at the movies with Nancy Belton and Julie Schwann—laughing, talking, flirting with the boys the way teenage girls do. My parents would be grateful I wasn't there, I knew, but it didn't make carrying the burden of grief and guilt any easier. Maybe it was that shared pain that bonded me with Dennis.

One thing Dennis had taught me—I had to let go of the pain. Work through it. Deal with it. Take the good from all the memories and experiences and allow them to make me stronger. It had taken Dennis forty years to be able to take that lesson to heart. I didn't want to make that same mistake.

I finally took a deep breath and opened the old shoebox, revealing Jeannie Sue's diary, which I had given him shortly after that night in the lot, a faded royal blue box, a packet of old envelopes neatly tied up with twine, and a few other odds and ends.

It took a long to time to work through the feeling that I was trespassing on private territory. It was the same feeling I had had before reading Jeannie Sue's diary. Again I prayed for the right to trespass on what felt sacred. But, then, surely this is what Dennis wanted, or he wouldn't have put my name on his safe deposit box account.

Slowly, I pulled out what turned out to be a velvet-lined box. I opened the lid to reveal Dennis's Purple Heart—a token of the living hell of a few, the inestimable bill of freedom they pay for the rest of us.

Gazing at the likeness of George Washington embossed on a heart of purple, I tried to understand what Dennis and so many others had endured in earning this token—one I was sure he never wanted but that must have held great importance for him.

The best I could envision was some vague feeling of ungodly noise and hellish screams of pain. *War,* I thought, *must be something like the droplets of hell I've felt when Milton forced himself through the mist to me.*

I shivered, imagining Dennis in the midst of a physical hell, then closed the case and placed it on the coffee table—this relic of faith and total commitment by the few to the world we have built ourselves.

Picking up the packet of letters, I found that one was not tied up with the others. I realized that the power of secrets had taken me on a long, wrenching journey that began with my own, all the way back when I was thirteen. I thought I had unraveled Dennis's secret and was surprised at the overpowering feeling that I was holding yet another. I grabbed the loose envelope as it fell to the table and got a jolt when I read the name scrawled on it. It said simply, "Molly."

Well, Dennis, I thought, *even now you're still surprising me.* I opened the plain white envelope, slowly pulled out the papers inside, unfolded them, and began to decipher Dennis's scrawling handwriting.

MOLLY,

NOW THAT I'M GONE, THERE'S SO MUCH I NEED YOU TO KNOW THAT I JUST COULDN'T TELL YOU BEFORE. I GUESS THE FIRST THING I NEED TO SAY, THOUGH, IS TO LET YOU KNOW HOW IMPORTANT YOU HAVE BEEN IN MY LIFE. YOU HELPED ME FINALLY FIND A WAY OUT OF THE MAZE OF PAIN AND GUILT I WANDERED IN FOR SO LONG. I WON'T SAY THANK YOU BECAUSE THERE'S JUST NO WAY TO DO IT, BUT I KNOW YOU WELL ENOUGH TO KNOW THAT YOU UNDERSTAND.

SO, WE GET TO THE OTHER THINGS I NEED TO TELL YOU. PLEASE BEAR WITH ME—THIS WILL TAKE A LITTLE WHILE.

AFTER THE FIRE THAT TOOK MY FAMILY, I LEFT OXBOW AND WANDERED AROUND FOR YEARS, DOING ODD JOBS, AS YOU KNOW. I WORKED A LOT OF CONSTRUCTION AND DID SOME COMMERCIAL FISHING. YOU KNOW THAT I ENLISTED WHEN THAT MESS STARTED UP IN KOREA—ENDED UP IN A VA HOSPITAL FOR ALMOST A YEAR.

BEFORE KOREA, I WAS WORKING FOR A CONSTRUCTION COMPANY IN WEST PALM. DOING PRETTY GOOD, TOO. HAD A ONE-ROOM APARTMENT—THAT'S ALL I REALLY NEEDED—AND I WAS REALLY PUTTING MY LIFE TOGETHER FINALLY. MET A GIRL TOO. SHE WAS REALLY SOMETHING. PRETTY. SMART. NICE GIRL, YOU KNOW? THE KIND GUYS TAKE HOME TO MOTHER.

ANYWAY, WE WERE GOOD FOR EACH OTHER. WE DIDN'T ACTUALLY SET A DATE TO GET MARRIED. WE DECIDED—WELL, I DECIDED—WE SHOULD WAIT TILL I GOT BACK FROM KOREA. I JUST FELT LIKE SHE SHOULD HAVE THAT TIME IN CASE SHE WANTED TO CHANGE HER MIND. SHE WAS SO YOUNG, YOU KNOW. I GUESS I WAS TOO, BUT I DIDN'T FEEL THAT WAY. BESIDES, THERE WAS NO WAY OF TELLING IF I'D EVEN COME BACK, AND

I DIDN'T WANT TO LEAVE A WIDOW BEHIND. IT JUST DIDN'T SEEM FAIR.

So, I ENLISTED AND GOT SHIPPED OFF, RIGHT INTO THE MIDDLE OF HELL. DID YOU KNOW THAT HELL CAN FREEZE A MAN'S SOUL?

Yes, Dennis, I think I do.

WELL, ONE AFTERNOON WHEN THE DEVIL HAD CALLED A TIME-OUT, I GOT A LETTER. IT WAS THE MIDDLE OF WINTER, AND A BUNCH OF US GUYS WERE ALL HUNKERED DOWN IN A DRAFTY, OLD TENT, TRYING TO KEEP WARM, WHEN THE MAIL CAME IN. YOU CAN'T IMAGINE HOW GOOD THAT FEELS, GETTING MAIL OUT THERE ON THE LINE. HOW IT CAN WARM A SPOT INSIDE YOUR GUTS WHEN THE WHOLE WORLD IS MADE OF ICE. WELL, I GUESS I'M GETTING SIDETRACKED HERE.

To MAKE IT SHORT, IT WAS FROM GINNY, MY GIRL. SHE TOLD ME SHE WAS CARRYING MY BABY AND THAT THEY'D BOTH BE THERE FOR ME WHEN I GOT BACK.

IT'S AMAZING. THERE I WAS, IN THE MIDDLE OF KOREA, HELL ON EARTH, AND ALL OF A SUDDEN THE SUN CAME OUT, AND MY WHOLE SOUL BLOOMED. I KNOW THAT SOUNDS DOPEY, BUT THAT'S WHAT IT FELT LIKE.

I HAD A REAL FAMILY AGAIN—SOMETHING I HADN'T HAD SINCE I WAS A SIXTEEN-YEAR-OLD KID. SOMETHING I DON'T THINK I REALLY BELIEVED I COULD EVER HAVE AGAIN TILL THAT MOMENT. ALL I HAD TO DO WAS STAY ALIVE AND GET BACK HOME. I GUESS YOU KNOW IT WASN'T QUITE THAT EASY.

I DON'T REMEMBER WHEN THE SHRAPNEL TORE THROUGH ME. THERE ARE A FEW CLOUDY "DREAMS," BUT THE FIRST THING I REALLY REMEMBER WAS WAKING UP IN THE VA HOSPITAL. FOR A WHILE I LAY THERE AND THOUGHT, Okay, when I get out of here I can go home and start my life again. THEN THE DOCTOR CAME

IN AND LAID THE REAL TRUTH ON ME—AND I GOT A GOOD, HARD LOOK AT MYSELF. I KNEW I COULDN'T FORCE THIS NIGHTMARE I'D BECOME ON ANYBODY I LOVED.

I THOUGHT ABOUT JUST NEVER GOING BACK TO THE GIRL I LOVED MORE THAN I WOULD'VE THOUGHT POSSIBLE. SHE WAS SENDING ME LETTERS ALL THE TIME, BUT I DIDN'T ANSWER THEM. BY THE TIME I FINALLY GOT OUT OF THE HOSPITAL, I KNEW I COULDN'T JUST WALK AWAY. I HAD TO GO TO HER AND LET HER SEE ME, MAKE HER UNDERSTAND THAT I COULD NEVER BE THE MAN SHE FELL IN LOVE WITH EVER AGAIN. I HAD TO MAKE HER UNDERSTAND WHY I HAD TO LEAVE THEM. I CAN'T TELL YOU ABOUT THAT DAY, JUST THAT I PROMISED HER I'D ALWAYS DO WHAT I COULD TO TAKE CARE OF THE TWO OF THEM.

AND I DID. I ALWAYS SENT MONEY WHEN MY VA CHECK CAME IN. SHE SENT ME LETTERS AND PICTURES OF HER AND OUR BABY. THAT'S WHAT THESE ENVELOPES ARE—THE ONLY LINK I HAD ALL THOSE YEARS WITH MY FAMILY. I NEED FOR MY DAUGHTER TO HAVE THEM NOW.

WHEN THE TIME IS RIGHT, PLEASE MAKE SURE MY BABY GETS THESE LETTERS. MAKE SURE DANA D'LORENZO GETS THESE PIECES OF HER LIFE.

YOUR FRIEND,
DENNIS

ABOUT THE AUTHOR

Patty Brant has been writing for a small community newspaper in south Central Florida since 1985 and served as editor since 1991. *Bitter Secrets* is her first book. She is a native of Canton, Ohio—think Football Hall of Fame—and has lived in south Florida since 1969.

CPSIA information can be obtained at www.ICGtesting.com
Printed in the USA
LVOW06s0709180713

343384LV00002B/82/P